CW00797129

The American Woman

R J Gould writes contemporary fiction about relationships using a mix of wry humour and pathos to describe the life journeys of his protagonists. *The American Woman* is his ninth novel and the third in the 'at the Dream Café' series. He has been published by Lume Books and Headline Accent and is also self-published. He is a member of Cambridge Writers, Society of Authors and the Romantic Novelists' Association UK.

Before becoming a full-time author he worked in the education and charity sectors.

R J Gould lives in Cambridge, England.

www.rjgould.info

The American Woman

R J Gould

To Gwennie

With very best
wishes,

R.Clark

Published by FeedARead.com Publications [2023]

Acknowledgements

There are several people I would like to thank for their help with the publication of this novel. Joss Alexander, Thure Etzold and Angela Wray, fellow members of the Cambridge Writers Commercial Editing Group, provide generous support, ranging from proof reading to consideration of plot and characterisation. In addition to giving valuable feedback on my final draft, my reader launch team – Alex Elbro, Dr Karen Jost, Gwen Nunn, Helen Appleby, Katy Dowling and Mary Robinson – offer inspiring enthusiasm and encouragement. For this novel, Karen, an American, has been a tremendous help, converting my perception of how Americans express themselves into a semblance of reality. Ken Dawson at Creative Covers has once again done a great job in designing the cover. Finally, a thank you to Terry Chance for her patience and support together with perceptive tough judgement of my wilder ideas.

1

Imagine a café that's a couple of minutes from your London home, a delightful walk through tree-lined avenues with Victorian houses of such elegance that you can't help stopping and looking even if you've stopped to look a thousand times before.

You arrive at the café for morning coffee, the aroma and the hiss of the milk steamer grabbing you on stepping inside. It's crowded – couples chatting, families with children sharing pastries to die for, singletons scanning their phones or reading a newspaper, student types with laptops and headphones.

You're back again that evening, tempted by the literature event when locals read extracts from their novels and poems – it's the sort of neighbourhood where every customer seems to be an author or a poet. At night the cafe has turned into a hub for the affluent middle aged. A welcoming soft light is bouncing off the pastel walls, plunging the scarlet coloured alcoves into shadow. The place is buzzing, alcohol is flowing, and the shoving to reach the counter is as polite as can be.

Bridget, the owner of Dream Café, is serving drinks together with Kelly, her deputy manager. Kelly lives round the corner from me. Whenever we cross paths she seems in a hurry, walking her dog or jogging, but she always manages a wave, a smile and a "Hi, Jennifer."

I'm alone at the café, of course, and I'm uncomfortable. I hate Gareth for that.

2

I was born in Idaho, on a potato and sugar beet farm a couple of miles out from a small town with a single main street that was even named Main Street. Running along it was a modest supermarket, a hardware store, and a bar that played Country & Western and blues. *Nellie's Ice Cream and Soda Parlor* was there too, open right through the year, even in midwinter when temperatures plummeted to minus fifteen. This was an indication of how desperate teenagers in the town and its surrounds were to find anywhere to go and anything to do. Later on when I was living in England, someone handed me a copy of Bill Bryson's *The Lost Continent*. That first line – "I come from Des Moines. Someone had to" – cracked me up. It could easily have applied to the place I grew up in and was lucky enough to escape from.

I guess we were a typical small-time farming family, Dad hard working, up at the crack of dawn and not back in until dusk; Mom the housewife, the Huckleberry pie maker and regular churchgoer; and my brother Daniel Junior, two years older than me. His childhood obsession was watching old westerns with the cowboys always beating the Indians, and sci-fi when the humans always got the better of the aliens. Later on he was outdoors whenever possible, helping Dad on the farm. He seemed comfortable with his destiny – to be a farmer in Idaho.

What about me? I suppose early on I fitted in. I'd be in the kitchen with Mom, happily stirring the ingredients for the pie filling. I remember being proud beyond belief the first time Mom trusted me to use a knife to core and slice apples. And nothing made me happier than sitting high up on the tractor with Dad when it was harvest time.

It's odd what you dredge up when thinking back to your childhood. In truth there probably weren't that many pies being made, but I was expected to help with the kitchen chores and housework, and I definitely did like the tractor rides.

I loved to read and filled many late afternoons exploring novels about American life in places that always seemed more exciting than Idaho. I discovered what girls got up to in *Sweet Valley High*. Judy Blume's books set in California and New York made the sad nearby town seem like it was stuck in a time warp.

For a while I held onto the belief that American life was wonderful and could never be beaten, even if the characters in the books I was reading had loads of obstacles to figure out. Then one year, it must have been when I was around sixteen, my best friend Rebecca's sister, Clara, started college. Returning for vacations she would lend us books that weren't easily found in the town library, books from way back like *On the Road* and *Catcher in the Rye* which got me thinking that maybe life wasn't quite as comfortable for everybody as I had been led to believe.

'Best keep it secret I'm lending you this one,' Clara told us one time.

'Why?' Rebecca asked.

'You'll see.'

The House on Mango Street had come our way. *The Handmaid's Tale* followed. They were dynamite.

Although nothing in particular triggered the thought, I knew that I had to get away from Idaho if I wanted to discover the real world. Rebecca and I would talk late into the night about an escape but deep down I knew she wouldn't do it. She had too many, "But what abouts."

'The only what about that matters is what about me,' I told her one stifling summer's evening when we were sitting together out on the porch.

Our pledge to lifelong friendship (we'd even cut our wrists and placed them against each other to seal the bond) turned out not to be the case after I said that. I suppose Rebecca saw me as a threat to how in her mind everything had to be. I was dropped in favour of girls who weren't the questioning types.

It took two years and more before I would escape. By then, I admit that I was making it difficult for my parents to restrain me. And as for my brother, he was accusing me of being possessed by the devil. The devil in question, though an absurd belief, was acting. I'd developed a passionate, some might say obsessive, interest in movies.

I signed up for the school drama group and was told that I had some talent. I discovered, too, that I could sing well with a natural ability for dance. Lead roles in the school productions of *Fame* and *Cats* followed and I worked hard to make them a success.

"Our very own star" ran the headline in the local paper.

"Jennifer has a dazzling career ahead of her" my drama teacher claimed in his interview for the article.

This was before internet went big and I was getting my information about the world of movies in magazines. While friends spent their pocket money on make-up I was using mine to get the glitzy Hollywood weeklies, *Variety* and *Movieline* being my regulars. And boy, was the lifestyle that was shown attractive.

I left in spirit way ahead of my actual move from home. There was no more helping Mom in the kitchen, no more duties on the farm. All I could think about was the glamour and pull of Hollywood.

I remember dressing up vintage style to playact star roles in movies that would one day be made just for me.

'I am NOT going out to get covered in mud,' I would tell Daniel, rigged up in his sensible boots, jeans and plaid shirts, when we'd been asked to pick vegetables from the garden. 'You do it.'

It didn't take much to get him into a rage. 'You are the most ungrateful, lazy person, you know that?'

'Yeah, I know. And you're wonderful.'

Daniel didn't take well to sarcasm. On the day when he completely lost it and gave me a hard slap, I saw that as the final straw. It was time to leave.

Telling my parents I was off to LA to become a star wouldn't have come as a surprise. We were all sitting at the breakfast table when I announced it. They stayed silent. Resigned.

It was left to my brother to voice his disgust. 'You're a disgrace, Jennifer. I hope everything goes wrong. I hope you die.'

'Don't speak to your sister like that, Daniel,' my Dad shouted. 'Apologise.'

But Daniel was on his way out, door slamming, and I never got round to thanking Dad for standing up for me despite me being such a disappointment to him.

I was eighteen going on nineteen when I packed my bags, gave Mom and Dad a peck on the cheek, ignored my brother, and headed west on a Greyhound bus. I had just enough money put aside to pay for the journey, with a bit left over to carry me through until I got my first part in a movie. Looking back, I wish I'd had the maturity to at least try to explain why I was leaving.

How many naïve girls still in their teens have turned up in Hollywood over the years chasing stardom? Thousands? Tens of thousands? And little me was one of them, a blue-eyed, blonde-haired girl with pale skin and a wide face who thought she only need appear at an audition to be discovered. I stepped off that Greyhound bus, found a place to stay advertised on a noticeboard at the station, slept a night, put on my best clothes, did my hair, made up with thick lines of mascara and scarlet lipstick, and headed off to the studios.

I didn't get past security; I was told it all had to be done through agents.

A miserable three or so weeks followed in an attempt to be signed on. Little chance of course, what with East Coast girls in competition, girls who had been to drama school since the age of three and already had a bio as long as my arm, who could probably play three musical instruments, and maybe were fluent in several languages. Mind you, I was soon to find out that it was tough for them too, unless they were prepared to do anything that the fat (they all seemed to be fat) middle-aged producers, directors and cast recruiters wanted. And by anything, I mean anything.

The agent who agreed to take me on, from a tiny outfit with no clout, made it clear that giving favours was a requirement for success. I was expected to start with him and to my shame, I complied. It didn't take long for me to realise that the "giving favours" in question was nothing more than a tempting carrot dangled before being pulled away. I wasn't going to play that game. I was not going to have sex with the last person in the world I'd choose to have sex with, in the hope of landing a role as an extra in a B-movie or a daytime TV sitcom.

What was there left for me to do though? Go home?

3

After a couple of drinks that Friday evening, being alone at Dream Café wasn't turning out to be so bad. I guess it doesn't matter whether you're by yourself or with a group of friends when all eyes are on the performers. However, during the interval with the lights on, I was scanning the crowd to see if anyone else was on their own – and it didn't look like it. I felt as awkward as hell, wondering why I was there rather than tucked up in my flat with the TV on and a few beers by my side. Going out alone was not something I enjoyed; it takes a lot of courage. But it would take a lot of stupidity to get into a relationship just because I didn't want to be by myself.

I'm a stranger, an outsider, I was thinking as I waited my turn at the counter. I have no connection with the district, the city, the country, the people.

'Same again?' Kelly was asking. She was the only person anything like an acquaintance, based on her friendly greetings as she was speeding past me in the street. We'd had a couple of brief chats when I was ordering drinks from her in the café.

'No. You know what, I'm going to have a whiskey. That one,' I said pointing to the bottle of Jack Daniels. At least, thousands of miles away from my homeland, I could capture a taste of the States.

She poured me a glass, precisely using a measure, which made me think back to LA where barmen just poured out from the bottle until the customer said "Stop." I took a sip, the unaccustomed heat burning the back of my throat.

A man was standing by my side. I'd seen him out and about with his wife, a baby and a dog.

'Andrew, this is Jennifer,' Kelly said. 'She's just moved here.'

The man smiled before turning back to Kelly, holding up his card ready to pay contactless and pick up his tray of drinks. Kelly placed a firm hand onto the tray and I figured out the hint she was giving him.

So did he. 'We're sitting over there. Why not join us?'

My smile was in appreciation of the invitation, but it was also because of the way the English say things, turning "Come join us" into the cryptic "Why not join us?" as if the offer and decision were mine alone.

I hesitated. 'I wouldn't want to impose.'

'Not at all. It would be a pleasure.'

'And I'll be with you as soon as Rachel turns up for her shift,' Kelly said as she slid the tray of drinks across to Andrew.

I followed Andrew to his table and was introduced to Emma, his wife, Darren who was Kelly's husband,

and Julien and Cecelia who described themselves as the in-between neighbours.

'See you later,' Andrew said and walked off from the group, leaving me confused until Emma explained that he was one of the performers.

'A published poet,' Darren added.

He was soon up on stage and I shared the crowd's enjoyment of the funny and thoughtful poems he read out. We cheered when Andrew returned, me joining in and for the first time wondering whether living in Muswell Hill might be alright after all.

It had taken three months.

4

No way was I going back home to Idaho, but without money and having put any attempt to find work in the movie industry on hold (forever?), I needed a job fast. Los Angeles is full of young women dreaming of being discovered, or more likely, aware that was never going to happen but unwilling to move on, especially if moving on meant returning home. I had joined their ranks and was about to find out that competition for waitressing jobs was almost as tough as it had been to get a film role.

It didn't take long to discover that some of the men running eateries were as single-minded as the Hollywood set – they expected favours in exchange for employment. Here were my two options, either a lousy existence living in a rundown shared condo but at least with a job, or destitution. Having opted for a roof over my head, with shame I admit that every so often I was enduring sex with impoverished restaurant owners having turned down wealthy men in the showbiz world. Some would call that stupid. It was never forced though; I chose who and sometimes it turned out to be an enjoyable if short-term fling.

There was a gang of us girls in a similar situation. We got to know the better places to work and those to avoid and we shared the information. Who were the biggest bastards, the violent ones? Which men stank of fat and grease? Where could you get the best tips? Which places were the safest to get home from late at night?

The years passed. I'd like to say they flew by with me getting the most out of living in such an exciting city. Sadly, the opposite was true. Time dragged on as I moved aimlessly between one post and the next. I was in between jobs as they say when a waitressing position came up at Giulio's Diner and I grabbed it. I had to thank my friend Kimberly for that. Having finally decided to pack in LA and return home, she let me know that she was about to hand in her notice. She said she'd put in a good word for me and I was waiting at the door as Joe was unlocking his place the next morning. There was no Giulio, there never had been, and there was no Italian connection. Joe simply thought it was a good name to attract diners. The only concessions to the Italian link were Spaghetti Bolognese on the menu and an espresso machine that kept breaking down. Apart from that it was an all-American diner with burgers, hot dogs and Cuban sandwiches. Pies too, but not as good Mom's.

Kimberly had told me that Joe was a good man and that turned out to be right. He had a wife and new baby and stayed loyal to his family.

I hugged Kimberly when I saw her off at the bus station a few days later and we both cried. "What am I going to make of my life?" she asked me, not expecting an answer because she knew I wouldn't have one. She said she'd write but we never did keep in touch until much later.

Ahead of my first shift at Giulio's, Kimberley's rhetorical question, "What am I going to make of my life?" hit home. I was in my late twenties, close to ten years on from arriving in LA with such high hopes. Giulio's would be my twelfth dead-end job waitressing.

~

The Englishman appeared a couple of months after I'd started working at the diner. Giulio's wasn't located in a good part of the city, and being well off the beaten track customers were from the neighbourhood.

It was late on a Wednesday evening and the place was almost empty when this guy walked in. He stood out like a sore thumb, smart in his tweed jacket and tie when the regulars wore jeans and tees. He had on thick black glasses like the ones Superman wore when he was Clark Kent. His twirl of red-blond curls pointed upwards like a meringue.

'May I sit down?' he asked which got me and Joe smirking.

'Sure Pal. Anywhere that's free,' Joe said, sweeping his arm across the now empty room.

We watched the outsider take his time to examine the menu. It was getting late and I was keen to leave. Joe used to let me start clearing up once the last order had been taken so as soon as the man dropped the menu onto the table I was by his side.

'What can I get you?' I asked.

'Burger and chips, err … fries, and a coffee please.'

Yep, he was English alright, his accent the giveaway though it wasn't cockney like Michael Caine or posh like royalty. He had an anxious smile like he was embarrassed to be there, embarrassed to speak to me.

'Thank you so much, this looks delicious,' he said when I brought his food over.

'Ketchup or mayo?'

'Both please. That would be wonderful.'

No one had ever suggested that a burger and fries dumped onto a plate without a thought about presentation looked delicious or that receiving packets of sauces was wonderful. I watched as he cut the burger into neat cubes using his knife and fork, rather than the usual grasping of the burger in a hand and stuffing it into a face.

He was taking his time eating and sipping his coffee which I wasn't happy about, though he was entertaining to watch. As soon as his cup was empty I waltzed across with the jug, the second cup being free.

'More coffee?'

'I wouldn't say no.'

This stopped me in my tracks because I wasn't sure what he meant. Was he politely turning down the offer but thought it was rude to actually say "no"?

He must have noticed my frown.

'I'd love another cup please.'

Gee, I'd learned some non-American English. "I wouldn't say no" meant "Yes".

I would test it out on Kurt for a bit of fun when I got home. It hadn't taken me long to realise that moving in with Kurt was a mistake. He was a car mechanic and definitely loved Chevrolets more than me. At first he'd included me in his social life but that hadn't lasted long. On the evenings when he wasn't slumped in a chair watching NFL matches he was out with buddies listening to hard rock bands at some downtown dive. There was a Crystal who was messaging him a lot. I'd lost interest in worrying about whether he was seeing another woman but what I did care about was him telling me off all the time and being suspicious if I was a minute late home after work. I knew the relationship was over and it had hardly begun.

That night was a TV night.

'You're late,' were his first words.

'There was a last minute customer.'

The commercials had come on, a giant pretzel crust pizza was on offer for six dollars. Kurt pulled himself out of the armchair and went over to the fridge. 'Wanna beer?' he asked me, holding up a can.

'I wouldn't say no.'

'What?'

'I wouldn't say no.'

'What the fucking hell does that mean?'

'It means yes, I'd love one, please.'

'Love a beer?'

'I'm being polite. Like the Brits.'

'Brits? You're fucking nuts.'

'Thanks a million, honey.'

'Fuck you. I'm going to watch the game round at Jim's place.'

I decided that was it with Kurt. There was a friend, Angie, who was looking for a flatmate. I called her, packed my bags and departed having left a brief note: *And fuck you too.*

5

We were all knocking back drinks that night at the Dream Café but I was downing them faster and more frequently than the others. I was nervous, an outsider to this group of close friends. Anyway, that was my excuse. It ended up with me being dragged home by Kelly and Emma, each clutching an arm to support me.

'Are you sure you're going to be alright?' one of them asked as I placed the fob against the keypad by the front door of my block.

The door buzzed open and we stepped into the hallway.

'Which flat is yours?'

I pointed upwards, dismayed that the steps were steeper than I recalled. There were more of them too. I braced myself in preparation for the ascent.

'I think we'd better help you. Let's get you inside your flat then we can leave you in peace.'

My guardian angels yanked me up and the next thing I knew I was lying on the bed in my underwear, the quilt over me, with daylight filtering in through the window.

Hangover aside, I was thoroughly miserable, devastated at having embarrassed myself and thrown away the chance to make friends.

Gareth would have talked me through this imagined disaster, reassuring me that no damage had been done and that all I needed to do was apologise for the poor behaviour. I'd been thinking a lot about Gareth lately; I missed his calm, quiet self. With him there'd be no reprimand for my stupidity, just a sympathetic smile, a cup of tea, and an Alka-Seltzer fizzing away in a glass of water.

Ignoring his favoured cure for hangovers I made an espresso, its bitterness aggravating my upset stomach. I was pouring the remains down the sink when my intercom buzzed.

'Hello?'

'It's Kelly. Just checking to see if you're alright.'

'I am thanks. Look, I'm sorry I was such a pain in the butt last night.'

'Hardly.'

'Except that I was … what did Gareth used to call it? … rat-arsed.'

'Gareth?'

'Yeah, a boyfriend. The reason why I'm in England. Britain.'

'But now it's over?'

'Over?'

'With this Gareth.'

'Yeah.' We were still talking through the intercom. 'Hey, wanna come up for a bit?'

'Sure, though I've got Tyson with me. Is that OK?'

'Tyson? I thought it was Darren.'

'He's our dog.'

'Oh, I see. Come on up. Both of you.'

Perhaps there might be a second chance, possibly my last chance to find a friend. I couldn't mess this up which gave me thirty seconds to race round tidying the living room. The kitchen could wait.

'Fancy a drink?' I asked when Kelly was sitting down.

'Water would be good. I'm about to go for a run as well as giving this thing some exercise.' She patted her dog. Kelly was wearing high-fashion running gear, navy and orange with trainers to match, the sort of stuff I'd seen the LA runners wear.

'Look, I really do want to apologise for getting drunk last night.'

'Don't worry about it.'

'But I do. We'd only just met and you and Emma ended up having to get me home. It wasn't fair of me to do that.'

'I've had loads of experience taking drunk people home. Well, drunk person. Darren.' She had a contagious broad smile. 'So, you came to England because of a man,' she continued. 'Gareth, didn't you say?'

'Yeah, Gareth. We met when he was working in the States. It's a long story.'

'I don't want to pry.'

'I'm OK talking about him. Us. But maybe not today.'

'No problem. I only wanted a quick check on you this morning.'

'That's kind of you.'

Kelly was on her feet, her dog pulling her towards the door. 'Tell you what, we have brunch at the café most Sundays. Why not join us if you're not doing anything special?'

On the assumption that "Why not join us?" meant "Join us" the invitation was a godsend: I'd been forgiven.

'I'd love to.'

'Great. Give me your number and I'll text you the details.'

I did and she called me, cutting off after a couple of rings. 'Now you've got mine, too. I'd best be off.'

'See you, Kelly.'

'Yes, see you, Jennifer.'

6

I was hit by a wave of relief as the cab pulled away from Kurt's place, despite this being the latest in a line of short, failed relationships with me having to be rescued by a female friend. I wasn't unique though, there were ten of us who were like in a never ending loop. Someone would rent a place and before long a friend would be turning up in floods of tears. Then the person with the condo would meet some jerk of a new guy and shack up with them. Soon afterwards they'd be escaping to another friend's home. Round and round it went.

Angie was now returning the favour, having stayed at mine for a few months after a cruel time with a guy. That evening we sat on her bed knocking back beers, laughing one minute and crying the next as we contemplated what was in store for us would-be actresses who had no chance of making it.

The next morning I was woken by a banging on the door. It was Kurt.

'What the fuck you doing, girl?' He pushed Angie aside and came towards me. 'Get your things and come back now.'

I knew Kurt's temper and was scared as he stood in front of me, our faces almost touching.

I might have done what he wanted, gone back, but Angie stepped in to separate us. 'She isn't going anywhere, so you get outta here!'

'But I love you, Jen,' Kurt said, having stepped away. He was facing me with those eyes that had got me interested in him in the first place. And maybe he really did love me because, and this was a big surprise, his anger had evaporated and he was crying.

'Go into my bedroom,' Angie ordered and I did what she asked. A couple of minutes later I heard the front door close and Angie joined me. 'He's gone. I didn't want you changing your mind.'

My head was pounding. I had one hell of a hangover and I was unsure whether I'd done the right thing with Kurt. I was that close to calling Joe to tell him I wasn't well enough to work that evening. I'm glad I didn't – I might never have seen the English man again.

He was back at Giulio's Diner around seven, sitting at the same table by the window. He ordered spaghetti bolognaise. This time he didn't say that his food looked delicious or that the packets of salt, pepper and parmesan cheese were wonderful. And I didn't blame him because the overcooked pasta and runny, greasy meat sauce looked as bad as it was gonna taste.

Mesmerised, I watched him twist the long strands neatly and tidily, not like the regulars who stacked up their pasta onto their fork and shovelled it in. I'd never seen anyone eat so slow.

'Jennifer!' Joe was calling me. 'There's food to collect!'

The man looked up and smiled as I dashed across to the counter to grab a couple of plates.

'Come on, concentrate. We can't be giving out cold food.'

'Sorry, Joe.'

And I was sorry because there were a lot of people out there ready to take my job if I wasn't delivering. I prided myself in being efficient, too.

'It's not easy this work, is it?' the English man said as I was walking past, having set the plates on a nearby table. 'Waitressing.'

'I'm not complaining.'

'Oh, apologies. I wasn't suggesting that you were.'

There was a pause that seemed to go on forever as we looked at each other. I broke the silence. 'Wanna drink to go with that?'

'That's not a bad idea.'

There was a further pause but I was getting it. The previous night, "I wouldn't say no" had meant "Yes" when I'd asked if he wanted more coffee. So now, "Not a bad idea" must mean it was a good idea. This was an order then, which was just as well because Joe was watching me, wondering what I was doing standing there when he had more meals ready to go.

'Wine? Beer?'

'A beer sounds good.'

'Right, one beer coming up,' I said loud enough for Joe to hear. 'We do Bud, Miller Lite or Coors.'

'The first one, if that means Budweiser.'

Well done, Sherlock Holmes. Of course I didn't say that; sarcasm had got me into enough trouble in the past.

'Sure does. I'll get you one.'

'Gareth,' he said as I handed over the can and a glass.

'You mean that's your name?'

'Yes,' he replied, with no indication that he'd registered just how stupid my question was.

'I'm Jennifer.'

'Jennifer! Counter collection. Now.'

'Coming, Joe.'

By the time my shift was over Gareth had long gone. He'd left a generous tip and I'd said, "Thanks, see you tomorrow maybe" as he was on his way out.

You know when you feel you have a connection with someone before you get to know them, even before they've spoken to you? Well, I sort of felt that about this guy. I'd had the same sense with some girls – at school in Idaho, at the casting studios in LA – but never with a man before. I saw all males as predators in search of sex with me deciding whether to let them have it or not. And let's be honest, I wasn't making a success of it, Kurt being the latest example of shit judgement. So my reaction to this guy was new to me.

When Gareth didn't show at Giulio's for the rest of the week I thought that was it, I'd never see him again. He was probably a tourist who'd somehow found his way to our side of town and had now returned home. Life went on and I wasn't particularly bothered, except that I was because ahead of each shift, in anticipation of seeing him, I was taking a bit more care doing my hair and putting on make-up than usual. Just in case.

I wish I hadn't mentioned Gareth to Angie, telling her that I was disappointed that he was a no-show, because she wasn't impressed.

'So let me get this straight. You're infatuated because of how he cuts his food.'

'I'm not infatuated, just curious.'

'But your only conversation has been to ask if he'd like more coffee or a beer and even then you don't understand anything he says.'

'He is kinda cute.'

'I remember you saying that about Kurt.'

'That was different.'

'And that other guy, the one with the big ears.'

'They weren't so big.'

'When I said they were you agreed.'

'OK, so I'm hopeless at finding the right man.'

Angie was at the fridge getting the beers. 'He'll be in tomorrow, this Gareth of yours,' she said handing me one. 'Take my word for it.'

'Yeah, right.'

7

I didn't hear back from Kelly following her brief visit the morning after my embarrassing evening at Dream Café, which meant no invite to the next day's brunch that she'd mentioned. Rightly or wrongly, even though I had her number, I intended to wait until she contacted me. It might be a long wait, an endless one, but no way would I be begging to join her group.

A week later, the last Saturday of September, I was still waiting to hear from Kelly. I felt let down and pretty fed up. The shit weather wasn't helping. Ever since I'd arrived in Muswell Hill in June, looking forward to what should have been the best days of the year, there had been close to zero sunshine or warmth. Instead, each day had been grey and damp, a pathetic excuse for summer.

Today, all of a sudden, came soaring temperatures to over ninety and a sky as blue as anything California could offer.

It was a day to be outdoors. After lunch I joined what looked like the whole population of Muswell Hill enjoying Alexandra Park. It was good to feel the sun on my face but it would have been nice to have a girlfriend to chat with as I strolled along. Or maybe a man, holding hands.

Despite the crowds it would be hard not to notice Kelly in her luminous jogging gear, her hair swinging from side to side as she ran. Emma was with her, her hair under close control in a pony tail, her leggings and T-shirt black.

'Hi,' Kelly called out, loud enough for others to turn their heads in case she was addressing them. 'Beautiful day isn't it?' she said as the two women came to a halt by my side.

'It sure is. I'm grabbing the sunshine before we get hit by more terrible weather tomorrow.'

'October can be lovely,' Emma declared.

'Really?' I was thinking of Octobers in LA, of the deep blue skies day-in, day-out.

'Haven't you heard of an Indian Summer?'

I think Gareth might have mentioned it but I hadn't taken much notice. I nodded and smiled.

'I'm done running,' Emma said. 'I'm completely out of practice and unfit.'

'I think you've done brilliantly considering,' Kelly said, giving her friend a firm hug.

'Considering what?' I asked.

'It's her first proper run since having Noah. He's six months old and he's a darling,' Kelly said.

There was a buzzing and Emma lifted her phone out of the pouch round her arm. She read the text. 'I'd better get back. Noah's crying and Andrew's struggling. Despite what Kelly says, he isn't always a darling.'

'No time for tea then?'

'Sorry Kelly, no.'

Kelly looked across at me. 'I was going to ask you to join us. Want to?'

'Sure.'

Walking along with the pair of them I had that sense of being the odd one out that you often get when there's three of you together. We reached The Broadway and Emma headed home, leaving Kelly and me to go in the other direction.

'Sorry I didn't contact you last weekend. I wasn't feeling great on the Sunday morning so skipped the brunch.'

'No problem,' I said, relieved that Kelly at least remembered her suggestion and could give a reason for not getting in touch.

We'd reached Dream Café. I'd never seen it so empty; I guess everyone was outside doing something or other in this Indian Summer of theirs.

'I quite like mint tea in the afternoons. Fancy?' Kelly asked.

'Sounds cool,' I said, the recollection of drinking iced tea on hot days back in Idaho popping up. The smell, the taste, the coolness as it slid down my throat; a memory so powerful that it startled me.

I watched Kelly chatting with the man who had introduced the performers the previous Friday night.

'Who's he?' I asked when she got back with the drinks.

'David. He's Bridget's business partner and the other type of partner, too.'

I lifted my glass, surprised by the touch having expected a cold drink. I took a sip. 'It's a great place they've got here. How long has it been going?'

'I'm not entirely sure; it was open by the time we reached Muswell Hill. When did you move here, Jennifer? Or is Jen better?'

'I prefer Jennifer.' Gareth had called me Jen and I kinda felt that it was reserved for him even though he wasn't around anymore. 'But if you want, Jen is fine.'

'I'll stick with Jennifer.'

I liked Kelly, she just said what she thought without any hidden meanings.

'I've been here for a few months though I left the States years ago.'

'To be with this Gareth you mentioned the other day?'

'Exactly.' I was all set to talk about my time with Gareth then realised that I couldn't. There was a lump in my throat and I was fighting off tears. Gazing down at my hands tightly clasped together, I switched subjects, my question mundane. 'How long have you lived here?'

Kelly surely would have noticed my unease but didn't make a thing of it. 'About two years.'

'Was the move to take this job?'

'God, no. Working here came much later. Darren's business is in the area and we were already living close by.'

'I've seen him in the *Stop Thief!* van.'

'Yep, that's the one. He fits security alarms.'

'The name's cool.'

'It does make people smile.' Kelly looked up. 'Hi, you two. Come and join us.'

Cecelia and Julien had entered the café and the intimacy of our conversation was lost.

Julien showed us what he'd bought in the secondhand bookstore, French language hardbacks by authors I'd never heard of.

Cecelia passed round her iPhone to show us the cover her publishers had chosen for some book she'd written – four shadowy men keeping a distance from each other on an otherwise deserted beach. They looked extremely unhappy.

'What's the book about?' I asked.

'How men cope with separation.'

That got me wondering how Gareth was getting on.

'Men tend to adjust in a different way to women,' Cecelia continued.

How did Cecelia think Gareth should be coping? I wasn't going to ask, of course. All I knew was that I was still finding the split with him impossibly difficult to deal with.

Julien had taken over, comparing the climates of LA and the South of France. Le Mistral. El Niño. La Niña. It felt like he was showing off and I can't say I was enamoured by the topic. God, I was using words like the English did. Actually, this conversation was as boring as hell.

Before we left there was a good outcome though: Cecelia invited me to the group brunch the next day.

8

Angie had many talents but I'd never regarded fortune telling as one of them, so I ignored her flippant comment that Gareth would turn up the next day at Giulio's Diner having been AWOL all week.

I headed downtown that morning for a painful wander past shop windows displaying all the things I'd like but couldn't afford – clothes, shoes, bags, make-up. I'd forgotten that it was Black Friday and everyone was there on the lookout for bargains. Everyone except me that is, because even bargain prices were way too expensive. My bus got caught up in traffic on the way home which gave me minus five minutes to get ready and dash round to Giulio's. I couldn't be too late so had to skip fixing my hair and make-up. Darting round the corner to the diner, I arrived sweaty and stressed.

I got changed in the back office, avoiding a glance in the mirror until the temptation was too great. I shouldn't have done, I looked awful.

'Come on, Jennifer. Move it,' Joe ordered. 'These are for Table 8.'

It was busy; Friday evenings were always the busiest. That's why I didn't see him at first because the tables were full and he was sitting on a swivel stool by the window. I only spotted him when he turned and raised his arm. Stupid me thought it was a wave so I waved back, but his arm stayed up as I headed towards him.

'Ever so sorry but I'm in a bit of a rush tonight. Do you think I could order now?'

'Sure. Something nice?'

'I hope so. What would you suggest?' he asked looking down at the menu.

'No, I meant are you doing something nice tonight?'

'Hardly. We've been working on a new system but there are some glitches to sort out before we present to the client. I'm taking a quick break for food then it's back to the grind.'

'Oh,' was all I could muster.

'I'll have the burger with a Diet Coke, please.'

'Right.' I was still stuck for words.

I took his order, returning with a burger in a bun, fries and onion rings, the fat from the undercooked burger oozing through the soggy bun.

'Thanks. Looks good,' he said as I set the plate down. He sighed. 'All I'm doing at the moment is working. Work, work, work.'

'Then let's go out one evening.'

Did I really say that?

'You mean out as in out?'

Yet more confusion from me. Was this another English expression? Surely the word "out" was clear enough, or did the English say things like "Sleep as in sleep" and "Eat as in eat"?

'I mean out as in not in, not in this place. As in when I'm not working here.'

'As in a date?'

'I didn't say that.' Jeez, I was that close to giving up.

'Sounds good to me.'

'I'm off work tomorrow,' I said as I watched him cutting the burger into small cubes. The bun was like a sponge. (Apologies to Joe because thinking back, I'm possibly being a bit unfair about the quality of the food.)

'Jennifer, to the counter. Table 4 waiting.'

'Coming, Joe. We can meet at The Oracle. It's a bar in Elysian Park.'

'OK. What time?'

'Nine. You will be there?'

'Of course I will. I'm looking forward to it.'

'Jennifer! Now!'

'Coming, Joe.'

~

Angie had been right about Gareth turning up at the diner after all, even if it was no more than a lucky guess. I told her where we were meeting, us girls having got in the habit of doing that to be on the safe side.

'Is it a date?' she asked.

'Date as in date?'

'What?'

'Only kidding. No it is not a date. The poor guy is over here for work. He's got no friends, no social life, so this is just me being neighbourly. I'll tell him all the good places to go, maybe better places to eat, too.' I was making all that up of course. We had hardly spoken so I had no idea about his situation.

'Not true, Jennifer. You've got the hots for him.'

Did I have the hots for Gareth I wondered as I was deciding what to wear the following evening? One thing for sure, I wanted to look good, but choosing wasn't easy. I had the boring stuff worn at interviews for restaurant work and the glitzy stuff left over from when I was trying to get into the showbiz world. I went for alluring because I could now that I was free from Kurt who'd told me he wasn't going to have his girl be a come-on whore whenever we were out. What a great guy!

I felt good in a navy sequinned dress and heels, but I was wearing this for *me*, not for Gareth who I didn't have the hots for.

The Oracle was fashioned in the Wild West style with a long wooden counter and lines of bottles on the shelves behind. I'd thought that if I was going to show Gareth something it might as well be a place with a bit of character. It was hardly authentic though and when I entered, hit by a blast of Bruce Springsteen, I had my doubts.

Gareth was already there, sitting at a table on the far side of the room. He leapt up when he saw me and we moved towards each other, meeting on the open space used as a dance floor, a silver ball casting dots of light onto us.

I was unsure whether to hug him or maybe shake hands with a "How do you do?" like I'd seen in old British movies.

There was no hug or handshake. 'What would you like to drink?' he asked.

'My treat,' I said. 'This can be your introduction to USA culture.'

'What does that entail?'

'Bourbon, I reckon.'

'Then bourbon it is. Please.'

'So take a seat and I'll bring the drinks over.' I smiled. 'Just like when you're at Giulio's.'

He laughed. That was nice. 'Much better than that,' he said, which was also nice.

While I was waiting to be served I was thinking about how the evening might work out. Gareth didn't strike me as a big talker which in a way was good because I hated guys bullshitting, but if true it did mean that it would be up to me to steer the conversation.

I didn't know a thing about him so there was an easy opening line as I was handing him his drink. 'So, you're English.'

'Actually no.'

'Yes, you are.'

'No, I'm not, I'm Welsh. That makes me British but not English.'

'I don't get the difference.'

'It's like Canada and USA. Both are in North America but they're hardly the same country. Americans don't know much about places beyond their own borders, do they?'

If he was waiting for agreement he wasn't going to get it. He was sort of saying we were dumb.

'Anyway,' he continued. 'Wales is a great place and England is shite.'

Why was he saying that about England? The English actors, stage crews and musicians I'd met in Hollywood were nice, not up themselves even though I was a nobody. And anyway, what was so great about Wales?

This might turn out to be a tough night. I knocked back the shot. 'Same again?'

'Why not?'

What was the matter with him, or maybe all the English? Welsh. What was wrong with simply saying "Yes" for fuck's sake.

By the time I was back with our drinks the place was filling and a band were setting up. They were caricatures of cowboy culture in their boots, jeans, check shirts and Stetsons. Embarrassing.

'Looks like they're about to play,' Gareth said as we watched the four men with 1970s haircuts tuning their guitars.

'Howdy folks,' the one with the moustache announced. 'I wanna see y'all on that there dance floor.' I think the man was deliberately using cliches, but I wasn't sure.

They started with *Bad Moon Rising* and in a flash there was a lot of dancing going on. I didn't expect to be joining in so was thinking maybe we should go somewhere quieter – or even go our own separate ways because to be honest this was not going well. *Ramblin' Man* was playing as Gareth made his way to the bar, having insisted that it was his turn to buy the drinks.

He returned during a lull in the avalanche of sound as the band retuned their instruments.

'Look,' Gareth said, 'an apology. I've been so manically busy at work it's like I've forgotten how to socialise. I'm really sorry.' He smiled as the music restarted, the volume up several levels. 'Come on, let's dance.'

He took hold of my hand and we were pushed together in the small space, bashing against bodies as the music blared.

The band played their first slow number, that Foreigner anthem *I want to know what love is*. I adored that song; I was crazy for it. Gareth pulled me close.

I'm liking this I was thinking as he held me tight in his arms.

9

Dream Café was heaving by the time I arrived for Sunday brunch the next day. The others were already there, tightly packed around an oval table.

'Hi, Jennifer,' Kelly called out and the others echoed her greeting. Andrew shuffled along to make room for me in between him and Julien. Sitting next to the two men wouldn't have been my first choice but at least I was with the group and I was thankful for that.

'It's so popular on Sundays you have to book a table, 'Andrew said. 'This place is a goldmine, packed from breakfast to late evening seven days a week.'

'And deserved,' Julien added.

Darren and the women opposite were chatting away as the three of us fell silent.

'How long have you been living in Muswell Hill?' was my boring ask to get the conversation going.

Julien got in first. 'A little over a year ago I moved in with Cecelia. Before that I lived closer to the city centre and before that, I was in France of course.'

'What made you move to England?'

'Work.'

'And you, Andrew? When did you move to Muswell Hill?'

'We've lived in the house for two years but were in a flat in the area for years beforehand. Emma's told me that you live in the plot that got bombed.'

'Pardon?'

Andrew proceeded to explain that the Germans had fired V2 rockets over London towards the end of the world war and one had landed in my street.

'I've seen photographs of the destruction; three houses were destroyed. It took years to do anything about it other than to clear the space. They finally put up your block in the early sixties.'

'Thanks for that. I was wondering why my building is in the middle of all the old ones.'

'Sadly your flats were built before preservation of character was considered important. It is rather … well, let's just say it's not my cup of tea.'

'You mean it's ugly, which I agree. It's OK to say that.'

With the arrival of the food the three of us sat in silence again with me enviously catching snippets of conversation across the table.

"It was an absolute hoot …"

"I bet it was, you must have …"

"And I'll tell you, I almost wet myself laughing …"

"So she told me that …"

Having eaten my poached egg on toast and drained my coffee, it was up to me to think of something interesting to talk about because I wasn't getting any help.

'I liked the poems you read the other night,' I told Andrew.

'Thank you. They were part of my new collection. I've shifted from dystopian to humorous themes recently, though I'm not sure that was a wise move.'

'Why not?'

'I can tell you why,' Julien said. 'This man, he thinks that dystopian is more intellectual. Which,' he added with a sly smile, 'makes him somewhat elitist. A snob.'

'Surely what matters is to write something that people enjoy,' I suggested.

'But which people? That, you see, is Andrew's dilemma. He would rather have a small group of intelligentsias admiring his work rather than a vast audience of common people.'

'Thank you for explaining my rationale, Julien, but I think I can do that for myself.'

'Peut-être.'

God, there was tension in the air.

'Is that your job then, Andrew? A poet.'

'Well, Jen, I –'

'Jennifer, if you don't mind.'

'Jennifer. I am a published poet, but I also teach.'

'And you, Julien?'

'I teach, though I am at a university not a school.'

Andrew reddened.

'Andrew. Earth to Andrew.' It was Emma calling across. 'Can't you hear your son screaming? I think we'd better head back.'

Emma had lifted Noah out of his stroller and was cuddling him but the crying didn't cease.

'You go, Emma. I'll catch up as soon as I've paid.'

'Don't worry about that,' Julien said. 'I'll settle and you can contribute next time.'

'OK. Thanks, Julien.'

I was kinda confused about what the men thought of each other – anything between loathing and affection it seemed.

Kelly was by my side. 'Hiya. Everything OK?' she asked.

I was fairly certain she hadn't overheard the conversation on our side of the table and it was a genuine question.

'Great.'

'Well, if you haven't got anything planned for next Sunday morning come along again.'

I wasn't going to tell her that it was my fortieth birthday the following Sunday and I wasn't going to add that I had absolutely nothing planned.

'Sure.'

I would join them I was thinking, but I'd arrive early to avoid sitting next to Julien and Andrew again.

10

As the band played *I want to know what love is* Gareth and I were clinging together like it was the most natural thing in the world and we would be on that dance floor until the end of time. When is he going to kiss me, I was wondering? Will I say yes to spending the night with him?

The music stopped and Gareth pulled away. 'Nice,' he said, just the one word, nice. I followed him back to our table.

'Another drink?' I asked, running a hand across his hair, across that bob of red-blond curls that wouldn't stay down.

'I'd like one but I'd best not. Bloody work. I've got that team meeting early tomorrow morning to sort out the blips before we present to clients on Monday.'

It was fair enough but I still felt cheated. 'Fine. No problem.'

'I'll get a taxi,' he said, taking out his phone. 'They can drop you off first and then go on to my place.'

'It's OK, I only live round the corner. I can walk.'

'Is that safe?'

'Not as safe as in Wales.' Cutting comments would be the death of me. I knew that but still out they came.

'You're right; probably not,' he said, not picking up the sarcasm. 'I'll walk you home and then pick up a taxi from yours.'

He was heading for the exit before I could choose between, "There's really no need" and "Thanks, that's great."

I chased after him.

'Left or right?' he asked as we stepped onto the sidewalk.

'Left.'

We were soon standing outside Angie's unimpressive condo with me waiting for him to do or say something. A hug. A kiss. A change of mind and a ride back to his place. An announcement that he was leaving LA the next day. Something. Anything.

'Look,' he began, his face again serious, his eyes kinda odd with a streetlight reflecting off his thick-framed glasses. 'I'll be away for a few days, there's a meeting in Alabama, but if you're up for it I'd like to see you again.'

'Sure, I'm up for it.'

'Good.' Just the one word.

'Let's swap numbers.'

'We can do that or else I'll see you at the diner when I get back.'

'I'm not in every night; sometimes I'm doing days,' I told him.

'I discovered that when I was there last Wednesday evening. I thought maybe you'd left.'

'I wish I could quit but I'm still there waiting to be discovered.'

'Discovered?'

'Surely you know that every young waitress in LA wants to be a movie star.'

'You could be one, you've got a great personality. And if you don't mind me saying, you're gorgeous.'

You'd be hard put to find a woman who would mind being called gorgeous. 'That's a nice thing to say. Thank you.'

It had taken a while but we were kissing. I liked it, playful, not like some guys who used their tongue like a missile.

Gareth must have had an eye on the road because he stepped back and lifted an arm to alert the yellow cab heading our way. 'I'd better take this,' he said as the vehicle slowed, 'and I'll see you as soon as I get back.'

I stood on the sidewalk until the cab was out of sight. My thoughts were a bit mashed. The dancing, the kisses, him calling me gorgeous, those were the positives. Against that were his obsession with work and turning affection on and off like a tap. And we never did swap numbers.

Angie was waiting by the door when I came in.

'Well?' she asked. 'And before you tell lies, I did see that kiss.'

I was open about what had happened that evening and she suggested that the things I found odd were maybe down to the Brits doing things differently.

'The jury's out,' I told her. 'I'm tired, I'm off to bed.'

'Sweet dreams, honey.'

~

Gareth had said he would be away for a few days and now I was wondering how long that meant? Three days? More? If it were four it would take us to Wednesday, my night off. Hopefully he'd remember that, having tried to catch me at work the previous Wednesday.

He came into the diner late on the Thursday, close to the end of my shift. I was wiping down tables.

'I've just got back,' he said. Joe looked across and I carried on wiping. 'And I've been thinking about you nonstop.' I wasn't going to tell him that he'd been on my mind nonstop, too.

'Good trip?' I asked.

'Who cares? When can we go out again?'

'As in a date?'

He laughed. He seemed more relaxed than I remembered from the last time. He'd had a haircut too, the curls cropped. It suited him.

'Definitely a date. What about tomorrow or Saturday?' he suggested.

Angie was planning something for the Saturday because it was my thirtieth birthday, even though I didn't see that as worth celebrating.

'Saturday's difficult, a friend's organising something.'

'A male friend or a female friend?'

'I'm done, Joe. I'll pick up my stuff and head off now. See you tomorrow.' I turned back to face Gareth. 'Wait here for me, will you?'

I changed and tidied myself in the back office.

'A female,' I told Gareth as we were leaving Giulio's. 'The girl I'm sharing with.' We paused on the sidewalk outside the diner. The breeze was refreshing after the sticky heat inside. 'It's my birthday on Saturday.'

As I said that I regretted it; there was no need for Gareth to know. But he snatched the news and made something of it. 'If your friend has booked you in for your actual birthday then I want to reserve your birthday eve.'

'Sorry, I can't. I work Fridays.'

Angie had insisted we do something to celebrate but as yet nothing was arranged. And it really was no big deal because birthdays, even milestone ones, were a time for commiseration not celebration for us gals, stuck in Hollywood with our fantasies about a career in movies. If I told Angie I was seeing Gareth on Saturday evening she wouldn't mind. She'd take me downtown during the day instead.

'I might be able to cancel my friend if you really do want to see me on Saturday.'

'Much more than really.'

'OK.'

'Great. I'll pick you up outside your place at eight.'

~

On the dot of eight there was a blast of a horn. I stepped out to be greeted by a cab with Gareth standing on the sidewalk. He opened the door for me. 'In you go, birthday girl.'

We drove to Santa Monica, stopping at a restaurant that overlooked the Pacific. The place yelled expensive from the pastel blue stucco exterior to the marbled foyer to the glass-fronted dining room with views to die for.

I had to say something when I saw the menu. 'This is crazy. It's way too expensive.'

'You're worth every penny. Every cent, I mean.'

Gareth was going to have to use a lot of pennies or cents to pay for his choice of wine, a Californian white that was near the bottom of a page that listed wines in price order.

Our conversation was all natural and easy-going, him asking about how I ended up in LA. I got to talking about my childhood on the farm in Idaho, my growing restlessness and the escape to Hollywood with a naïve certainty that I would be discovered. Me and thousands of other hopefuls.

'What's so special about the ones who do make it?' he asked.

I wasn't going to mention "giving favours".

'I guess it's largely down to luck,' I told him.

He paused, sweeping up paté with his knife and spreading it onto a thin rectangle of toast. 'If you were starting again would you do anything different?'

'No.' A short, honest reply.

He seemed OK with that and sort of took on the role of a school counsellor. Assuming waitressing wasn't going to be my lifelong career, did I have any longer term plans he wanted to know.

There was no answer to give. Stalling for time I took a mouthful of Waldorf Salad which, despite the huge cost, tasted no different to any other Waldorf Salad I'd eaten.

'That's enough about me. What about you?' I asked.

11

It had been another shit day at work. Heading home past Victorian splendour, I reached my ugly apartment block which seemed uglier than ever. Once inside I collapsed into an armchair with a beer by my side.

In a roundabout way it was thanks to Gareth that I was living in Muswell Hill, managing the catering teams in local care homes. When we were in the States and I was stuck doing dead end waitressing jobs, he'd encouraged me to get a qualification.

I should be grateful but that day I'd happily have served food and wiped tables rather than have responsibility for recruitment at the care homes. Finding staff and enough money to pay them was a constant struggle, but with three people quitting to work in supermarkets on a single day, I was right back to square one searching for assistant cooks. If the worst came to the worst I'd have to step in as temporary cover and that would be on top of carrying on with my regular duties.

The intercom buzzed. I was that close to leaving it but when you don't have any visitors even the possibility of an Amazon delivery sends you rushing to respond.

It was Emma.

'Hi, Jennifer. Can I pop in?'

'Sure,' I said, pleased despite having been geared up for a chill out hour alone.

'Delivery for Jennifer,' Emma announced as I opened the door. Kitted out in running gear, she was holding a bunch of flowers wrapped in newspaper. 'They're from our garden. It's been a brilliant summer for flowers, we're overloaded. So here you are.'

'Thanks, they're lovely.'

'That's probably it for healthy looking flowers now that autumn's arrived.'

Hadn't she gone on about Indian Summers a few days earlier? I let it pass.

'I can't stay though. I've grabbed some time for a run but I'm back on baby duty soon. Actually, apart from giving you these, I wanted to check that you're OK for brunch this Sunday.'

'Yeah. It's nice of everyone letting me join in.' I was trying to look enthusiastic while remembering the previous time, a dull morning sandwiched between two of the men.

'Andrew did tell me that last Sunday was a bit awkward. Apparently Julien was in one of his confrontational moods. He can be a pain.'

'It was fine. Really.'

'I'll make sure you sit somewhere where there's interesting gossip going on this time. That will definitely involve Kelly because she's always got amusing stories about the café to tell. Darren's fun too, what with his adventures of a security alarm fitter.

'When I see him out in that *Stop Thief!* van it always makes me smile.'

'Me, too. I'd better be off or I'll have a grumpy Andrew. See you on Sunday.'

Emma paused having spotted the small collection of cards on the cabinet to the side of the door.

'Forty! When was that?'

'Not quite yet, my birthday's on Sunday. The cards from the States arrived early, I suppose people wanted to make sure I got them in time. I wish they didn't splash my age in sparkly silver font though; I really don't want to be reminded every time I leave the apartment.'

'That's silly, forty's a great age. I'll be the same as you in a few months' time.'

You have a partner, you have a baby, you own a house in Muswell Hill, so it's not quite the same. 'If you think it's great you're a better person than me.'

'Well, I will be letting everyone know about this and we'll decide what to do to celebrate.'

'Please don't, Emma. I'd rather let it pass by quietly.'

'We'll see,' Emma said as she edged towards the door.

As soon as she'd gone I collected a bag of chips – packet of crisps that is – from the kitchen to go with the beer I had yet to start drinking. I streamed random chill music on Spotify while glancing at the birthday cards. They stared back. There were four of them, one from a friend I'd left behind in LA, one from Mom and Dad, and even one from my brother Daniel, now married with three kids. That left one more. I'd recognised the handwriting on the envelope, making me part furious, part inquisitive and part desperate to hear from him. I wasn't going to wait until my birthday – I ripped it open – and having opened one of the cards it seemed pointless not to see them all early.

I walked over to the cabinet, picked up that fourth card and for the umpteenth time read it.

A special day, ten years after our own special first day together. I miss you, Jen. Love, Gareth.

12

You couldn't ask for a more romantic setting to celebrate my thirtieth in style – that magnificent view from the stunning Santa Monica restaurant with the lights low, the table candlelit – and there we were talking like at a business meeting. Having been interviewed about my own background I was now finding out about Gareth's childhood.

For the record he was Welsh, although I already knew that, raised in a village near a small town where his dad was a postman. He didn't dwell on it but I could tell life hadn't been easy; there'd been difficulties in the family. By the time we were being served our desserts along with another bottle of wine, we'd reached Gareth getting a place at university. That was when he was around eighteen which meant another half of his life to plough through. Of course I was interested, but surely not tonight I was thinking. I turned away from Gareth to admire the spectacular sunset.

'Let's skip a bit,' I said, looking back. 'How come you're here in the States?'

'My company is part-American, part-British owned. This isn't the first time I've worked over here but it is the biggest project I've been given, a nine-month job so I've got about another six to go.'

I made a mental note of that, it gave me the time frame if we were ever going to be in a relationship. I was hoping we would because I liked the guy, I was attracted to him, but he seemed tense and that tension was rubbing off on me.

'What sort of project?' I asked, unable to think of a topic away from his work.

'Designing IT systems to solve business problems.'

'Mmmm, that sounds complicated.'

I lost the plot fast once he started going on about terabytes and coding options and was stirring the leftovers of mango ice cream and raspberry coulis together on my plate when he burst out laughing.

'I am completely mad. Talking about work when I'm with a beautiful woman.' He was speaking loudly, almost shouting, maybe because there was a lot of noise around us, maybe the alcohol was getting to him. We were on our third bottle. 'I'm really sorry, Jennifer,' he continued. 'It's been so hard lately. I think I've lost the ability to have a normal conversation.'

'It's OK, don't worry about it. And anyway, you had to listen to me go on about my life.'

'Yeah, true,' he joked. 'So do you want to hear about the coding options I'm installing on a mainframe?'

'I'd love to.'

He had a nice smile; we were connecting at last.

'Seriously though, do you want to come back to mine tonight?' he pretty well yelled.

At that precise moment there appeared to be a lull in conversation at tables close by, maybe a coincidence, though probably because fellow diners couldn't avoid hearing his question. Looking across at us they were waiting to catch my reply.

'I wouldn't say no,' I said teasingly, and being English or Welsh, he knew exactly what I meant and started laughing again.

We took a cab back to his place, a half hour or so drive. There was some light-hearted chatting, some kissing and a bit of looking out the windows in silence as we passed through the outskirts of LA. It wasn't exactly an embarrassed silence but I was struggling to think of appropriate conversation and I imagine Gareth felt the same. We were on our way to his place to have sex, so what was there to talk about? What type of foreplay do you like? I suppose we could have messed around more on that back seat but Gareth didn't seem the type which was fine by me. I'd been mauled enough in cars by insensitive men to last me a lifetime.

We reached Pasadena. I do love the part of the city that has those crazy 1920s buildings that look like cakes covered in pastel-coloured icing. Moving on from downtown we stopped outside a sleek modern block. Gareth took my hand and we made our way upstairs to his condo. Stepping inside you could tell it was a rental and a place where a single guy lived, meaning functional with little personal stamp or flair.

'Nice place,' I said as we stood by the entrance. I didn't quite know what was to happen next. Most men I'd slept with tended to pounce once they knew I was up for it. They'd be taking their clothes off fast, maybe taking mine off too, and we'd be groping each other before you could say lickety-split.

We were still in the hallway, entwined and kissing but not progressing. I think Gareth was nervous and he was making me nervous too.

'I'll just go to the bathroom,' I told him.

'That door,' he said, pointing.

I didn't need the bathroom but it would give me time to think. I looked in the mirror at a world-weary face that perhaps no longer attracted him now that we had moved to the point of love-making. OK, I'd reached thirty, but that wasn't going to make me uninviting compared to when I was twenty-nine. Should I add a layer of make-up? Or I could take my clothes off and reappear naked. I lifted off my dress.

OK, this is it I said to myself ahead of stepping out in my bra and panties. This was either going to be an exciting sensual moment or I'm going to feel like an absolute idiot and want the floor to swallow me up.

One. Two. Three.

Gareth was standing outside the door naked except for Calvin Klein boxers and his Clark Kent glasses which got me giggling. He was laughing, though only for a couple of seconds before we lunged at each other, stumbling towards the bedroom in an intoxicated tangle and falling onto the bed.

It was a great night. I can't speak for the whole male population of England, Britain or Wales, but this sex with Gareth might well have been better than anything I'd ever experienced with an American man. Intense, unselfish, sensitive – what a combo.

Lying there early morning, still dark outside with me wide awake and him by my side out for the count, I was considering whether it really had been so special. Maybe it was just the wine, the improvement on Kurt (not difficult), or the thrill of him being foreign (even though not a hot-blooded Italian or French man). I dismissed these thoughts because it had nothing to do with any national characteristic. It was about one man, a man who had cared about my enjoyment ahead of his own and that was lovely. Often in the past I'd been made to feel that my body was redundant immediately after making love, but Gareth had taken me in his arms, pulled me close and held me tight all night.

Sitting together chatting away over breakfast, Gareth was again apologising about feeling the pressure of work, the tight deadlines, his clients' unrealistic expectations, the long hours. It was easy to see that it was really getting him down.

'You've made me realise how obsessed and uptight I've been. Thank you.'

'Thank you for what exactly?'

'Well, for being with me today, for last night, for showing me that there are far more important things than work.'

It was an honest thing to say and seemed true because I could sense the change in him that morning and I was liking what I saw.

'And for being you,' he added, which made me blush. I don't think anyone had ever said anything like that to me before.

'That's such a nice thing to say.'

'It's only the truth. But hey, what shall we do today?' he asked.

'Bad news. On Sundays I'm on day shift at the diner. I'm going to have to leave soon.'

'Can't you call in sick?'

'It wouldn't be fair. Sunday is our busiest day, it's when we get the families in. I can't let Joe down.'

'Tomorrow then.'

'I don't have to be in until early evening but I guess you'll be working during the day.'

'You know what, I'm going to skip work. The others know what they're doing and they can get on without having me around.'

'You sure?'

'Absolutely. It's time for me to ease up. And besides, there's no way I'm going to go for over forty-eight hours without seeing you again.'

'OK, let's do something together. As in a date.'

'Yep. As in a date.'

13

Emma texted me early Sunday morning. *Happy 40th Birthday!*

Thanks.

Doing anything special?

Not really. I'm not being negative but I don't feel like celebrating.

But is it OK to pop over early evening to drop something off?

Please not a present, there's no need.

I've got you something small. Otherwise it will end up in the bin.

OK then.

Rereading the texts I felt guilty about being abrupt. It was a nice gesture and good of Emma to care. I thought about texting an apology but that might make things worse.

Here's what I did during the day of my fortieth birthday – I cleaned the flat from top to bottom which, despite the small space, kept me busy for over three hours. Next I did the ironing before nipping out to the shops on The Broadway to pick up something for dinner. Chicken Kiev.

It was six-thirty and I was wondering what Emma had meant by early evening. Should I put the Kiev in the oven or wait until after she'd been round? It took thirty minutes to cook so the likelihood was that she'd turn up just as I was about to eat. Maybe best to wait.

The decision was made for me; the intercom buzzed. I pressed to open the door without speaking. Immediately I knew something was up because it sounded like a herd of elephants were making their way up the stairwell. I should have realised – the whole gang were there. Darren started the Happy Birthday song, Emma gave me an enormous bouquet of flowers and Julien handed over a bottle of champagne.

'A toast. Then into your glad rags, Cinderella, because the restaurant is booked for seven fifteen.'

For a nanosecond I was angry, but that dissolved to be replaced by the delight that these almost strangers cared enough about me to organise something.

The women were in dresses, the men in jackets, and I was wearing jeans. 'You're right, I do need to get changed.'

'First a drink though. Show me where the glasses are,' Kelly said.

'And a vase for those,' Emma added.

Having led them into the kitchen and pointed at cupboards, Kelly flung her arms around me. 'It's lovely to see you smiling. We're going to have a great evening.'

'I'll make sure I won't get drunk this time!'

'No problem if you do. We know where you live and there are six of us to carry you home if necessary.'

We crammed together in the small living room space for the drink before I left them to quickly get changed. It was weird dressing up; I hadn't had a reason to since the job interview ahead of my move to London.

'Wow, stunning,' Darren said as I joined the others.

I'm not sure about stunning but I did feel good in my Jigsaw dress. I couldn't afford and didn't need it but had fallen in love with it in the window display.

'See,' Darren added, 'women can still look great in their forties.'

A short, stunned silence ensued, broken by Cecelia. 'You mean like me?'

'You might not realise it, Darren, but you're being highly offensive,' Kelly told her husband.

'But why? Isn't it a compliment to say that Jennifer looks smashing.'

'Apologies everyone, see what I have to put up with.' Kelly took hold of Darren's hand and dragged him towards the door. 'Come on everybody, let's go.'

'How are we getting to wherever we're going?' I asked.

'Walking. It's that Italian place with the real pizza oven.'

Ten minutes later we were sitting at a round table, Emma having made sure that I was in between her and Kelly with Darren as far away as possible.

The evening raced by. I forgot that I was a stranger in a strange city. I forgot how difficult the recent past had been. I forgot I had turned forty.

When my phone buzzed my bag glowed as the screen lit up. I considered leaving it. I was enjoying myself, and besides, I have this thing about people looking at their phones when they should be focusing on the company. However, in the remote possibility that there was a crisis in one of the care homes, I did have a responsibility to have a quick check. It would have to be a major crisis to call me out over the weekend though, a kitchen fire or an accident with a chopping knife.

By the time I got the phone out the call had terminated, chased by a text message. *Please call.*

'Anything important?' Kelly asked.

'It's only my brother.'

'Calling from America?'

'Yeah.'

'That's nice. See, everyone wants to wish you a happy fortieth.'

'I think the last time he called to wish me a happy birthday was on my thirtieth. We don't get on well.'

Another text. To the point. *Call back NOW.*

'I'd better see what he wants.'

There was no reason to move out of earshot from the others. On the rare occasions when my brother called me it was for a curt telling off, leaving me feeling intimidated. But now, being with newfound friends, a little drunk and separated by five thousand miles, I was ready to take anything he might want to throw at me. I called him back.

When the brief call ended I couldn't make eye contact, I couldn't say a word.

'What's up, Jennifer? Why are you crying?' Kelly asked.

'It's my dad,' I managed to utter. 'He's been rushed to hospital. He's in ICU.'

14

Our Monday daytime date was back in Pasadena – my choice. I'd already visited a few times and loved walking around the cute town with its parks, museums and trendy cafes. To be honest there was another reason why I wanted to be there – so that we could end up at Gareth's apartment with plenty of time to spare before I had to leave for Giulio's. I called Gareth on the Sunday evening after work to confirm arrangements and guess he had the same idea about what we might be doing once the sightseeing was out the way. "A day here is a brilliant idea; I've hardly had a chance to explore the city. And then maybe back to my place afterwards."

Gareth offered to collect me from LA but I told him the train was easier and that I'd meet him at Memorial Park Station. He was there already but didn't spot me because I came out from a side exit. It meant I could check whether he was as gorgeous as I had thought. He was. That hairstyle of his made me smile and having sneaked up to his side, I ruffled it.

'Here I am.'

'Hello, Jennifer,' he said. 'Or better still, Hi there, Jen,' he added with a terrible attempt at an American accent.

'I hope you're not considering acting as a career!'

He frowned; his eyebrows sinking low behind those Clark Kent glasses. 'I'm sorry, I …'

'Dreadful joke. Ignore. Kiss me though. Please.'

Gareth obliged and I wondered whether we should abandon the sightseeing part of the day. We didn't though and I led him to wedding cake buildings with exaggerated architecture like from a Disney film set.

We took our time wandering around, frequently lingering to comment on our favourite buildings. It was all so natural and relaxed and I'd only been with the guy for a few hours in total. We left the historic centre of the city and headed over to Brookside Park, peering into the grounds of the palatial dwellings, imagining what sort of people lived in places like Gamble House and Bentze House. It turned into a game of creating fantasies. A recluse sitting in a single room in a vast Gothic home, the furniture covered in dust sheets. A host drunk and drugged to near death following his nightly wild parties. A tiny, old lady spending her day making herself cups of coffee and baking biscuits to feed the birds in her garden.

I felt secure and comfortable, with escalating thoughts of what was to come. By the time we had paused outside the Museum of History I was sizzling.

'Do you want to go in or shall we head back to my place?' Gareth asked.

'Get a cab. Now!'

'But what about lunch?'

'You're joking …'

He was. He'd already hailed a cab and was smiling.

When we reached his building we scampered up to his place, falling into each other's arms as soon as we were inside.

Have I built up expectations way beyond the reality I was thinking? He was running his hand up my thigh. Hell no, this was reality alright.

I was woken by the chime of nearby bells: it was three o' clock.

'Hungry?' he asked.

'Sure.'

'I'll make us lunch.'

'I'd like a shower first.'

Gareth joined me in the bathroom and it was gone four before we reached the kitchen.

I flicked through *The Economist* which was on the table while he was preparing the food. Definitely not my type of read.

'You're going to love this,' he said, handing me one of the two plates he was carrying.

'Thank you, this is absolutely wonderful.'

'But you haven't tasted it yet.'

'You don't remember, do you?'

'Remember what?'

'You're always calling Giulio's food wonderful. Those were the first words I heard you speak.'

'Really? Anyway, you will love this.'

'It's a sandwich.' I lifted up the top slice. 'With cheese in it.'

'But not your usual cheese; this is Gorwydd Caerphilly. Once you've tasted it you'll never be able to eat American cheese again. And remarkably, they sell it at the deli round the corner because it's almost impossible to get hold of over here.'

I wasn't convinced that the only store in the whole of California that sold *go with carefully* or whatever was his one, but I was more thinking about that word "remarkably." It sounded so old-fashioned, so English.

'Remarkably decent weather we're having at the moment,' I joked, my attempt at an English accent quite possibly as bad as his earlier try at an American one. I took a bite of the sandwich. It was OK.

'And?'

'Remarkably flavoursome.'

Isn't it funny how one minute you're pressed against each other, ecstatic and gasping, and the next you're sitting down eating a cheese sandwich? I'd always felt edgy with a guy immediately after sex, it took me a while to switch moods. But now I was totally chilled. Sex followed by a conversation about *go with carefully* cheese was fine by me.

Another chime of the nearby bells got me looking at my phone – it was five o'clock and I had to be at the diner by six-thirty.

'Five minutes then I have to go,' I said.

'Call in and apologise for a no show,' Gareth suggested.

I didn't hesitate. Lifting up my phone I dialled.

'Hi Joe,' my voice low and subdued. 'I've gone down with something and I've been sick. Obviously I won't be coming in tonight, it's too risky. Hopefully I'll be fine by tomorrow though. I'll call you first thing to let you know.'

Good old Joe, hoping I wasn't too bad and that I got well quick. Although feeling guilty, Monday was the quietest night and I knew there was family around to help out in an emergency.

'Done,' I said.

'Great. What shall we do? We could hang out here for the rest of today or else head into LA.'

'I'm happy to chill out here. It's a nice change and relaxing being somewhere quiet.'

'I suppose Pasadena is pretty dull compared to LA. I thought it would be a good idea to live away from all the noise but it's turned out to be a pain. The journey to where I'm working, it's near Giulio's, is a nightmare despite a six-lane highway which still can't cope with all the commuter traffic streaming in.'

'Why don't you take the tram? It's faster than driving.'

'I tried but I'd need a taxi to get me through the centre after the tram. Driving is still quicker.'

'So are you saying you're sorry to be out here?'

'Not after what you took me to see today. I do live in a concrete cube though, but you can't have everything.'

'This place isn't so bad.'

'I'm afraid it is and the interior doesn't make up for the exterior. It's like I'm living in a clinic, everything white, functional, boring.'

'Not the bed!' I'd assumed the décor was his taste or lack of it, but of course being a rental he wouldn't have had any say. 'What colors would you choose?'

'Dark shades – maroon, purple, navy.'

This was unreal; these were the moody ones I loved. I told him so.

'Well, who knows, Jen? Maybe one day we'll be deciding on colours together.'

I was torn between thinking things were going too fast and that it might be wonderful. Hang on though I told myself, excluding taking his orders at the diner I'd only been with this guy three times.

'Don't worry, I'm not pushing anything,' he said.

I was regretting not responding fast enough; I definitely didn't want his apology.

Say we did stick together and at the end of his six months in the States he asked me to come back with him to … would it be to Wales? Would I go? I had little idea who he was yet; it's not as if you get the full picture in the whirlwind first days of a relationship. But say he was as nice as I was thinking, would I go then? I weighed up what I'd be giving up. Life in LA. The job at the diner. Family in Idaho. Friends. The loss of friends was the only one that mattered. I wish I could have added Mom and Dad, too, but there was a lot of making up needed for that to be the case.

'What's Idaho like?' Gareth was asking like he was tuned into my thoughts. 'I've never been there.'

'There's no hurry unless you want to be a farmer.'

'Is that really what you think?'

'Sort of. Where I was brought up it's all farms and not much else. There are some nice parts if you head out to the mountains, but most tourists are passing through on their way to Yellowstone or the Rockies rather than stopping anywhere in Idaho for long.' As I said this I realised how unfair I was bring; it was the teenage me speaking. The mountains, the skiing, the forests, the rafting and fishing – there were some beautiful places.

'Maybe one day I'll visit. I'd like to – with you.'

I changed the subject, wary of exposing too much about my family. 'Idaho does have one claim to fame. We make a lot of the processed stuff that us Americans call cheese.'

He smiled, a lovely smile that was kinda laid back. 'Really? I'll look it up later. Do you go back to see your family much?'

I didn't want to answer that one either. Although my escape to LA hadn't gone down well with Mom and Dad, I'd never intended to break the bond because I loved the pair of them. At first I went home every Thanksgiving and Christmas. Comments like, "Surely you aren't gonna be a waitress forever" bugged me but I would bite my lip, smile at the right times, help in the kitchen and ask how things were going on the farm.

'I used to go a couple of times a year but then things got difficult,' I told Gareth, hoping he would be leaving it at that.

'Difficult? In what way?'

'I guess we just drifted apart. We ran out of things to say to each other.'

We'd be sitting at that old wooden kitchen table decked in the same red gingham tablecloth that I'd seen as a child, and there'd be long periods of silence. I'd drink as much of their rationed sweet wine as I could before making off to my bedroom for a shot of bourbon and a sniff of coke. I was into drink and drugs in those early years away.

'They must be happy whenever they do see you though,' Gareth persisted.

I used to keep out of everyone's way as much as possible, hungover in my bedroom each morning; off into town in the afternoons with nothing to do but wander round aimlessly as darkness descended early; then back home for another silent evening. I'd stay two or three nights before escaping back to LA.

'We sort of fell out one year so I haven't been back for a while.'

I wasn't the good little girl anymore and I saw my parents' concern about my future as an imposition. "It looks like your dream of being an actress isn't gonna to happen," my Dad said one morning, having tapped softly on my bedroom door. He'd come in even though I'd called out for him to go away. He offered to help me that day, said he wasn't sure how but maybe paying for training for something. Would I think about it? "Look," I snapped, "I'm alright, I'll find something without your help." I wasn't nice back then in my early twenties. I'd like to think that I'm not a bad person, that it was a period in my life when I was full of frustration, fearful of failure, uncertain about the future, scarred by a couple of awful relationships, all that plus the effect of the drugs and alcohol. It was a long list. "Fair enough," I remember Dad saying, looking real sad. He left me to it; there was a gentle click as he closed my bedroom door and I felt so shit I needed something to calm me down.

Minutes later Daniel burst in. He'd seen Dad upset and was there to get at me. We'd never got on well but while I'd found LA and all that went with living there, he'd found God which made the divide worse. He caught me sniffing and with the palm of his hand he slammed the white powder across the floor. I thought he was about to hit me and screamed at him. He was screaming back as Mom and Dad came rushing in.

'What's going on?' Mom asked.

'It's nothing, we're good,' I said.

'Hardly good. Your daughter is an addict. My sister is a cokehead.'

I couldn't deny it, Daniel was pointing towards the floor, the navy rug looking like a starlit Idaho sky.

'I'd better leave,' I said and no one was rushing to stop me as I pulled my belongings together.

'I'll take you to the bus depot,' Dad said.

'It's OK, I'll walk.'

'Don't be juvenile, it's pitch black and freezing cold out there and it's way too far.'

We drove in silence until we reached the parking lot. Dad got out first and opened the door for me. He was holding my bag.

'Whatever you do, Jennifer, you make sure you take care of yourself.'

'Sure, Dad.' We hugged and part of me didn't want to let go of him.

I sat there sobbing in the otherwise empty waiting room until the morning bus arrived, then I sobbed some more all the way to LA. What to do was racing through my head; maybe turn right round and head back home. Call them to apologise? Write them a letter like people did in the old days? I sniffed some coke on the near-empty bus and decided to sleep on it.

I slept on it for days, then weeks, then months, and then it was too late to do anything.

'Haven't you seen them since when you fell out?' Gareth was asking me.

I wasn't going to tell him any more about the past, it was too painful and too private. 'We do call and we send each other the usual cards, but no, I haven't gone back for over five years.'

'Surely it's time to move on. Let me come with you to see them.'

I took hold of his hand and squeezed it; that was a kind offer. 'Let's see,' I said.

He didn't ask again for a long time. Maybe he was hoping that I'd suggest it once we got to know each other better, but I wasn't planning to do that.

15

Kelly was a star when I told her that Dad had been rushed to the hospital. She took me home and was soon on her phone arranging flights. At 10.30 the next morning I was up in the sky on a Delta flight to Salt Lake City. Ten hours later I'd landed and was in a cab on my way to the hospital in Pocatello.

I was too late: Dad was dead. My strong, kind Dad who had worked so hard on that farm, never complaining about the summer heat or the winter snow, the long hours of toil to get crops out the ground, the struggle to make ends meet when competing with the giant farms further south. He was eternal: it was impossible, he couldn't be dead.

My distraught Mom was saying the same thing over and over again. 'It happened so quickly. There wasn't even a chance to say a proper goodbye.'

What is a proper goodbye, I wondered? All my latent guilt about leaving the family behind, deserting them, came gushing in. 'I'm sorry I wasn't here, Mom,' I apologised as we hugged.

Despite the grief she was generous with reflection. 'There's nothing to forgive, Jennifer. You have your own life to lead and that's fine by me. I am glad you're here with us now though.'

We hugged some more and cried as we reminisced ahead of the funeral. I got to know Mom as a person rather than Mom as the parent, a woman with hopes and dreams and feelings just like everyone else. She had spent her entire adult life on the farm, for months each winter in near isolation. That was where Dad toiled so that was good enough for her. Was it though because she was probing me for stories about my travels and experiences?

'What adventures you've had, Jennifer. What excitement.'

'Hardly,' I said because it had never felt that way to me. I could have told her that adventure didn't always bring happiness, but although she never said it, I did sense that she would have liked to have made more of her life. When I added, 'Mom, it's never too late to take on something new,' she shrugged and smiled.

I guess the funeral was like any other funeral – awful. Dad must have been a popular guy judging by the number of mourners at the church. I knew so little about him; who were these people offering their condolences and asking me how I was getting on living in England? It was like I'd missed several chapters in the middle of a book, a good book, and it got me questioning whether those decisions I'd made over my adult years had been the right ones.

'What are you going to do now, Mom?' I asked after the well-wishing acquaintances had departed and we were alone in the kitchen tidying up. My return to

England was booked for three days later but I was having second thoughts. Should I stay over longer to support her? When I offered to, her answer surprised me. She had a plan which she must have been mulling over immediately after Dad died: she intended to stay with her sister. 'Just for a short while,' she said.

Maisie lived in Wilmington, North Carolina. I'd met her a few times when I was a kid and liked her a lot. She seemed the exact opposite to Mom, a career-minded woman with strong views about everything. I remembered her peppering me with questions about my future and it's just possible that she sowed the seed for my flight from the farm. She'd never married and was living alone in the heart of the action downtown where she ran the city's Visitors Bureau.

'What do you mean by a short while, Mom?'

There was a pause. 'Who knows? Daniel's taking on the farm and his family are moving to the house. They won't want me around so I guess there'll be no hurry to get back.'

Two things crossed my mind. Number One, was Mom considering a move away from the farm and Idaho for good? And Number Two, if yes, was it because she was made to feel as unwelcome and awkward in my brother's company as I was? Actually there was a Number Three. Was Daniel driving her out?

I needed to find out.

Daniel's long silences and sour looks had made me suspect that according to him I was in some way to blame for Dad's death. I didn't want to talk to him but for Mom's sake it was essential.

I found him sitting at the dining room table watching a game on his iPad.

'Can we speak, please?' How crazy that I had to make a request on the day that our Dad had been buried.

'What, now?'

'Yeah, now.'

'Not in here then.' He stared at his iPad for a few seconds before closing it with a sigh. I followed him into what had been Dad's office, I guess his from now on. 'Shut the door,' he ordered.

I left it open and sat opposite him. 'What's going to happen to Mom now that Dad's gone?'

'She's going to stay with Aunt Maisie.'

'I know, she told me, but that's only for a while. What about when she gets back?'

'I believe it might be permanent.'

'But is that what she wants?'

'There's enough money coming her way because I'll be buying her portion of the house, but you'll have worked out that Dad's left running the farm to me.'

I already knew this from Mom.

'There's a small amount coming your way too,' he continued.

It was evident that Daniel would be getting the majority of the inheritance, which I accepted even though I could have done with some money. But what about Mom? 'How much is there for Mom?'

'I'm not going into that now, there's a lawyer dealing with it. Of course, you'll be gone by the time we meet him so you'll find out through an email or a letter.'

'Give me a hint.'

'Sorry, Sis. Can't do.' He hadn't recognised my attempt at a smart-arsed tease. Had we really originated from the same parents?

'I'm here for a couple more days. If nothing's sorted before I go that's fine, but I do want to know that Mom's going to be taken care of.'

'Her welfare hasn't bothered you up 'til now though, has it?'

With that Daniel got up and left me in the room.

For the rest of my time there I made an effort to get on with Daniel's wife. I can't explain why, maybe I was thinking that if I could get her to like me it would annoy my brother. A worthwhile enough reason, I suppose.

Ashleigh was like out of a 1950s home-sweet-home sitcom. She wore her hair in a tight ponytail that emphasised her frowning countenance. She was a slim woman, her long, loose dresses concealing what could well have been an attractive figure. However, middle age had definitely arrived early in spirit. She was super strict with her children, offhand with me, and formal and cold towards Mom. I dread to think what Daniel had told her about me but I was determined to get her to make up her own mind rather than accept my bullying brother's dirt.

Was I successful? Hell no, but I kept at it indirectly by spending all my free time playing with her three children. When we did stuff like face painting and collecting critters in jars they were asking me if they were allowed to, which I thought was real sad. I did catch Ashleigh smiling one time when we were making up stories about well-behaved grizzly bears, a small victory soon over with Ashleigh's frown returning when she noticed me looking at her. I loved playing with those youngsters and hoped that they'd one day break free without having suffered emotional damage.

The day before I was due to leave I got a text from Kelly to check if I was OK and would I like to be collected from the airport. I appreciated the offer but texted back that I'd be fine taking the train. Kelly was shaping up to be a good friend but she alone couldn't be the reason for me returning to London. So what exactly was I going back for? Somewhere better than this place – that was all.

On my mind the whole time I was in Idaho was whether to let Gareth know that Dad had died. When we split I'd told him I wasn't going to keep in contact. He didn't want that and I accepted a compromise to not get in touch for at least six months. I suppose he'd broken our agreement by sending me a fortieth birthday card and despite what had been decided, I was pleased to receive it.

The news about Dad was different though because I had taken Gareth to Idaho to meet my family and jeez, he'd been a huge hit with Mom and Dad.

~

We arrived late summer when the sun was still high in the sky and the fields were rich with crops soon to be harvested. The farmhouse had been painted since my last visit and the place was looking good. I was proud to show Gareth around. Mom just loved to see me happy and that this man was treating me well. Dad liked the interest Gareth took in the farm. Their discussions about what to grow, crop rotations, tractors and the markets for the produce left me behind, but I was pleased they were getting on.

'How d'ya know so much about farming?' Dad asked.

'I grew up in the countryside, though it's mainly sheep where I come from.'

Dad took me aside early on to tell me that Gareth was a great catch and that he was happy for me.

'I know, Dad. Early days but I know.'

Daniel was morose from the start of the visit and things got worse by the day. I couldn't make out why he was so angry that Gareth had an interest in the farm. Did he think we were going to move out there and take the inheritance from him?

One morning we were sitting around the kitchen table. With breakfast over Daniel asked Gareth if he could have a word in private. He agreed and followed my brother outside.

'Wonder what that's about,' Mom said as we sat at the table hearing voices raised by the minute.

Before long there was shouting and then Daniel came bursting into the kitchen.

'You're perfect for each other, Jennifer. Your man is as much of a disgrace as you are and I think it's time you both left.'

'I'll decide when it's time for my guests to go, Daniel,' my father said. Daniel headed back outside, crossing paths with Gareth who was by the door on his way in.

'What's going on?' I asked.

'As far as I can tell, nothing at all. I don't think it's fair to give my side of the story to your parents. I don't want to create a difficult situation.' He turned to face them. 'If you don't mind, Mr and Mrs Kroll.'

He took my hand and led me upstairs to our bedroom. We sat on the bed.

'Apparently we should not be fornicating until after marriage according to God's Law. Perhaps I was wrong but I burst out laughing when Daniel said that. "We're not in the nineteenth century," I told him. "It's the twenty-first." He didn't like that and I got a sermon, quotes from the bible included. Honestly Jen, I was keeping my cool until he started going on about your reckless lifestyle, about how you'd abandoned your family in favour of a life of sin. And then stuff about how God would be seeking revenge, hell and all that. I'd had enough. "You're talking bollocks, man. Stop dissing your sister," I said. It looked like he was all set to punch me but then he lowered his fists and headed indoors. I didn't know what lies he might be telling your parents so I followed him in, almost colliding as he was on his way out again. I'm sorry Jen, I really don't want to create any difficulties.'

'Don't worry, it's not your fault, I know what he's like. We'd better get down and tell Mom and Dad something, but let's keep it short.'

'I'll do it.'

Gareth did keep it brief and straight, explaining that Daniel didn't approve of us not being married.

'Daniel has strong religious beliefs,' Mom explained, 'but that doesn't give him the right to impose them on others.'

'He's hardly righteous,' Dad added.

'We don't need to talk about that in front of our guest,' Mom got in before Dad could say more.

'No, you're right. Gareth, this doesn't change what we think of you. Keep caring for Jennifer the way you do, we're happy with that.'

'I will, Mr Kroll. I don't want today to spoil things. I'll apologise to Daniel for getting angry.'

My Dad snorted. 'Good luck with that, son.'

~

Yep, Gareth and my Dad, Mom too, had hit it off like a house on fire. Of course I had to tell Gareth about Dad dying even if it broke our agreement to not communicate.

My message was brief and to the point. *Hi Gareth. I have some sad news, Dad has died. I'm back home for the funeral.*

He texted straight back even though I'd deliberately sent mine when everyone in Britain should be asleep. It was a kind, thoughtful message and fuck it, it made me cry.

Can I call you? chased his first text.

No, best not. Sorry.

16

It was a whirlwind of a relationship.

Four weeks after our first weekend together I moved out of Angie's place to live with Gareth in Pasadena, convinced that this wasn't like previous relationships loaded with hope and quickly ending in failure. Yeah, I'd been just as convinced in the past, as Angie reminded me, but this really was different. Maybe.

Getting to the part of LA where Giulio's Diner was located on a daily basis wasn't realistic so I quit. I was sorry to leave, unlike at every other waitressing job when I couldn't wait to get away. Joe had been a great boss and the diner would always have a special place in my heart because it was where I'd met Gareth.

On my second day in Pasadena I headed downtown in search of a job. Gareth was being generous, letting me know that there was no hurry to find work, insisting that he wouldn't accept a contribution towards the rent or the running costs of his apartment.

'It's not as if I'm paying for anything; the company is,' he told me.

However, I've never been shy of hard work and I valued my independence, so I saw getting a job as an immediate necessity. And anyway, with Gareth out, what else would I be doing alone every day?

Gareth's comment did mean that I could be choosy, I didn't have to grab the first job I was offered out of desperation. I only went into the places I liked the look of to ask if there was a position open. I struck gold at my second attempt, getting hired with an immediate start at a deli that doubled up as a chic café. It was crushed avocados on sourdough rather than hot dogs on soggy buns that I was now serving. Sue was the wonderful, laid back owner. I'd never met anyone like her before, running a business single-handed, by the looks of things making a huge success of it, while being as generous as you could ever imagine to customers and her staff. There was always a free coffee available for the homeless and us staff could come in early or stay on at the end of a shift for a free breakfast, lunch or dinner.

Gareth was working from home some of the time and got into the habit of joining me for lunch at the café. We'd then have time to wander through one of the parks before I headed back to the deli. I was loving my Pasadena life, getting on amazingly well with Gareth while enjoying my job. I wasn't missing the LA buzz; everything was calmer here but there was still loads going on in our city.

You know how right at the start of a relationship it all seems perfect then you realise it isn't and you have to decide whether it's worth continuing. So I guess I was waiting for that time to arrive with Gareth but it never did. It just got better and better and I knew it was the same for Gareth because he told me so. I was head over heels in love with this kind, fun-loving, sexy man.

My big worry wasn't about whether I'd stay happy in our relationship, it was the fear of what would happen when Gareth's time in the States was over. His comment soon after we met about having six months to go had stuck with me. The months were racing by and I was counting them down.

Shouldn't we be discussing this I was wondering as the clock kept ticking? I wasn't going to start the conversation because I was too scared that it would be bad news. But why was Gareth keeping quiet?

Three. Two.

One month to go. The last month.

When I got home from the deli one evening, the table was set with a cloth, proper napkins, wine glasses and candles.

'What are we celebrating?'

'Hang on.' Gareth lit the candles and pulled out a bottle of sparkling wine from the fridge. Hell no, I saw the label. It was the real thing. 'I've been doing some negotiating,' he began as he poured the drinks. The fizz from the first glass shot over the rim and oozed onto the tablecloth. He laughed, I didn't. I wanted to know what was up.

'Negotiating about what?'

'About me staying on over here. I asked my boss if I could and he's absolutely fine with it if that's what I want.' He handed me a glass. 'And I do because I can't imagine life without you, Jen.'

He held up his glass and we clinked. I was speechless, up on Cloud Nine. There should be a Cloud Ten for the best news ever.

'You're not saying anything.'

That was because I was crying. Daniel used to tease me whenever I cried when we were kids. I'm sure it wasn't because of him but I sort of got out of the habit in LA. I reckon all those knocks hardened me. Now I was crying again, but these were tears of joy.

Gareth put his arms around me. 'This is good news, isn't it?'

'Yes, yes, yes! I was so worried about what was going to happen when you had to leave. About our future,' I whispered.

'Our future is always to be together, wherever we live, whatever we're doing.'

That was such a lovely thing to say. Brits have such a nice way with words.

~

I could park the fear that once Gareth's time in the States was over our relationship would come to an end. Any worry about having to leave my homeland if I wanted to stay with him was on hold.

We had a great weekend together and when I came bounding into the deli all smiles on Monday morning, Sue asked me what I was on.

'Only happiness,' I told her.

'You're not expecting, are you? I can't lose you, Jennifer, you're much too valuable.'

'No, not expecting. Just happy.'

Just four weeks later she did lose me. When Gareth had said that our future was always to be together wherever we lived, I was fixated on the being together bit and ignored the wherever we live part. I should have realised that to carry on working in America, Gareth would be moving around the country to wherever there was a new contract. He hadn't mentioned it because to him it was obvious that staying in the States didn't mean staying in Pasadena.

Our next stop was to be Connecticut, pretty well as far as you could get from LA, and we had only ten days to organise our move.

At the end of my final shift, Sue organised a farewell party for all the employees and their partners. It was fun, there were people there I'd have liked as friends, but it was too late.

When everyone else had gone and Sue and I were alone, she said I was the best employee she'd ever had. I told her she was the best boss ever and I meant it. She'd taught me how to treat employees decently, something I never forgot and would put to good use later on.

The following day we were all packed up and ready to go, flying across the country with the essentials in a couple of suitcases, our other possessions to follow.

Gareth and I became nomads, staying somewhere for a few months before moving on across the country. Colorado. Virginia. Delaware. New Jersey. Texas. Sometimes Gareth's contracts were so short that we stayed in a hotel, but if a project was going to run for more than a couple of months his company found us an apartment. At least then we could put in some effort to make it feel like home. I can't say it was easy to be uprooted so often and there was little opportunity to make friends. After all, what would be the point when we'd be leaving them behind soon after getting to know them? Of course, I had Gareth, though there were days when I hardly saw him because of his work schedule.

Our first argument, we were in Missouri at the time, was because of all that moving around. I guess I started it, complaining about not being able to find a decent job. Temporary work in catering is easy enough to get but you're always at the bottom of the pile when you're a fill-in.

'Then take a break from work,' he suggested.

'I like working.'

'But you don't because you keep going on about how boring it is.'

'So what do you think I should be doing if I'm not working?'

'Getting to know a place.'

We were in Springfield, Missouri, and there wasn't that much getting to know to do. 'So I wander around all day long and report back to you about all the exciting places I've seen each evening?'

'There are parks, places like that.'

'Great idea, a park one day then another park the next day, and then what? I know, I could spend the third day in a park!'

'Count yourself lucky, Jen. I wish I had more time to relax.'

'Well, I wish I had less time to relax.'

'The zoo's meant to be good.'

'Are you deliberately trying to annoy me? Don't you get it? I want to explore new places with you, not by myself. And a zoo isn't top of my list. Anyway, I want to earn my own money.'

I left the room, I left the apartment and went for a long walk, the joke being I ended up strolling through one of the Springfield parks, the one that bordered the zoo.

By the time I got back I'd cooled down and I was fine with Gareth telling me that he'd only been trying to help.

'I'll find something, even if it isn't the job of my dreams.' As I said that I realised that I had no idea what a dream job would look like having completely abandoned the idea of acting.

'You don't have to …' Gareth stopped, just as well because we'd be back with the original argument.

I didn't get a job in Springfield because Gareth was told he was needed in LA for a short while to supervise a team who were messing things up. It was only going to be for a couple of weeks so we kept hold of the apartment in Missouri and booked into a hotel in good old Pasadena.

'See this as a holiday, Jen. Catch up with some old friends.'

17

When I arrived back to my small apartment in Muswell Hill after Dad's funeral I was feeling down. Seeing those wide open spaces in Idaho, the ones I'd hated in my teenage years, was making me feel trapped in congested London. The argument with my brother had rattled me, I hated him for his selfish and unkind manner. As ever, Gareth was in my thoughts. Why hadn't I accepted his offer to talk, there would have been no harm in that? He could have come over for the funeral, no harm in that either. Then there was Mom. Would she be happy if there was a new start away from the farm? And Dad was dead. I hadn't been mature enough to get to know him before leaving for LA and now it was too late.

I put all my energy into work. My deputy had been competent enough to manage day to day affairs while I was away but she had avoided dealing with accounts and recruitment until I returned. There was a lot of catching up to do. Pronouncing that I was madly busy was my excuse for keeping away from Kelly, Emma and the others for a while. I couldn't face answering questions about the funeral, about how I'd got on back with my family.

It wasn't even as if I was enjoying work, in fact I regarded managing the care homes as being back to square one. In the States I'd seen waitressing as a stopgap ahead of deciding what to do in the future, having realised I wasn't going to make it as an actress. Now I was sucked into another stopgap job, desperate to find something better. But what? My whole life seemed to be an unsuccessful search for a better future – a rewarding career, close friends, escape from a tiny apartment in the ugliest building in the area. I suppose a new relationship, too.

So yeah, I was not in the best of spirits. When Emma called to invite me over for a meal the choice was simple, either carry on wallowing in lonely self-pity or snap out of it and do something. Anything. I was so lethargic I was struggling to decide.

'Is it a special occasion?' I asked Emma.

'No, we just get together every so often and I thought it would be nice for you to join us. I suppose we could make it special; the delayed celebration of your fortieth.'

I glanced at the cabinet by the door. The cards were still there. Maybe it was time to chuck them but I wanted to check something first.

'I'm not sure about making it to do with my fortieth but thanks for thinking of me and I'd love to come.'

'Great. We start at around seven-thirty. You do know where I live, don't you? 38 Brookland Gardens, the house with the lovely stained glass panel on the door and a front garden nurtured to perfection by Andrew.'

'I've been past it; it is impressive.'

'Don't tell him that or else he'll be talking about what he's planted all evening.'

As soon as the call ended I picked up the card from Mom and Dad. On the front was a photo of a herd of bison. If I hadn't known them I might have regarded it as a tongue in cheek depiction of the Wild West to get me smiling, but this was simply a picture that they liked. I opened the card to see who had written the message. I thought it would be Mom and that was the case; it always had been. Dad had signed it though and I was grateful to see the last thing he'd ever written to me. I'd be keeping the card.

~

By the time the evening of the dinner party had arrived, an excuse not to attend because of work would have been truthful. It had been a horrendous week with severe colds among staff leading to absences in one care home and an accusation of bullying in another. I was doing twelve hour days.

I wouldn't cancel though because a break might take my mind off things. I'd even buy something new to wear. With plenty of clothes stores in Muswell Hill the choice was considerable, the challenge being to decide between five different outfits. I ended up returning home with far too many carrier bags.

When I stepped into Emma's house the first person I saw was Bridget, the owner of the café. Standing by the hosts, she had on the same dress as me. Our embarrassed giggle broke the ice and I immediately felt relaxed at this first meeting since Dad's death.

There were seven of us there in addition to Emma and Andrew: Darren and Kelly, Cecelia and Julien, Bridget and David, plus me, all too aware that I was the only one alone.

I was placed next to Bridget who might have regretted it because I fired questions at her about how she'd got round to setting up the café. There was a purpose beyond general chat because running my own business was something I'd started to consider.

Bridget was open about what had happened. The café had been David's idea. Soon after they'd started their relationship he told her about his dream of an escape from a job in accountancy that he hated. At first she thought an arts café was a mad idea.

'And how wrong I was because it's been an amazing journey. It just goes to show, if you really want something there's always a chance of making it happen.'

I didn't challenge Bridget but knew it wasn't as simple as that. My early investigations about opening a restaurant had indicated that there would be a long and risky path to success. Nevertheless, I nodded and smiled in the right places as she told me about how she'd had a eureka moment while working in a gallery selling pretentious art to ignorant customers. She decided to pack it in and help David to fulfil his dream.

'It worked for us from the word go. I guess we're lucky to have complementary skills.'

'Meaning?'

'David's accountancy and business knowledge combined with my creativity. I suffer from impulsiveness and he from procrastination, but usually we manage to meet somewhere sensible in the middle.'

We looked across to the other side of the table when Kelly burst out laughing, a shrill, raucous laugh.

'Kelly didn't work for you at first, did she?' I said. 'She's told me that.'

'Correct. She joined after we'd been going for about a year. Despite our hard work we hadn't realised how time consuming it would be. By then we were desperate to add to the management team and struggling to find the right person until Kelly came along.'

'I heard my name, what are you two saying about me?' Kelly shouted.

'I'm telling Jennifer what a pain you are at the café.'

'At home, too!' Darren added.

'Oh, that's alright then. I thought you were bad-mouthing me!'

'Would I do that?' Bridget turned back to me. 'Where do you work?'

I told her about my job at the care homes, that it was barely OK and not what I wanted to do for the rest of my life.

'So what would you rather do instead? If you had a free choice?'

'Act if I had a completely free choice, but it's probably best to stick to things that are realistic.' I paused to reflect. I'd had plenty of internal debate about what I'd like to do but never during a conversation. 'I've got the skills and experience to work in the hospitality sector and I can't see myself doing anything outside of it. What I dislike about the current job is that I have no direct contact with customers, or in my case the residents. I'm fine with the office work but I'm a people person.'

'One of our café customers, well more than that, a friend really, is setting up a boutique hotel near here and they're about to hire staff. They're not opening until spring but they want the senior people in place to help with the planning. If you like I could mention you.'

'Yes, please. I haven't thought about working in a hotel but actually that sounds exciting.'

'Melissa and Shaun, they're a lovely couple. I think I've got your number; I'll pass it on to them.'

18

Gareth had suggested that I should treat the short time in LA as a holiday and I did just that, revisiting favourite places in Pasadena and catching up with old friends still living in LA.

Over three crazy days I took the tram into downtown LA to meet Angie, Suzie and Belle. I'd decided to see them individually because I thought that openness and honesty about how they were getting on was more likely that way. Their stories were depressingly similar, a series of failed relationships and failed attempts to get into the world of showbiz. Was Belle trying to impress me or did she really believe that a five-second, non-speaking role in a commercial was a major triumph. She took out her phone and showed me an ad that had her sitting at a table behind the lead actress who was ordering a pepperoni pizza with extra cheese topping.

'I look good, don't I?' she said, her subdued tone a giveaway.

'You sure do,' I said, forcing a smile.

'I've got an agent now so hopefully that'll lead to more work.'

'Cool.'

She knew what I was thinking and I knew what she was thinking. She was still waitressing in some dive.

Each catch up got me appreciating how lucky I was to have moved on. It could have been me there hanging on to unrealistic dreams while serving and wiping down tables. But then, reflecting following the three meet ups, it struck me that apart from being with a man I loved, what was I doing that was any different? Gareth aside, maybe things weren't so great after all. OK, I'd moved on from the naïve dream, but I was waitressing just like the friends I was feeling sorry for. At least they had a big friendship group to mix with while I was never in a place long enough to make friends.

My final get-together was with Scarlett who had been my closest friend in LA. She was one of the first I'd met after moving from Idaho, a drop dead gorgeous gal with a sparkling personality to match. Perhaps we'd hit it off because we shared awareness of how fake the Hollywood scene was. Maybe, too, because we were both from country backgrounds though our families couldn't have been more different. My parents were conservative, modest and happy with their quiet life. Scarlett's mother seemed to have devised a plan before giving birth, even the name was part of the mapping out of her daughter's path to stardom. Scarlett had told me about the Toddlers and Tiaras pageant shows she'd been in, showing me photos of a little girl in a suggestive dress with frills, buttons and bows, the sweet little face wrecked by make-up. It was sick we agreed.

I'd delayed catching up with Scarlett until last in the hope of capturing at least one success story. We'd kept in touch a little through Facebook but I had no idea what route she'd taken until we met in the lounge of an exclusive hotel.

She was an escort.

'It's OK, Jennifer, don't look so alarmed. The money's great and most of the guys are fine.' Her faded looks and sad eyes said otherwise. She'd gone full circle I guess, back to the layers of make-up and seductive dresses of her childhood.

I was feeling sad so decided not to see any of these old friends again while in LA, despite having my second week filled with offers of meals, gigs, and a movie premiere that Scarlett had tickets for. Instead I revisited the old haunts in Pasadena, strolling through parks and visiting some of the museums Gareth and I never got to see. He took time out some days to join me which was nice, but I was missing having close female friends to gossip with.

I'd been looking forward to LA but by the time the two weeks were up I was happy to leave, even if it was to go back to Springfield. I didn't feel like there was a place I could call home and that wasn't a nice thought.

In Springfield I found a job in a Greek restaurant, a low-ceilinged room with bare brick walls covered by giant posters of ancient ruins which you could tell must have been spectacular at the time. It made me want to visit the place, to step into those avenues and courtyards, to look up towards the temples, to imagine what it was like to live there all those thousands of years ago. The restaurant owners were a lovely couple, as polite and friendly to their staff as they were to their customers. I was doing nights and weekends so what with Gareth working long hours on weekdays, we weren't getting to see much of each other.

Yeah, the Greek place in Springfield was good but it wasn't killing off my worry about what the future held. I thought about how Mom had been content to tie her existence to where Dad worked, but this wasn't good enough for me with Gareth. Maybe the world was changing and women were less accepting, or maybe it had to do with personalities and mine made me restless. I took to reading some new wave feminist books and got angry because if society had changed it hadn't changed enough. I didn't take my anger out on Gareth though because he wasn't responsible for what the world was like and was nothing like how some guys behaved. Quite the opposite – I knew he'd encourage me to do anything I wanted. The trouble was, I had no idea what that anything was.

Despite the easy relationship with Gareth, all the frustration was still boiling up inside of me when he was given the location of the next project. We were off to Burlington, Vermont, a contract with a start-up company which would take a minimum of six months to complete. At least that meant living in our own place rather than a hotel and the accommodation we were given was the best yet, a large single-storey house with a rocking chair on the porch where I could read and a sizeable yard to putter around in.

There was another bottle of champagne, another fancy meal out, another week of shopping and sightseeing together before Gareth started the new work. What was this, the seventh, eighth, ninth place since LA? I'd lost count and had little interest in working it out.

I got a temporary daytime waitressing job at a restaurant, a nice place but well off the main drag. It was heading towards mid-winter and the place was quiet; I was struggling to find things to do to fill my six-hour shifts. One day when we hadn't had a single customer in I was expecting the worst – why would the owner hand over good money for nothing in return? I was instructed to take the dry goods off the shelves in the store room, wipe them down and put everything back. That took three hours, there were still one and a half to go. I scrubbed the bathrooms and mopped the floors. I was too quick, too keen.

'You might as well go home, Jennifer. Perhaps don't come in again until I text you.'

I took that to mean I'd been sacked.

The snow was thick outside and I slipped on the top step, jarring my ankle. I stood under the neighbouring store awning and texted Gareth. *Can you pick me up, I've hurt my ankle? Not serious but not fun walking in this.*

I had to wait in the freezing cold for a reply. *Can't get out of meeting for twenty or so minutes. Best call a taxi and I'll meet you back.*

Yeah, great idea, Gareth. The rest of the population of Burlington had the same idea and every cab passing me was taken.

I started walking, home wasn't too far, but by the time I got back, wet and in pain, Gareth was there.

'You look like a drowned rat,' he said.

You know when someone tells you something, trying to be humorous and friendly to lighten the mood, and you don't find it at all funny and see red? I was seeing red.

'Get changed and there'll be a drink waiting for you,' he continued, not picking up that he was in dangerous territory. The patronising pat on my shoulder did not help.

'I don't want a drink. I'm fed up doing fucking waste of time jobs.'

'Whoa, steady on there. What's got into you?'

And he still didn't get it and I was getting madder and madder.

'Yeah, and it's fine for you, driving off in your aircon car every day with music of your choice blaring out. Stepping into your cosy office with any drink you'd like served up by some submissive woman.' I took a deep breath. 'Then you can chat away about terabytes or whatever with male colleagues before your next drink's served. I've fucking had enough.'

I stormed past Gareth; I was not going to give him a chance to be the calm voice of reason. I showered and got into a tee shirt. I sat on the bed for a while to calm down. I changed back into daytime clothes as I tried to work out whether this was simply a bad day or if it was the never-ending nomadic life that was doing my head in.

'Sorry,' I said when I came back into the living room. 'It's not your fault. I was wrong to lay into you.'

Gareth was sitting on the sofa not doing anything, just sitting.

'Will you say something?' I asked.

The thing is though, I didn't want to hear what I thought he was going to say, the sort of thing he usually said. "We can work this out, Jen. Let's reflect on how to make things better." If he'd said that I might have screamed.

'Then stop being a fucking waitress.'

Where did that come from? 'What?'

'Do something different if you don't like what you're doing now. It's the sort of work youngsters do, not someone your age. In fact if anyone is still waitressing at your age then maybe they aren't too smart. But you are smart.'

'I know what, I can be a big-time lawyer or I could sort out terabyte problems for corporates!'

'Sarcasm doesn't help. Get a qualification in hospitality then you can manage other people.'

'Are you serious?'

'You're the one who's got to be serious. Do you want to do better?'

'Yes, I do.'

I'd never thought about it but those three words made me believe it big time. It was like a mist had lifted and I could see a purpose beyond being Gareth's girlfriend.

19

I bought a smart, mid-grey, two-piece suit and a white blouse for my interview with Melissa and Shaun. In heels and stupidly without a coat on this bitter fall day, I scuttled round a couple of blocks to reach the double fronted house that was to become a hotel. You could barely recognise its beauty since it was swamped by scaffolding, ladders and planks of wood, but a look at the buildings on each side made it clear what was hidden from view – a quirky Victorian edifice with turrets, stained glass and ornamental brickwork.

The front door was open – on closer inspection it was missing – and I stepped onto a plastic sheet sprinkled with plaster broken off from walls that had been stripped back to brick.

'Hello?' I called out, and then a little louder to be heard above the upstairs hammering.

A woman came out of a side room to greet me. She was in jeans and a sweatshirt splashed with a rainbow of paints. 'Hi. I'm Melissa.'

'Jennifer.' I extended my arm for a handshake.

'Best not,' she said, showing me a hand streaked with red paint flecks. 'Oh, I should have told you not to dress up, the plaster dust is getting everywhere.' True enough, my jacket was speckled like a sparrow's egg. 'Come into our sanctuary.'

I followed her down a long corridor, sidestepping between lumps of plasterboard, blocks of brick and pieces of wood. The hammering was loud, echoing from wall to wall, and there was a builders' sing-along to a song I recognised but couldn't name.

'Sorry about the mess,' Melissa continued. 'We're opening up the downstairs to make a lounge, breakfast room and reception area. And that's the easy part. We're gutting the upstairs so that we can fit in ten en-suites.'

The singing was becoming ever rowdier. 'How many have you got working up there?'

'Five, maybe six. Their building skills are better than their ability to sing.'

'Phew, that's a relief.'

There was no response to my quip though there was so much noise Melissa might not have heard me. She opened a door and gestured me inside.

The man behind the table stood. 'Hi, I'm Shaun.' He shook my hand. 'Is it Jennifer, Jenny or Jen?'

'I prefer Jennifer.'

'OK, Jennifer it is.'

It hit me that a lot was at stake. I was hating care home management and this was possibly my one opportunity to escape. In a flash my heart had started thumping, my mouth had gone dry and my head was pounding.

I took a deep breath and forced a smile. Another deep breath to restore clear thinking because surely I had nothing to fear. I'd prepared meticulously for this interview and was ready to utilise all the expertise I'd gained while being on the other side of the table, interviewing and recruiting catering staff.

Yes, I was prepared for anything they threw at me – except for what they were about to throw at me.

'Before you sit down, Jennifer,' Melissa said as she handed me a cloth. 'I gave the chair a wipe to get rid of the dust but it's already covered again. You might want to clean it.' I wondered whether this was part of the interview as I wiped.

Shaun took over. 'Thank you for coming in today and apologies for the mess.' There was a loud thud as something above us crashed onto the floor. 'And the noise.'

The upstairs destruction had sent a layer of fine dust gliding down and the crystal light fitting directly above my head was rattling.

Shaun must have noticed my upwards glance. 'Perhaps move your chair a little this way. Just in case.'

I shuffled across.

'Let's start, shall we?'

I nodded and smiled.

'Jennifer, you've got thirty minutes to convince us that we should employ you. This is your interview; you can manage the time however you'd like.'

A single question, I hadn't prepared for this at all.

How I used that thirty minutes! I was the accomplished actress, finally able to star with an Oscar-winning performance. Jennifer Kroll as the homespun girl with wisdom beyond her years and a heart of gold as she captivates the English couple.

'I've used twenty minutes so far and that's enough from me. But I always see an interview as a two-way process so I have some questions for you.'

They'd told me I was in charge of the interview so I'd taken control and boy, were they in for a hard time.

'The place is in a dreadful condition. How confident are you that all will be ready in less than six months?'

'What research have you done to estimate the size of the market?'

'Do you have a five-year plan available for the me to see?'

'What exactly is the job you have in mind for me?'

'What salary are you offering?'

They knew their stuff. Their answers were direct and I was confident they were honest. I wanted this job badly.

'Right, my time's up. Thanks for your frank answers to my questions and I'm definitely interested. All that's left to ask is when will you be making your decision?'

Melissa and Shaun looked across at each other and smiled. 'Now,' Melissa said. 'Would you accept our offer of deputy manager? Subject to the terms, of course.'

We discussed terms there and then, a salary far higher than anything I'd previously got and they even offered a two percent stake in the business on completing my probation period.

'We believe in a culture of treating our employees well,' Melissa said.

'That's not just because we're nice – which we are – but if you treat your staff well they respond by working hard and being motivated. It's a win-win situation,' Shaun added.

'And in the hospitality sector having motivated staff is hugely important.'

'I agree, Melissa.'

I was keeping my cool on the exterior, the actress still playing her part, but internally I was shaking with excitement and joy. I'd forgotten what it was like to feel happy.

The three of us hugged then laughed as another thump generated a cloud of dust and sent the ceiling light shaking again.

Stepping outside my future workplace I brushed myself down and paused. The dream of bringing some happiness into a miserable life had perhaps been realised.

Left was home, right was The Broadway.

I turned right. What better place to celebrate than at the Dream Café, hopefully to see Bridget to tell her the good news and to thank her for the introduction.

20

As soon as Gareth said "Get a qualification" he had his laptop open and was clicking keys while I was still thinking about it.

He chatted as he searched. 'I've got at least another three months of work here, enough time for you to start by taking a short course. Look. There are loads here.' He flipped the screen towards me. 'I've found something in hospitality if you think that's what you want to do.'

I hadn't caught up with him yet. He'd asked if I wanted to do better and I'd said yes but that didn't mean that I was ready to act. 'It's as useful as anything, I suppose.'

'That's not good enough, Jen. You have to really want whatever you choose.'

I started reading information about a Certified Professional in Catering and Events Diploma on offer at Vermont Tech. 'This does look interesting.'

'See, Jen. It's a mix of online and in-person which seems ideal.'

'It takes six months to complete. You said you've only got another three here.'

'Maybe a bit more, but if I can't extend the contract with the client I'll take time out while you complete it.'

'Would you do that for me?' Tears welled up; where did they come from?

'For you I'd do anything. You know that.'

And I did.

'I am interested but let me sleep on it.'

'Only for one night then decide either to do this or something else. Keep searching while I cook.'

My heart was thumping; I was that excited, but nervous too. I'd left school without any qualifications even though I'd always received good grades from elementary to high without much effort. I lost interest between 11th and 12th grades and never considered AP exams or college.

I carried on investigating to the background sound of clattering pans as Gareth cooked, googling back and forth and finally settling on that first course he'd come up with which looked the best on offer by far. I liked that it included two weeks of practical experience with local businesses. I would do it. I would make a success of it. And I loved Gareth for forcing me off my butt to try for something worthwhile.

'How are you getting on?' he asked as he came out of the kitchen carrying two rice dishes.

'I'm going to do the one you saw – the catering diploma at Vermont Technical College.'

The course was starting in mid-January which only gave me a couple of weeks to prepare, probably a good thing as that meant no time to allow doubts to get me chickening out.

With a few days to go I was trying to work out travel because the college was in Randolph, a sixty-mile journey from Burlington. When Gareth came into the living room I was surrounded by sheets of paper, most of them screwed up on the coffee table.

'What ya doin' doll?' he asked, his attempt at an American accent as bad as usual.

'Finding out which bus is gonna get me from here to the college.'

'How long would that journey take?'

'Four hours, I think.'

''It's only an hour to Randolph by car so it's a no-brainer. You can use mine.'

'No, I can't do that.' The only cars I'd ever driven got me praying they weren't going to give up on me during the journey. Gareth had a top of the range rental. 'You'll be needing it.'

'No I won't. I can work from home on the days you're out and if I do need to get somewhere it'll be local so I can take a taxi. It's not a problem, just do it.'

It was looking like I would need to take a night bus to get there for the eight thirty start. 'Maybe for the orientation day.'

'Orientation day! You make it sound like a map reading expedition. Americans!'

'What would you call it then?'

'Induction, I suppose.'

'Well, whatever. And I accept your kind offer as long as you invite me to an induction session for your vehicle,' I said, my accent based on a recent viewing of Emily Blunt in *My Summer of Love*.

114

The following Monday I set off double nervous – driving that car and starting that course. The controls looked like in the cockpit of an airplane. I was panic-pressing the info screen to turn the air conditioning down and the windshield wipers on, to open the trunk, to access GPS, to switch from Gareth's lack of taste in music. At least it took my mind off being a student. Would I be able to cope?

Having checked in, I joined a group of about twenty on a tour of the facilities – the library, the classrooms, the computer lab, the café, the lecture hall. Finally, we were back in a classroom where we received handouts of the syllabus and all of the requirements were explained. I was at the front writing down every single word spoken. Glancing behind me, I saw the late teens scanning their phones and whispering while the instructor was talking. On the tour they had oozed confidence and coolness, indifference too. I smiled at the woman around my age who was in the front row a couple of seats down from me. I guess her look of irritation matched mine.

We sat together at lunchtime and complained a little about "the youngsters". Rosemary was a local who'd been married and divorced three times and was now all set to "get serious".

'I guess they aren't any worse than I was at that age,' she said.

'I suppose me too.'

'I didn't care about anything then but I do now. I'll tell ya though, it isn't gonna be easy back studying after ten years.'

'That's exactly how I feel,' I said, wondering whether she was puzzled why I was there given the look she was giving me.

After lunch we were taken to the computer lab where we logged in to set up student accounts. 'This first assignment is for you to do online,' the teacher informed us as we studied the information on our screens. 'You need to send me your answers by Wednesday and we'll be sharing them when we meet in person again next Friday.'

I left the room with Rosemary and we walked to the student parking lot together. 'I'm here,' I said, stopping by Gareth's sleek model and pressing the remote key.

'This one's mine,' Rosemary said, pointing to a battered vehicle with fading red paint. 'I have to put a key in to unlock it! See ya Friday.'

'Yeah, see ya Friday,' I said, strengthening the drawl for her benefit.

I drove home in a tizz, this a Gareth word describing the state I was in. There was a problem. My ancient tablet wasn't going to be good enough to do the coursework. I needed a laptop and fast.

'And?' Gareth asked the instant I stepped indoors.

'It was good.'

'So why the frown?'

I told him why.

'No need to get in a tizz. Do an about turn.' He took hold of my shoulders and spun me round.

'What are you doing?'

'We're driving out to that mega electronics store in the mall to get you a laptop.'

'I need to sort money out first.'

'No you don't. It's my gift for starting the course.'

Gripping me tight he was steering me towards the car, insisting we were going to the store and that he would be paying.

'I'll drive,' he said as he opened the passenger door for me.

Although he never seemed short of money and I didn't have much, it was not in my nature to take advantage. 'This is a loan, Gareth.'

'No it's not. It's a gift.'

'I can't accept it.'

We were close to having an argument about him being incredibly generous and me being incredibly reluctant to grab. Sitting in the car the absurdity of the situation finally dawned and we burst out laughing. I accepted his offer knowing that he'd made it out of his love for me and I loved him all the more for that.

Over the next few months I worked like I'd never worked before. It turned out that Rosemary and I weren't the only mature students in the class, there were two men in their late forties or early fifties, too. The four of us stuck together at first even though I wasn't happy that the men were flirting with us. Rosemary went along with their flirting and was soon organising evenings out at local bars. I let them know I was taken but that didn't stop them so in the end I kept my distance, becoming a bit of a loner among three oldies and fifteen or so teens. That was fine, I was there to study, to take in every word the instructors uttered like it was straight out the bible. I was the one who always handed in assignments early, irritated that the youngsters were getting the highest marks despite their lack of interest. Competitiveness kicked in – I wanted to be the best and before long I was, in part thanks to Gareth's help with the Math and IT.

All this time I was working at the Burlington restaurant, re-employed full time now that the spring to summer trade was kicking in. Coping with the study and holding down a job was exhausting.

'I'm leaving now,' I told Gareth as I was about to set off for work. 'And sorry but I won't be much company tonight because when I get home I've got an assignment to finish.'

'You should quit that job you don't like and concentrate on your studies.'

'That's crazy.'

'No it isn't, I mean it.' Gareth came over and did what he liked to do when we were talking about something serious; he put an arm round my shoulder and pulled me closer. 'You know that I can support you while you do your studying. We're fine for money.'

'I can't accept that.'

'Yes you can. When you get through the course with top marks and the world of catering is there for you to conquer, that's when I get my payback.'

'It's a kind offer, but still no.'

'So tell me, how are you going to do your two weeks of practical experience if you're still working full time?'

That had been on my mind and I was yet to come up with a solution. 'I'll sort it out.'

'Sort it out by telling them you're quitting. Tell them today.'

That's what I did.

I never knew such unselfish kindness could exist in a man until I met Gareth. Or maybe, now that I'm thinking of it, perhaps his generosity without expecting anything in return was matched by my Dad. I'd been too young to appreciate it at the time. It might explain why Gareth and Dad had got on so well the one time they met. It might also explain why Daniel had been so bitter during our visit. Jealousy.

I had the first of my work experience weeks a little over half way through the course. The intention was for a host organisation to provide training in exchange for our unpaid labour. It hadn't crossed my mind that hospitals needed catering management, but of course they did and that was where I ended up – at the community hospital. It was an eye opener. The staff were chasing shadows, so busy that training was not going to happen. I was thrown in at the deep end, getting the food onto trolleys to be wheeled into wards and corridors as fast as possible. I recognised how important the job was and was full of admiration, but I knew that working in a hospital wasn't for me.

In the final month of the course I had my second placement with Dine Fine, a national chain of restaurants serving mid-range food. It wasn't one of the giants but the company was big enough to have two restaurants in Randolph and another two in Burlington. I did a bit of everything, accepting deliveries, preparing food, processing accounts, creating staff schedules – I even did a shift waitressing – and I loved it all. I must have impressed them because I was called into the manager's office on my last day and told there was a job waiting for me if I got my qualification. By then I knew I would pass, my marks had been that good.

Gareth reserved a table at the classiest restaurant in Burlington on the day I received my diploma, not quite at the Santa Monica level but pricey enough though the food was great.

When we'd finished eating he signalled to the waitress. 'Could we have the bill, please?' He was still calling it that.

'I'll take the check,' I said as the woman came up to us with the card reader.

She hovered but when I held out my hand she passed it over. I decided not to look before inserting my card. I might be about to go into debt to cover the cost, but soon I'd be earning good money.

Gareth was smiling; he got what me paying was all about.

21

Striding along in the opposite direction to home on this bitterly cold day when I'd gone out without a coat, I was regretting the decision to head for the café after my interview. The final few steps became a run to get inside as the heavens opened up and a stinging hail fell from an ever darkening sky.

Would sitting alone drinking a cup of coffee really be worth the effort even if I did treat myself to a cake? No, I reckoned. And if I was going to celebrate, because I was truly ecstatic, shouldn't I be drinking champagne? Another no because alcohol at 11.00 am on a dismal fall day ahead of having to walk home without a coat in the torrential rain didn't seem like a great idea.

So it was pointless being there, but there I was. At least there was Kelly behind the counter to say hello to.

'Hi Jennifer. What can I get you?'

'I've got the job!' It just came out.

'I forgot, today was your interview. That's brilliant news – well done! Take a seat and I'll bring your order over. I can take a quick break so I'll join you for a bit.'

When Kelly came towards me carrying a tray, it seemed to be resting on her belly, a belly that hadn't been there when I'd first seen her eight or so weeks ago.

She set the drinks onto the table and collapsed into a chair. 'I'm absolutely shattered.'

'Kelly, are you …' I paused. Should I be asking? It might be a sensitive topic. Some illness even.

'Yep, I'm pregnant.'

'That's wonderful news.'

Something at the back of my mind kicked in. Soon after we'd met, Kelly had apologised for not contacting me about a Sunday brunch, telling me that she'd given it a miss because she was feeling sick. I hadn't asked what the problem was in case it was something private and I barely knew her, but it could well have been early pregnancy morning sickness. 'When's it due?' I asked.

'Another four and a bit months. I haven't gone round telling the world but now that it's starting to show I will be. I've got a scan next week which is when we find out whether it's a boy or a girl.'

'I'm so pleased for you. And Darren of course.'

'He's treating me like a piece of bone china. You name it, he's doing it – cleaning, loading and unloading the washing machine and dishwasher, insisting on carrying everything.'

'That's lovely.'

'It is. I'm hoping it'll be the same for the rest of our lives. Hi, Cecelia.'

'This weather is mad,' Cecelia said as she dropped down onto a chair. 'My one hundred percent waterproof coat has failed me; I'm soaked through.'

'I don't think anything could offer total protection when it's like this,' Kelly said. As if to prove her point the windows were hit by what sounded like a burst of machine gun fire. 'I'd better get back to work. What do you want, Cecelia, and I'll bring it over?'

I was left alone with Cecelia. We'd hardly ever spoken; I regarded her seriousness as a bit intimidating.

'I got the job,' I began.

'Job?'

'At the hotel, the one Bridget mentioned when we were having dinner over at Emma and Andrew's.'

'Oh yes. Apologies, it slipped my mind. Congratulations.'

'Thanks. I can't wait to start.'

'You've been working in care homes, haven't you?'

'Yes, that's right. Not the easiest of places to be in.'

'I'm sure not, but extremely valuable.'

I lifted my cup and took longer than needed to drink, considering what to say. I think Cecelia noticed.

'How long have you lived in England?' she asked.

'About six years.'

'What brought you over here?'

'The usual reason I suppose. A man. Gareth.'

'And I assume, since we haven't met him, that it's over now?'

'Yes.' This was awkward. Cecelia's questions were closed, preventing anything resembling a flowing chat.

'When did it end?'

'That depends on whether you mean the drift, the arguments or the actual split. The latter was about five months ago.'

'It's never easy, is it?'

'No.'

I wasn't feeling comfortable, I wanted to get home, but Kelly had arrived with Cecelia's drink and I thought I needed to stay out of politeness. It struck me that finally I was able to talk about Gareth and me splitting, but not with Cecelia.

'Anything else for you?' Kelly asked as she lifted up my plate, cup and saucer.

'Sure, same again, please. The drink, not the cake.'

Cecelia took a sip of her flavoured tea. I could smell the fruit but was unsure what it was. Maybe raspberry.

She rested her cup in its saucer, swivelling it in the groove. 'Separation, what a minefield. It's what my current research is about; the difference between how men and women respond when a relationship ends. Did you know I lecture in psychology?'

'No, I didn't. Does that mean you're always analysing as you chat with people?'

'Absolutely not. Mind you, I could write a book about some of the people I know. Several books.'

She smiled and I responded which somehow made things easier between us.

'To be truthful, I'm finding it difficult,' I admitted, as much to myself as to her.

'That's understandable because it is difficult – and it's still early days. How long were you together?'

'Almost exactly ten years. We met on my thirtieth birthday when he was working back home. Not exactly my home. In LA.'

Cecelia took a sip then another sip of her tea. For an instant I was annoyed that she was so slow to respond, but when she continued I was respecting how she measured what to say instead of spouting out the first thing that came to mind.

'Let me tell you what my research suggests. It is only a generalisation but men tend to move on more quickly than women, whether it be to a new partner or even to buying a new car. Or they might be in denial that the relationship had ever meant anything to them. On the other hand, women find it much harder to break from a past relationship.'

'That's interesting, though with Gareth and me I'm not sure that's the case. As far as I know he's still single and finding it really hard to let go. I have no idea about the car though!' One of Gareth's friends had recently emailed me, urging me to reconsider, letting me know that Gareth remained devastated. I hadn't replied and I wasn't going to because at the time of the split this friend (who I'd never much liked) had suggested it was all my fault and that I was, relayed at different times, either a bitch, a cow, a slag or a cunt. I should have blocked him but part of me wanted to keep a connection open for news about Gareth, however twisted the messenger was.

'Like I said,' Cecelia continued, 'those responses are only generalisations. Separation is complex and loaded with irrationalities. Of course, I don't know your boyfriend.'

Kelly was back at the table with my drink. 'Talking about boyfriends are you? All men are bastards as the saying goes,' she added, unaware that Julien had come in and was making his way towards us.

He stooped to kiss Cecelia. 'I missed what you said – all men are what? Were you talking about me?'

'Yes, definitely,' Kelly said with a wink directed at me.

I'd only ever known men to wink – another generalisation I suppose.

22

We were on the move again just weeks after I'd got my certification and started work at the Dine Fine restaurant in Burlington. Gareth's job would be taking us to New Jersey. In the short time I was with the company I must have made my mark because the manager gave me a great reference and there was an assistant manager's post waiting for me at the Dine Fine restaurant in Atlantic City.

We moved there in late spring, just as hordes of tourists were beginning to flood in. The restaurant was in one of the busiest spots, on the Boardwalk, across from the casinos, nightclubs and glitzy hi-rise hotels.

I had a bit of a love-hate relationship with Atlantic City. The love was the buzz, I hadn't seen anything like it since my time in LA. But even with its casinos and shows, this was no Las Vegas. There was an air of neglect with poverty visible just a short distance away from where the action was.

During our five or so months in the city we moved three times. Initially we were in a small hotel in the thick of it that was noisy 24/7. The first move was well away from the crowds, but in a district that I never felt safe in. When we complained, Gareth's company agreed to cancel the lease for us. Finally, like Goldilocks and her porridge, we found a place along the coast that was just right – attractive, quiet and secure. I could have happily stayed put there for a long spell but knew that after a few months we'd be on the move again.

I've always been a sucker for hard work and was happy to be rushed off my feet at the restaurant. I can't say I liked all of the customers though, brash New Yorkers who treated us staff like trash, demanding their meals be served in an instant, and complaining that the food was either too hot or too cold, though never just right (Goldilocks again!). I soon realised there was a reason for the unwarranted dissatisfaction, a demand for a reduction when presented with the check. Unsurprisingly, tips were minimal.

'What do you think about Maine?' Gareth asked me on one off-duty morning when we were still in bed.

'I've never been there; I've heard it's a nice place. Why are you asking?' Obviously I did know why.

'That's where my next project is.'

I looked across the bedroom, a pleasant room with its china blue walls, high ceilings and whitewashed furniture. Apart from clothes there was little evidence of our presence there though, not a photo or an ornament, not even a vase of flowers or a plant.

All this moving was so tiring. 'When?' was my resigned question, the only one that mattered really.

'I've got another three weeks here, maybe four. Are you alright with another move?'

It was hardly a question that merited an answer since there would be no choice. I tried to be upbeat. 'Sure, no worries. I am wondering about my job though.'

'We'll be living in Portland and I've already looked it up. There's a Dine Fine there, right by the harbour which is meant to be the best part of the city.'

Yeah, it was nice of Gareth to do the researching but I had a surge of irritation that he hadn't left it to me to investigate.

'There might be a restaurant there but that doesn't mean there's a job opening.'

'You're such a star, if there isn't one they'll create something for you.'

I suppose that was intended as a compliment but it added to my irritation. I pulled back the covers and sat on the edge of the bed.

Gareth put a hand on my shoulder. 'Don't get up yet, I thought we could …'

I was about to say no thanks, but when he sensually trailed his fingers from my shoulder down my arm I stopped thinking about our next move and lifted off my T-shirt. Gareth, already naked, was in kissing and stroking mode which was fine by me.

~

The next day, when I told my boss I was handing in my notice ahead of a move to Maine, he told me that he would speak to the head office rather than me contacting them. I'm not sure what he said but a couple of days later he let me know that there was a job as manager at the harbourside restaurant in Portland waiting if I wanted it. Boy, did I want it, a promotion.

Although I liked our home, that was less the case for Atlantic City, so I wasn't disappointed to be leaving, particularly once I'd done some research on Portland. It looked like a cool place to live.

You never know what somewhere is really like until you're living there and I was in for a pleasant surprise. Immediately, I fell in love with the Old Port waterfront. It was like a scene from a movie with its fishing wharves and converted warehouses filled with boutique shops and cafes. On that first day we discovered the Dine Fine restaurant right in the hub. From there we took the short walk to Western Promenade Park and sat on a bench to admire the arrival of fall. The hillsides were ablaze with golden trees with striking views over to the distant mountains.

'Happy?' Gareth asked.

'So far, very,' I said taking hold of his hand. But I was already thinking about having to leave the place however much we liked it.

'We're only booked into the hotel for a week, so tomorrow we should start seeing what's available to rent.'

'Sure. Somewhere only a walk away from here would be nice.'

The first dwelling we were shown was a condo in the West End, part of a converted house with spooky features – turrets, towers and fancy brickwork – that reminded me of the Addams Family's house in the TV show.

I hummed the tune and clicked my fingers when I saw the place.

'Don't you like it?' Gareth whispered before the agent took us inside.

'As long as it's not haunted.'

'It's Victorian. Mock Gothic.'

'I'm not sure what mock gothic means but it is kinda cute.' Of course, I had no idea that one day I'd be living in an oasis of Victorian gothic splendour in Muswell Hill. 'Come on then, let's have a look.'

We took the place, which we worked out would be a twenty-five minute walk to my restaurant. Gareth suggested we get bikes and I was soon cycling to work, an enjoyable journey with me always on the lookout for some new, quirky feature on a building. Sunday bike trips into the countryside whatever the weather became a bit of an obsession. As much as I enjoyed our excursions, I couldn't get out of my head the fear that it might be the last time we saw a particular destination before another move.

The Portland restaurant was the best of the three I'd worked in, an attractive wooden barn-like structure with a high beamed ceiling and an interior which Gareth described as minimalist western. I was initially concerned because several of the staff were older and more experienced than me, but they turned out to be a great team, hardworking and willing to go with my decisions without a fuss. They were as polite as could be with customers which worked fine because the diners were equally polite in return. It made me wonder what made a community so at ease with itself, friendly and laid back, as seemed to be the case in Portland. I guess income and education had something to do with it.

I loved the variety of my job, right down to discussing menus with the chefs. Although Dine Fine across the States had a standard menu, each restaurant was allowed to break free with seasonal local specials. Our Lobster Pie and Monkfish Fra Diavolo used fish sourced fresh from the harbour. I even got to cook the spicy monkfish recipe a couple of times. Fun!

I was happy; I had a career even if it wasn't the one I'd most wanted. And I had a boyfriend who I could trust. He most definitely was the one I most wanted. Yep, life was good despite that niggling ache of never being able to lay down roots and form friendships because of moving from place to place.

'Let's make more of an effort to socialise,' I suggested to Gareth one evening when we were sitting alone in a bar by the harbour, me conscious of groups of friends laughing away around us. 'We shouldn't use the excuse that we won't be here forever as a reason not to.'

We started mixing with colleagues from both our workplaces, leaving me regretting that we hadn't done the same in all the other places where we'd lived. I put aside concerns about leaving Portland; Gareth would tell me when our time was up.

One thing I'd entirely put aside was that Gareth's work in the States wasn't going to last forever. So that came as a shock – Portland was to be our final destination.

'That gives us two options, Jen,' he said, having broken the news. 'One is to stick with the same outfit back in Britain, the other is for me to find a new job here. I'm happy to try for that if you want to stay in America.'

Over the next days and nights we went round and round in circles until something Gareth explained made up my mind. 'There have been loads of IT start-ups recently, too many, and I think there's a bubble that's likely to burst. Having a new job might be risky compared to staying with my company. It's well-established, profitable and has a high market share.'

As far as I could see the decision was made – Gareth had to stick with his secure job with us moving to England. The fretting vanished, replaced by excitement. Living in England, that would be an adventure and a half.

'England it is then.' I threw my arms around his shoulders. 'When do we go?'

'There's flexibility but I reckon in a month or so.'

'To London?'

'I'm afraid not. The head office is in Salford.'

'Where's that?'

'Near Manchester.'

'Where's that?'

23

I got a call from Cecelia a couple of days after our conversation in the café.

'It's my turn for our Saturday night dinner party the week after next. Would you like to join us?'

'That would be lovely.'

'I might ask one or two others to come along; I'll see. Anyway, the usual time, half seven.'

'Great, and thanks for –'

Cecelia had cut the call.

I should have guessed I suppose. The other guest, just the one, was male, around forty and single. As we were introduced I sensed all eyes were upon us – will they, won't they eyes – and surprise, surprise, we were placed next to each other at the table.

Having got over the discomfort of being set up for a blind date, I did enjoy Will's company, his relaxed and friendly tone as he questioned me. How was I finding life in Muswell Hill? Had I visited the usual London tourist sites yet? What films had I seen recently?

It took a while but I managed to switch the focus to him to discover that Will was an academic at Cecelia and Julien's college. At some stage he must have asked what had brought me to England and I mentioned that it was a man.

'Who you're still with?'

'No, it's over.'

'Same with me. My wife and I separated ridiculously soon after the mammoth celebration of our tenth anniversary.'

He fell silent and looked sad but I wasn't going to probe and I certainly didn't intend to go into detail about my own relationship with Gareth. So, with no personal revelations forthcoming and having dealt with general stuff, I was wondering what was left to talk about through the upcoming main course, dessert and coffee. Will turned the other way to speak to Emma, leaving me facing Darren for a brief account of a football game he'd seen that afternoon. He might as well have been speaking in a foreign language, even more foreign than the usual English English.

'We drew level with a cracker from outside the box but then VAR disallowed it.'

'VA what?'

'R. VAR.'

'What does that stand for?'

'I don't know exactly but it's the thing they use to check if decisions are fair or not.'

'So if this VAR disallows something it means it was unfair. That's good, isn't it?'

He shook his head and sighed but I thought what I said had made perfect sense.

'Only if the VAR is correct,' he explained.

'Jennifer?' Luckily Will was back facing me. 'I'm fascinated to hear what you think about current American society. I lecture in American Studies so I do know a little about what's going on there and the recent history.'

'Which will be more than I know.'

'Can I ask you a couple of questions though?'

I nodded.

'Where are you from?'

When I told him Idaho I reckoned that would be it because there's not much to say about Idaho that's of interest. I was wrong as far as Will was concerned. He covered the history of the Oregon Trail; the appalling treatment of the Shoshone tribe; how the state was one of the worst suffering during the Great Depression; and why, despite the hardship of so many, it was a diehard Republican bastion. He knew his stuff and it was interesting the way he described things, though at one point I was guilty of stifling a yawn.

'I'll stop,' he said, 'because I'm actually an extremely boring person.'

'You sure are,' I said with a smile as broad as the Mississippi River. Clearly it wasn't broad enough because he looked forlorn, devastated. 'It's OK, you're not boring. It was a joke.'

Later on I discovered that I'd hit a raw nerve. His wife had walked out on him three months earlier and the reason she'd given was, yep, you've guessed it, that he was boring. I think she was wrong; he was fine and I quite liked his earnestness. Mind you, I wouldn't be telling him that I'd lived in LA for a while in case he launched into the history of a state that had far more to say about it than my home one.

I asked him about his weird accent. I didn't find it appealing, in fact quite the opposite and definitely not at all sexy, so I was baffled when he gave me the answer.

He laughed and put me right. 'No, not erotic. Rhotic.'

I remained clueless. 'But you said erotic.'

'No I didn't. Rhotic. R-H-O-T-I-C.'

'Never heard of it. Where are you from to be R-H-O-T-I-C then?'

He laughed. 'Bristol.'

That got us chatting about favourite cities and I said how enjoyable it had been living in Portland. I found myself judging Will as a blind date rather than a neighbour's dinner party guest. He was pretty good looking in an unassuming way. He wasn't all muscle, but he wasn't too thin. His face was well-proportioned, but not memorable. His hair was lightish, but not quite blond. His accent sucked though.

I think I took him by surprise when I whispered an invitation to come back to my place as we were about to leave Cecelia and Julien's. He dithered. 'I'm not looking for a relationship,' I added, 'but I am happy for you to stay the night.'

He stopped dithering. 'I'll walk Jennifer home,' he announced unnecessarily loudly as the six of us stood by Cecelia's front door. The four other guests had no distance to go home, of course, but I sensed them staying put to watch us as we headed down Brookland Gardens.

The sex was enjoyable if nothing special, but the next day was a let down. After all, I wasn't a counsellor so how did he expect me to respond to his outpouring about why the relationship with his wife had deteriorated so rapidly. He couldn't understand what he'd done wrong. The topic really wasn't first date material.

'Maybe it wasn't that rapid. Perhaps she'd been dissatisfied for quite a time and was building up the courage to tell you.'

I guess that was a bit harsh because it led to a further torrent of blaming himself.

'Will, I'm starting my new job soon and I have some preparing to do, so can we call it a day?' We'd only just finished breakfast.

'Can I see you again?' he asked.

'Sure, but I think as friends.'

Wanting Will to leave wasn't because of an unwillingness to hear about his separation. His contemplation had got me reflecting on the parallel between him and Gareth and I needed time alone to process my thoughts. Will had expected answers from his wife when there were none to give, as had Gareth with me.

'What do I need to do to get us back to where we were?' Gareth had asked me.

'It's not as simple as that.'

'But what can I do?'

I'd cut him short. 'Nothing. You can't.'

Maybe I was too quick to say that. Perhaps I'd been wrong.

24

We arrived in Salford mid-winter, not at all like the icy cold, blue sky winters I remembered from Idaho or the pleasantly mild ones in LA. Salford was all mist and rain for days and weeks on end.

While searching for a place to rent we stayed downtown in a bland hotel that was part of a large American chain. During Gareth's couple of weeks off work we got my visa sorted and had a fun time getting to know the city. We were shown apartments by an over-enthusiastic real estate agent who told us that everything we saw was wonderful, fabulous and fantastic. Finally we settled on one in a converted quayside warehouse, a cavernous open plan space which we fell in love with, right down to the bare brick walls and exposed brightly coloured piping.

When I looked online to see how much our penthouse cost, with its whirlpool on the balcony overlooking the city, it was scary. But Gareth seemed able to afford it, not that we ever discussed money. I wasn't going to take advantage though; I was forever telling him how grateful I was and I intended to find a job as soon as possible.

The only downside to our new home was being surrounded by those so-called wonderful, fabulous and fantastic new glass and steel hi-rises that we'd rejected, their size shutting off much of the light to our place.

A short walk away from our neighbourhood with its chic shops, galleries and restaurants, took us to an area with small independent eateries serving food from a kaleidoscope of countries – Lebanese, Moroccan, Spanish, Turkish, Israeli, Jamaican. I sampled Indian cooking for the first time and got addicted to it.

'Where's the traditional English food though?' I asked Gareth. It was the evening before he was due to return to work and we were strolling through the area deciding where to eat.

'Fish and chips is about it,' he replied with that smile I loved. Sometimes when he said something, I wasn't sure whether he was serious or joking until he broke into that mischievous grin of his.

With Gareth back at work I was left to organise the move to the apartment. Our small shipment of belongings arrived on time and I spent my days unhurriedly sorting and putting stuff away while listening to music on Gareth's playlist. I put *Goldfrapp* and *Florence and the Machine* on a loop.

You could tell we'd been nomads because we had little beyond clothes and books to organise. There were no photos of me as a kid in Idaho or Gareth in Wales.

One morning, out of nowhere and for no obvious reason, I burst out crying when thinking about that. It got me wondering how come Gareth at least knew about my time on the farm whereas I knew so little about his background. I'd tried to find out but he always dismissed my questions by saying that there was little of interest to tell.

Having unpacked and sorted out the apartment I decided to take a day or two break ahead of finding a job, using the time to explore the city away from our usual walks. In one respect what I saw was no different to American cities – rundown neighbourhoods only a short step away from the wealth.

'It was interesting when I was out today,' I told Gareth that evening.

'Was it?'

'Gareth, could you stop looking at your screen please?'

'There's something I need to finish by tomorrow.'

'So I can't have a minute of your time?'

'Sorry, of course you can.'

'Never mind.'

What I didn't get round to telling him was that Salford seemed divided according to ethnicity. There was an Indian district, a black one, and one neighbourhood that appeared to be all white. Gareth had said that Salford was a cosmopolitan city but it looked the same as in the States with people living where they felt comfortable.

My walks weren't just for pleasure, I was investigating what jobs might be available. Something in the area filled with independent restaurants was my preference, but going from door to door enquiring wasn't getting me anywhere: there were no vacancies. That left the branches of restaurant chains right by where we lived. There were plenty of waitressing jobs advertised in the windows – I could start immediately – but I wasn't going back to that.

'Do you think I can't get anything because I'm foreign?' I asked Gareth after a frustrating day trekking from restaurant to restaurant.

'No, of course not.'

'Then why?'

'Because the economy's tight. People are hanging on to what they've got.'

'When will it stop being tight?'

'If I knew the answer to that I'd invest and end up a millionaire. But look, be a tourist for a bit, discover the world beyond Salford. There's Liverpool for a start, that's where the Beatles are from.'

'I know that, everyone knows that. I want to work though.'

'You might need to look beyond restaurants then.'

I visited Liverpool later that week. It was interesting enough but it would have been far nicer to have gone there together. What was I meant to do, discover England as a lone tourist?

After another few days of trekking round restaurants without success I took Gareth's advice and went into an employment agency to get help. Having established that I wasn't a chef and didn't want waitressing work, the woman who was interviewing me asked if I had considered other opportunities in the hospitality sector.

'Like what?'

'Hospitals are recruiting.'

The memory of my uncomfortable work experience week at the Burlington Community Hospital was still strong so I dismissed that option.

There was more clicking on her keypad ahead of letting me know that if I wanted management responsibility then care homes were a possibility. Apparently they were desperate for staff, hardly an inviting observation.

I didn't respond with enthusiasm; in fact I didn't respond at all.

She misinterpreted my silence. 'Don't worry. You wouldn't be expected to do any of the actual caring.'

She printed out the details of a post as catering manager across two large homes in the city.

'Definitely go for it,' Gareth said when I talked it through that evening.

I applied online and was called for an interview the following day. The meeting was brief, I could sense their desperation, and I was offered the job there and then. I accepted it.

OK, we had a nice place to live, I had a job lined up even if far removed from the ideal, so the next step was to find friends now that we were close to Gareth's head office so surely long term settled.

Who though and how could I connect? It was hardly like going into a store to find a pet dog or into a supermarket to buy bread. Ahead of starting work, alone in the apartment, I'd been wondering whether there was anyone there to meet. It was pathetic really, hanging around at the entrance to monitor the comings and goings. All the residents I saw were youngsters who left home first thing in the morning and didn't return until late at night. They drove expensive cars and power dressed; I guess you had to be earning a top salary to be able to afford to live in our building.

I used much of my first month's salary to join a gym, in search of friends as much as to get fit. It was nowhere near a state of the art place and I wasn't optimistic on first entering the cramped ugly space with its small coffee bar. I did try though, chatting to fellow treadmill runners, but I got minimal response. They probably thought I was mad, attempting to converse when all they wanted was to connect their earphones as they thudded and grunted. The café was usually deserted apart from people picking up a takeaway before heading off as soon as they'd got their exercise out of the way.

Thirty-something American woman from Idaho seeks friends. Her interests include potato farming and dreaming of acting.

I wrote this on a scrap of paper while at work when there was little to occupy me. Of course I'd never be using this plea for friendship, but in the past I would have shown it to Gareth for fun. I crumpled it up and tossed it in the waste basket. It was time to process a fruit and vegetable order for the care home.

On weekends our apartment building was deserted, the exodus beginning on Friday afternoons with a convoy of cars streaming out of the underground private garage.

'Why don't we go somewhere this weekend?' I asked Gareth.

'I'm going to have to do some work tomorrow and Sunday.'

'You said that last weekend.'

'And money's a bit tight at the moment.'

I held eye contact.

'Don't worry, nothing serious,' he continued.

I'd been working full-on for peanuts in a not particularly enjoyable job for half a year and whenever I came home moaning and exhausted after a twelve-hour shift, Gareth would remind me that I could quit because he could support me.

Now that I was thinking about it, he hadn't said that for a while. I didn't dwell on his comment though; maybe I should have done.

~

When did I first notice that Gareth's stellar career might not be quite as glittering as he implied? When did I realise that things were not at all right?

The trouble is, when behaviour changes imperceptibly day by day, you don't notice a shift in circumstances until you're suddenly hit by a cataclysmic event.

The signals were there and I should have picked them up. All my ideas for a weekend away were being turned down. My suggestions to eat out or see a band, movie or a show were being rejected, the excuse being that he was either too busy or too tired to do anything. Gareth rarely went into the office anymore, instead staying at home with his eyes glued to his laptop screen. He'd stopped talking about work and as far as I could tell, visits to clients had dried up. He downsized the car. He was drinking too much. Worst of all, that lovely smile of his had disappeared and I was subjected to long periods of sullen silence.

Despite all the signals, it came out of the blue.

'We need to move, Jen.'

'To a cheaper apartment?'

'No, more than that. To a new region.'

'Where?'

'I was thinking back to Wales, it's much cheaper living there. Maybe we could move in with my parents for a while.'

'Wales! Your parents! I thought you hated the place and you didn't get on with your family.'

'I never said that.'

He had, many times.

'Nothing's definite. We'll only go there if we have to.'

25

I started work at the *On the Hill* hotel only three weeks after my interview. This was way earlier than I expected but Melissa presented me with an option when I'd popped in for a chat. I could see that a lot of progress had been made but there was still a fair bit to do.

'We think the renovation work will be completed by the end of this week but that leaves the decorating and we've decided to do it ourselves to save on costs.'

'That makes sense. I guess it'll just be a case of rolling paint onto smoothly plastered walls.'

Melissa nodded. 'Exactly.'

'So when do you think you'll be finished and when do you want me to start?'

'We were wondering whether you'd be interested in assisting with the decorating. It's hardly deputy manager work so it's completely up to you and we'd understand if you're not keen. No need to answer now; have a think about it.'

I didn't need time to reflect, it would be fun helping to get the place ready. 'I'd love to.'

'Oh, I so hoped you would say yes. You can help me choose furnishings and fabrics too if you like.' Melissa joked that Shaun had no taste or judgement so it was essential to have me as an ally to cast the deciding vote on paint colours and fittings. 'We'll need to get going though, there are supply chain problems for everything.'

I felt privileged that Melissa wanted me involved at the planning stage. We parted with a hug and although I was an employee I felt very much part of their team.

Each morning when I turned up in old clothes that I'd happily splatter with paint, the three of us had a pre-start meeting to decide what to tackle that day and who was going to do what. We worked in neighbouring rooms with Shaun's Sonos speaker turned up high to play streamed tracks from his youth – *Pulp*, *Manic Street Preachers*, *The Verve* and *Massive Attack* – all of it new to me. He was particular about his music, knowledgeable too, keen to tell me who played in which band and which concerts he'd seen. Melissa would roll her eyes when his enthusiasm edged close to nerdism.

Those days together were physically hard work but hugely enjoyable. We were choosing fabulously bold colours and to see the walls transformed from insipid off-white plaster was exciting. Most days one of us would pop down to the French patisserie on The Broadway to get something delicious to go with our coffee, made with a *Nespresso* machine that would eventually end up in one of the bedrooms. Usually I left Melissa and Shaun to have a short lunchtime break at home, then it was back to decorating in the afternoon. It was taking longer to get everything done than anticipated and it was touch and go whether we'd be ready to open in early May. We had no choice though because Shaun had set up the website and established the links with the various hotel booking companies. With a few weeks to go reservations were rolling in.

As the opening day approached it was common to still be working until eight or nine at night. Melissa would order takeaways, travelling round the world with our food choices, and we'd sit together in the office chatting. There was lots of laughter, possibly explained by the supply of wine in the mini fridge in the office.

When it became apparent that we would be on schedule for the opening, Melissa suggested that a celebration dinner was deserved. 'Bring a change of clothes tomorrow, Jennifer. I'll book something nearby for around seven thirty.'

By the time I stopped working late afternoon the next day I was splattered with Farrow & Ball's Card Room Green paint, this being the splash wall colour in the breakfast room. Even my hair was covered with flecks of the emulsion; that's a roller for you. I went into the office to collect my bag with a change of clothes, towel and soaps.

Shaun was sitting behind the desk, his laptop open. 'You look like a female version of The Hulk,' he joked.

'Which is why a shower is needed.'

'Me too,' he said, lowering his head. I had chosen the paint he was showing me; it was the Kittiwake Blue emulsion for behind the reception desk that covered his scalp.

The showers were a dream, giant rainforest nozzles overhead and pulsating jets on the sides. I could have stayed in that cubicle for hours.

'Oh God, sorry, I thought you'd finished.'

I turned to see Shaun standing there naked, a towel over his shoulders.

The extractor fan was doing its job so there was no blurring of his or my view because of the glass steaming up. It seemed pointless to whip an arm across my breasts and a hand over my pubes. I simply turned my back on him, assuming he'd leave immediately. When I turned back, admittedly fairly quickly, he was still standing there – with an erection that he was making no attempt to cover up. Dropping his towel in front of him would have been easy, but he didn't.

'I'll use another room,' he said and left.

OK, men get erections I was thinking as I was dressing. I'd seen naked bodies, he'd seen naked bodies, so this was no big deal. He'd been slow to leave, that was all. Maybe so, but I was also thinking that Shaun must have heard water running when he came into the bedroom so why did he continue into the bathroom? I suppose if he wanted to see a naked woman he was no different to other guys I'd known. It's not as if he'd tried anything.

In the restaurant that evening there was no embarrassment or tension as the three of us chatted about how well we were doing with the decorating. As we were leaving Shaun suggested that we took the day off tomorrow.

'That's a great idea,' Melissa said, kissing him on the cheek. As we walked towards our homes, Shaun put his arm round Melissa and she leaned into his shoulder.

I didn't give the shower incident another thought.

26

It was our final week in Salford and there were a few packed cardboard boxes in the living room and in the bedroom. It struck me how little we had accumulated since coming to England as if we'd known all along that the stay in Salford was to be yet another short one.

Initially Gareth had told me that we might be moving in with his parents, a surprise because as far as I could see he had avoided contact with them for as long as I'd known him.

When he announced the move would be to Cardiff I wanted answers.

'Why not your parents' house then?'

'It wouldn't work. Their place is too small for a start.'

I wasn't going to let him get away with that alone. 'And also, as you keep telling me, you don't get on with them.'

'Yes, that too.'

'Which as a result has meant that I haven't met them and don't know anything about them. Do they even know that I exist?'

'They must do,' was his infuriating response.
'Clairvoyant are they?'

~

We followed the moving van along motorways all the way from Salford to Cardiff, pulling up outside a terraced property in a narrow street. The houses butted against the pavement, so no front gardens or trees to soften the squat red brick buildings. I'd seen the place on the internet so there were no surprises either outside or in and I wasn't looking forward to living there.

Neighbouring doors had opened as we arrived and women and children were on the sidewalk watching as we unloaded the car and directed the movers. I waved and smiled, both gestures reciprocated.

A girl of around ten came up and started chatting, telling me that her name was Bethan, that she lived at number twenty-seven and would be receiving her first mobile phone on her birthday which she was keen to let me know was on August 27th.

'It's easy for you to remember because of the two twenty-sevens,' she said. 'And there are only two weeks to go.'

'A phone's a great present. You're a very lucky girl.'

'I'd better go,' Bethan said before running down the road screaming to those still out on the street observing us, 'She's American!'

Soon afterwards, when we were indoors, there was a succession of knocks on the door with offers of mugs of tea, cakes and sandwiches. I sensed that the providers were hoping I'd say a little more than a thank you to test the accuracy of Bethan's claim.

'Gee whiz, this is mighty nice of you,' I said as I opened a wedge of sponge cake wrapped in silver foil, acting out a highly inaccurate perception of the true American.

'Yes siree, it's my first time in Wales and I sure am impressed,' I said with an accent I'd never used except in drama class. I was aware of being patronising and decided to stop the game.

The mug of tea she handed to me had Welsh words on it that made no sense, though why should it?

There was a pause between visitors, leaving us in peace until about six o'clock when there was a ring on the doorbell.

'I was thinking you won't have had time to cook tea. So I made extra, like. Here you are.' The woman handed over a saucepan and lifted the lid.

'It's pasta,' she said. 'If your cooker isn't connected I can heat it myself and bring it round hot. Plates too if yours are hiding in boxes.'

The woman was wearing a shiny navy track suit that had seen better days and the saucepan she'd passed over was battered and discoloured. As I got to know our neighbours over subsequent weeks, it was evident that many on our street, this woman included, faced considerable hardship which made their generosity all the more touching.

There was a community room at the end of the road. Before starting to look for a job I joined some of the other women for tea in the mornings. These women, and it was always only women there, were blunt about their plight, recounting awful events that had shaped their lives. I couldn't be as open about my own situation so I told my neighbours that Gareth was a computing consultant, that he'd been working in America and was now in Cardiff to help companies solve their IT problems. Living there didn't fit with my portrayal of Gareth as a senior executive and I couldn't look anyone in the eye as I spoke.

Although I knew what I was telling them couldn't be correct, I had no idea what the real truth was because Gareth was hardly communicating. His working week consisted of being tucked away in the spare bedroom, its tiny north-facing window casting a depressing gloom into his office, even during the daylight hours.

'Isn't it a problem being so far away from your head office?' I asked, not for the first time.

'Not in the IT world. I can meet online.'

'But what about visiting clients like you used to do?'

'Things have moved on. As I said, meetings are online.'

'I don't get it though. I thought you had to be with them to work on their computers.'

'Trust me, Jen.'

'Of course I trust you. It's just that I'm curious.'

There was a look that I couldn't place. Possibly anger? Disappointment? Fear? Could a single look convey such contrasting emotions?

One thing was for sure, our quality of life was nothing like in the past. It wasn't simply where we were living, it was the getting out and doing things – concerts, restaurants, weekends away – all that had gone.

When we were in the States I had loved Gareth's spontaneity. 'I've had such a tough week,' he would say. 'Let's head off somewhere this weekend.' We'd find a hotel on the coast, a cabin in the forest, a mountain lodge. Wherever we went it was good with the two of us together, putting aside all worries.

That was back then. In Salford there had been much less adventure and so far in Wales, none.

I googled places we could visit near Cardiff and there was loads to see. The coastline to the west looked gorgeous. I showed Gareth photos of the scenery and a list of budget hotel possibilities.

I got one of those anger-disappointment-fear looks. 'I know it's lovely there, I'm from Wales remember.'

'But I'm not, that's why I've been looking. Can't we go?'

'It's not on at the moment. I'm sorry though, I didn't mean to snap at you.'

Slowly my brain was catching up with the reality – we had serious money problems.

~

Finding a job to supplement Gareth's income was a priority. Having spent a couple of weeks trying and failing to get restaurant work, I took a post managing the catering team in a large care home. The place was dismal, stinking to high heaven and in need of a total refurb. At least it was a job and I was going to put away some money each month to save up for a weekend break.

Returning home one Friday afternoon three months into the job, I was all set to present Gareth with some options for the surprise trip. When he came out of his den he suggested that we eat out. I was pleased, it would be the perfect place to present him with the good news.

We took a bus into the centre of Cardiff where he had reserved a table at what looked like quite an expensive place. The waiter poured our first glass of wine, dropped the bottle in the ice bucket, and left us in peace.

'Here's what I'm going to do,' I announced.

'Me first, Jen. I'm sorry, but we're going to have to move again.'

That stopped me in my tracks. 'Move? Why? When?'

'As soon as the six-month tenancy ends.'

'Where to?'

'One of the villages around where my parents live. Anyone with sense is abandoning the area so there are lots of empty houses. It's dirt cheap to rent there.'

'But why?'

My brain had finally caught up with reality – I think I knew the answer but pushed ahead. 'If everyone with sense is escaping why are we thinking of moving there?'

'I've lost my job. I was made redundant.'

'Oh no, you poor thing.' I took hold of Gareth's hand. He wasn't making eye contact. 'How much notice have they given you?'

'I was dumped a while back, when we were still in Salford.'

'That was nearly five months ago. Why didn't you tell me then?'

He shrugged his shoulders.

'So, what have you been doing in that little office of yours all this time?'

27

The hotel had been open for a couple of months and as usual I was rushed off my feet on duty at the reception desk.

'That's everything done, sir. Here's your key card and your room is to the right when you go upstairs.'

'Thank you, you've been most helpful.'

'A pleasure.'

The phone rang and I accessed the calendar on the computer as I made a mental note of the request.

'I'm afraid we're fully booked that week but there is some availability the following one … You're welcome to get back to me once you've checked but don't take too long because we're down to our last room. If you go online there's a real-time view of when we have vacancies … I'm glad you enjoyed your last stay here … I hope we'll see you again.'

I caught sight of Belinda by the storage cupboard and called across.

'Best if you change the cleaning schedule this morning. The people coming in to Number Six have asked if they can get here early, they have some do to go to mid-afternoon. I've said yes so we need a quick turnaround as soon as the current couple leave.'

'No problem, Jennifer. Just text me when the room's free.'

Zahra had arrived. Great, she could take over at reception while I went to the office to process invoices.

The hotel was madly busy, I was madly busy – and I was loving it. Looking back though, I think my obsession with work was a substitute for socialising. Of those I could call friends, Kelly and Darren were now overwhelmed with their brand new baby, Andrew and Emma likewise with their son Noah, and Cecelia and Julien seemed to spend their lives at conferences or on courses when they weren't tied down at the university. So that left me with no one to hang out with except for Melissa and Shaun who were often asking me to join them for something or other – a movie, a concert, bowling, a meal. Although I enjoyed being with them, I usually turned down their offers. I didn't want to be the odd one out with a couple and I didn't like to impose on their private lives. After all, they were still my bosses.

I bumped into Cecelia on my way back from work one day and we lingered on the sidewalk chatting about this and that.

'Remember Will?' she asked.

I reddened. Had she found out that we'd spent the night together, that I was the one who'd triggered it and then made it clear that it was a one off? Not my

162

proudest moment. 'Yeah. How is he? I haven't seen him since the evening we met at your place.'

She did know, I could tell by her look. 'He's trying to get back with his wife and it's looking promising.'

'Good. Tell him I'm rooting for him, will you?'

'I will. I'd best get going, I've got to meet Julien at the college this evening for some presentation or other.'

'Enjoy.'

I was happy for Will if things worked out, but what were the chances of that? He'd made it clear that he loved his wife and maybe it was right for him to try to win her back. But from what he'd said she was pushing for a divorce as soon as possible and wasn't going to change her mind. So couldn't he recognise that it was over and he needed to move on.

What a simplistic solution I'd come up with – move on. So easy to say if concerning someone else but who was I to advise what to do when I was failing to take my own advice. It was over nine months since I'd split from Gareth and despite one relocation and two jobs, I was nowhere near moving on from him. I'd be kidding myself to believe I could wipe away the fond memories of our time together. One minute I'd be smiling as I recalled the first time I saw him at the LA diner when he apologised for taking too long to decide what to choose from the menu. Then I'd get tearful as I reflected on his gentle nature and kindness. So many memories – the excitement as we moved from state to state, the fun as we explored new cities together, and then my anger, my justified anger together with sadness.

I tried to shut down the memories by reminding myself that the Gareth I first knew was not the same as the person by the time we broke up, but it didn't work. I was missing him.

If I had more of a social life would those memories fade? If only I could find friends in Muswell Hill, by that I meant single friends, or perhaps even a partner. But it wasn't happening and I was sliding into the view that reaching forty was a barrier to meeting a new man. I wasn't into pubbing or clubbing or gaming or online dating (and definitely wouldn't be sexting). What was left because I wouldn't meet anyone while sitting alone in some cinema watching a romcom that wasn't funny?

And that's why for me it was work, work, work with Melissa often telling me to slow down.

One afternoon as I was about to leave reception Shaun handed me four fifty-pound notes. 'For you.'

I'd never seen a fifty pound note, everything was by credit card. 'What for?'

'I've just finalised the first quarter accounts; they're off the radar.'

'Great, but I get paid for doing my job so …' I held out my arm ready to hand back the money.

Shaun took hold of my hand and wrapped my fingers round the notes. 'It's for you to go out and get some glad rags because the three of us are out celebrating tonight.'

'I can't accept this, Shaun.'

'I, we, insist.'

I wasn't going to make a fuss so took the money despite embarrassment. However, once I'd left *On the Hill* my attitude shifted. My hard work had contributed to the success so why not accept the gift gracefully? I was soon in the Muswell Hill boutiques trying on clothes and ending up spending far more than what Shaun had provided.

Back home I pampered myself in advance of the evening out. I couldn't help thinking about Gareth again, of having him there to tell about how successful the hotel was, having him admire the off the shoulder tight-fitting dress that I'd bought, having him join me for Melissa and Shaun's celebration.

Well, there was no Gareth but I was determined to make the most of the evening and enjoy myself.

28

Obviously I was dismayed that Gareth had been made redundant, but I was also furious that he hadn't told me for so many months. All sympathy went into hiding when I discovered that he'd lost his job soon after we moved to Salford.

'That makes it ten months of you keeping me in the dark. That's disgraceful.'

'I'm sorry.'

'But why not tell me?'

It was like we barely knew each other, hadn't shared everything for years, because he couldn't or wouldn't say. He simply shook his head.

Gareth became increasingly withdrawn as the days passed by, refusing my increasingly harsh and desperate demand for an explanation. I persisted; how else would I be able to make any sense of our time in England then Wales?

With my questioning veering between hard-hitting and at times conciliatory, a breakthrough finally came on one of my calmer days.

'Gareth, didn't it cross your mind that I might have been able to support you, maybe by suggesting that we shouldn't be spending a fortune renting an apartment in the most expensive part of Salford?'

He nodded.

'So, I'm assuming you got some severance pay and we were living off that in Salford.'

'I had savings.'

'But also severance pay?'

'No.'

'What do you mean no? I thought businesses had to do that.'

'I was never on the company's books. I was engaged as a contractor which meant they could terminate whenever they felt like it.'

'What I don't get is why you spent ten months hiding away in an office at home with the door closed. What were you doing?'

'I was looking for a job and I did have some independent consultancy work. Not much, but a bit.'

'So another thing I don't understand is why the company stopped using you. I'm assuming you told me the truth when you said you were the best person they had for tackling certain specialist tasks.'

'I was.'

'Were you actually working all the time we were in the States?'

'Of course I was.'

'So why did they get rid of you?'

'There were some irregularities in my expenses account.'

'Is that the English way of saying you were swindling them?'

'Yes.'

'Is that all I'm going to get; no explanation of exactly how and why you'd cheat on expenses when you were on a good salary?'

'Maybe like father like son.'

'Meaning?'

'I'm done with explaining, Jen. Sorry.'

And I guess I was done with asking for explanations now that I knew he was sacked for dishonesty rather than made redundant. Until hearing that I would have said that dishonesty and Gareth was an impossible mix.

What was I meant to do now, prolong the periods of silence that could last for a full day or make an effort to restore our relationship? I chose somewhere in the middle and slowly things began to improve. We were able to chat about anything not to do with his work and that was fine by me because there seemed nothing left to say. We went to the movies and a nearby pub a few times, and together we packed up in preparation for leaving Cardiff. The sweet natured Gareth seemed to have returned. Maybe a weight had lifted having told me what was going on.

Despite this improvement I was pretty dejected. We were on the move again and God, had I had enough of moving, enough of following Gareth's lead and ending up in ever worse situations.

Researching the village where we'd be living didn't help. OK, renting a place there was dirt cheap, but how would we ever find work?

'What's it called?' I asked Gareth, bemused by the name beginning with a double L. He tried to get me to pronounce it which was impossible and at least that got us laughing.

The day of our move arrived, a move to a tiny place in the middle of nowhere with just two lines of houses along the main road and a single side street at right angles to it. A tiny house in a backwater village, both of us unemployed with me wondering whether Gareth would ever get another job following his dismissal. And then I had Gareth's parents to look forward to meeting, parents who he'd never wanted to talk about.

As we drew close, driving through undramatic though pretty enough countryside, I thought about how I'd escaped a similar landscape to launch my career in Hollywood.

Dream on!

~

'Well, we're here and for now there's nothing we can do to change that, so at least let's make an effort,' Gareth said after we'd entered our new home. Perhaps he'd seen my grimace.

There was a musty smell and I could see patches of damp on the walls under the front facing window in the living room. I opened the french windows and stepped into the back garden which was longer than I expected. Beyond was a field with cows grazing. It looked like it was about to rain which reminded me of what I'd been told when a kid – those cows should be sitting. Dad had said it wasn't true. Beyond the cows were yellow-brown squares of some crop close to harvest and further still was a woodland. I liked the view and imagined sitting out in the sunshine to admire it.

A dog barked, the first sound we'd heard since our arrival.

'Come on,' I said, as upbeat as I could muster. 'Let's unpack and move the car to make room for when the moving van arrives.'

29

We took a cab to Mayfair and dined in one of those expensive places where the menu with prices on was only handed to the person who they expected would be paying the bill. There was no hesitation. They assumed it was Shaun – the man.

I hadn't been to such a classy restaurant since the special occasions out with Gareth. It was one of those places where they serve tasters between courses, small bites on giant plates. We drank pink champagne, a lot of it. I recognised the label and dread to think how much it cost.

At the end of the evening we squeezed onto the back seat of a black cab, Sean sitting in the middle, an arm around each of us. He leaned across to kiss Melissa. I turned the other way and watched us pass through Regent's Park then on towards Hampstead.

I felt a pull on my shoulder and faced Shaun.

'We're lucky to have you, Jennifer. Thank you for everything.'

He drew close and kissed me on my lips, not lingering but not a single peck either. I would rather he hadn't have done that.

The cab dropped me off first and we said our goodbyes. Tottering up to my apartment entrance I was relieved to be off duty the next day. I reckoned I'd be spending it dealing with a hangover.

~

I woke the next morning with the imagined feel of Shaun's lips against mine, pleasant but disturbing. That got me thinking about Gareth all over again, about the kisses with the only man I'd ever loved.

Usually I would be working on a Saturday. I decided to take this rare opportunity to do what had been habitual before the hotel had opened – morning coffee at the Dream Café. First a quick shower, the power and heat of the water substantially clearing my head, before dressing in what turned out to be inappropriately thick clothes for this warm, sunny day. I was still hopeless at gauging English weather and by the time I'd reached the end of the street my jacket was off.

As ever, the café was crowded and there were three serving behind the counter, Bridget, her son Andy, and David's daughter Rachel. The two youngsters were helping out during their university holidays while Kelly was off on maternity leave. No one looked happy.

It was Bridget who served me. 'I'll see you tonight unless I've been arrested for murder,' she said looking across at Rachel.

172

'Tonight?'

'At Kelly's. For dinner.'

'Oh, of course.'

I had forgotten but it was in my diary and I would have got a reminder text. I drank my coffee quickly and headed off to buy flowers for the hosts.

It was Bridget who opened the door that evening with the others in a tight circle around Darren. He was gently cradling Lily in his beefy arms, serenaded by a chorus of oohs and aahs.

'She's smiling,' Cecelia declared.

'It's probably wind,' Kelly called out as she came over to greet me, her navy apron speckled with flour.

'You're always saying that. I think it is a smile,' Darren said, his own smile taking doting to the highest level possible.

'Come on, the food's ready; sit down everybody.'

'Good of you to fit us in,' Andrew said. 'You must both be exhausted.'

'It's nice to do something other than feeding the baby and changing nappies,' Kelly said as she returned from the kitchen area having collected a stack of plates. 'She should be a happy bunny now so hopefully we'll get an hour or so of peace and quiet.'

Darren carried Lily upstairs; the man had a permanent smile on his face.

'Is everything going well at the café?' Kelly asked. 'Are you missing me?'

'We are, but everything's fine,' David said.

'Hardly,' Bridget countered. 'I really am going to kill those two soon.'

'It's not that bad,' David said.

'Rachel plays the little girl with you. With me it's full on defiance. She refuses to take notice of anything I ask and I'm the lucky one compared to Andy who gets the undiluted force of her assault.'

'I told you we should have made them equal status rather than have Andy line managing her. I knew Rachel wouldn't be happy with that.'

'But he's the methodical one, the one who can organise time sheets and make sense of the ordering. Rachel's too scatty to do any of that.'

'Not scatty, it's simply not the sort of thing that interests her. She's great with the customers.'

'True enough, but that's no good if there isn't any food or drink to serve when they come in.'

There was an abrupt halt and an embarrassed silence. Perhaps David and Bridget were realising that they were being unprofessional in front of friends who were also customers.

Kelly broke the silence. 'Well, it's only a month before they're back at university and then my maternity leave will be over.'

'Both of us can't wait for that,' David said, stressing the both and taking hold of Bridget's hand.

'Agreed.'

'Although we haven't quite decided what to do, have we pet?' Darren said. 'Lily must come first even if it means Kelly delays returning to work or does fewer hours.'

Kelly shot up. 'Stack the plates will you Darren. I'm going to check the oven.'

There was no further mention of the café that evening but there was tension in the air.

30

I was determined to make an effort in that village, to tolerate even if not to love the place. It was either doing that or wallowing in self-pity. Or a return to the U.S.

Our house was located on a side street. Rephrase – we were in THE side street, a cul de sac called Millers Lane. There were six other houses there, the nearest and largest was directly opposite and named Miller's Nest.

On our first morning I yanked Gareth out of bed early and suggested we go for a walk to explore the place. There wasn't much to see. The main road at the bottom of our street was little more than a throughway connecting our village to civilisation, Cardiff to the south and a small market town fifteen miles further up into the hills.

I counted as we walked. There were eighteen houses unevenly spaced, a mix of styles and ages, and a general store which was currently closed. The village shouted poverty, the buildings small, ugly and uncared for, the broken sidewalk slabs a hazard. One house stood out, the last in the village, set back from the road and partially obscured by a tall hedge. It was detached, double-fronted and three storeys high. Two expensive cars were on the driveway.

I stopped to snoop with Gareth by my side.

'That would cost a fortune in some places but here it's probably worth peanuts,' he said.

'However cheap it is, I still couldn't live here.' The absurdity of the comment hit me because I *was* living there, and in a house that would have comfortably fitted into the space taken up by their double garage.

I was glad Gareth didn't comment on my idiocy, or maybe he wasn't listening.

We crossed the road and headed back to our home, stopping at the end of someone's path by a rough wooden table piled high with carrots.

'You wouldn't find honesty like this in a city,' Gareth said, pointing to a metal container with a weathered and barely visible handwritten sign behind it: *50p a bunch, please leave money in tin.*

I lifted it up.

'What are you doing? You can't steal it!'

I fought off the inclination to make a sarcastic retort as in, "You're a fine one to talk."

'I'm checking to see if anything's in it,' I said. I shook the tin; it was empty.

'Now what?' Gareth asked.

Opening my purse, I took out the single pound coin I possessed, the one kept in reserve to unlock supermarket trolleys. I dropped it into the tin, a clang of metal against metal, and picked up two bunches of carrots. They had a pleasant earthy fragrance.

'Carrot soup for lunch today,' I said as I flicked a bug off the foliage.

It had taken ten minutes to walk the length of the village and back again and we hadn't seen a single person.

We returned to Millers Lane. As we were stepping into our new home I turned for one final look at the deserted landscape, resigned to this being my fate at least for a while. I caught sight of an elderly woman coming out of Miller's Nest carrying waste to her bins. She didn't notice me and I suppose I could have run across the road to introduce myself. She might become my only friend in the village.

I closed our door with a firm click.

~

'So, now that we're here …' I began as we were sitting at the pine table slurping carrot soup. Although this was our first full day in the village, I was determined not to let decision making drift for a minute longer than was necessary. 'What happens next?'

'I'm not intending for us to stay here for long, Jen. It's an affordable stopgap for a short while because of the low rent, that's all. I'll get a job, maybe you can too, and we'll take it from there.'

'We're in the middle of nowhere. How are you, how are we, going to find any work?'

'Don't worry, I've already been looking. We're not far from the train line to Aberystwyth which is having a bit of an economic revival and I've seen some jobs going there. If that doesn't work out, in the other direction is Shrewsbury, or even Birmingham isn't a million miles away.'

'And work for me?'

'I'm not sure to be honest, but as soon as I start working we can think of moving.'

Well, at least there was a plan even if I wasn't as convinced as Gareth that jobs were easy to find. I'd had such a shock discovering that he'd lost his job nearly a year previously, together with the reason why. Could I trust him? In fact, did I love him after what had happened, the moving from place to place, being fired, where we had ended up? Yes. Despite the frustration and the state he had got us into, I did.

We watched some TV that first night with lots of laughter when Gareth put on a Welsh language programme. I played along as he kept pausing to get me to repeat the words. Finally he switched on the subtitles and we rewatched from the start, a pretty good detective series ironically set in some backwater village in Wales.

'Do you think they shot it here?' I joked.

'Quite possibly, so you'd better not step outside after dark!'

'Not even in the back garden?'

'Especially in the back garden. There'll be wolves out there!'

I did step outside that evening, with Gareth, and we marvelled at a sky ablaze with stars. It reminded me of Idaho nights.

Gareth broke the tranquil silence. 'I've told my parents that I'm back. I suppose we should visit soon and then you can meet them at last.'

'You're not making it sound enticing.'

He picked up the empty glasses and stood. 'It isn't. Let's go inside.'

31

Dear Bridget

I hope you don't mind me emailing you rather than having a person-to-person conversation. I'm highly embarrassed about what has happened and I'm going to have to quit my job at Melissa and Shaun's hotel. I realise that they're friends of yours and David and that it was thanks to you that I got the job which makes it doubly awkward.

Best wishes
Jennifer

~

Dear Jennifer

Thanks for the message. If you decide to leave the hotel then that's your choice, David and I being friends with Melissa and Shaun isn't an issue. I did think that you were loving it there though and I know that they are really happy to have you as part of the team, a hugely important part Melissa tells me. I don't know what you see as embarrassing so I can't pass comment on your decision.

Regards
Bridget

~

Dear Bridget

I'm finding the situation impossible because I have no one to turn to for advice. I wish I could tell someone what has happened and talk it through with them. I feel isolated and I hate it. I'm stuck having to lie to Melissa, telling her I'm not well enough to come into work. When she calls to see how I am and asks if she can do anything to help I feel awful. Shaun knows why I'm not in and I have no idea what he's telling her, if anything. Sorry, I'm rambling.

Best wishes
Jennifer

~

Dear Jennifer

I'm sorry that whatever has happened is causing you so much distress. It remains impossible for me to consider giving advice when I don't know what's been going on, though I take your hint about it being something to do with Shaun, I'm assuming Shaun and you. If you do want to tell me more I would be happy to listen and keep our conversation confidential, it's up to you. We are seeing them in a couple of days' time and Melissa might mention something but I won't raise it.

Regards
Bridget

—

It was a Wednesday evening and I'd finished my shift. It had been an easy day with no new guests, no food deliveries and no staff issues to worry about. I liked to be kept busy but it was good to have the occasional day when I could take it easy. Melissa was away, she was visiting her parents somewhere "down south" as she called it and would be staying with them overnight.

I was in the office. We used it as our changing room, the three of us often discarding our smart gear before heading home. The door was usually kept open with an understanding that if closed someone might be getting changed and it was a good idea to knock before coming in. We didn't always stick to that; it was hardly a big deal if one of us saw another partially dressed.

The door was closed that evening, I'm positive I'd closed it. Having taken off my shirt I was about to slip on a tee when Shaun came bursting in.

There was no apology, no fast exit. 'Wow, I'm lucky,' he said.

'What do you mean?'

'Seeing your lovely body.'

I took hold of my tee and stretched the neck hole.

'No need for that, Jennifer. Leave it off.'

'Don't be silly.'

He was by my side. 'You do know that I fancy you like mad.'

He placed his hand on the wrist of my arm holding the tee and pushed down to obstruct me lifting it up to put it on. Not full force but enough to make the point.

'Let go, please.'

With his other hand he cupped my breast through my bra.

'What are you doing, Shaun? Get off!'

Strangely, I didn't feel threatened – I was confident I'd be able to handle this but the aftermath with him being my boss and my friend Melissa's husband was another matter.

'There's no harm having sex with me, Jennifer. It's no big deal, just fun.'

'You'd better step away this second or else you'll be in deeper shit than you can possibly imagine.' He did step away. 'And now you'd better leave the room fast.'

He edged out with one last look of desolation. Fuck that, I was hardly going to feel sorry for him.

Shaun was waiting outside the office when I opened the door having got changed.

'Go away, Shaun.'

'You won't tell Melissa, will you?'

'I'm going home.'

~

Dear Bridget

Thanks for offering to help but I think the best thing is for me to drop it because nothing good can result from anything I say or do. I'll tell Melissa that I've been feeling the strain and need to take a break from work for a while.

See you at the café soon.

Best wishes

Jennifer

~

Dear Jennifer

Whatever you decide is fine by me and I'm sorry something so difficult for you has cropped up. I won't report back unless it looks like there's a crisis brewing.

Regards

Bridget

32

Gareth's parents lived in a neighbouring village, somewhat larger than ours though at first glance equally unexciting. We drove into a small estate with a maze of cul-de-sacs, Gareth muttering and swearing as he reversed out of a wrong turn.

'Why are you so tense? Calm down.'

'You're right. Anyway, we're here.' We had pulled up outside a semi-detached cube with tiny windows. 'These used to be council houses,' Gareth explained.

I had a vague understanding that council houses were for the poor and that a past government had sold most of them. I had no idea whether this was a good or a bad thing and didn't ask for clarification because my attention was on the visit. 'You're sure I should call them Mr and Mrs Edwards and not use their first names?'

'Like I said, they'd prefer that.'

Gareth hadn't provided any information about what to expect and I was shocked to be confronted by such a dowdy couple. I'd dressed up for the occasion (though Gareth hadn't, he was wearing an old pair of jeans and a creased shirt) whereas these two looked like they hadn't changed clothes for half a century.

'Hello Mum. Dad. This is Jennifer.'

I stepped forwards, unsure whether a hug was in order. 'It's lovely to meet you both, I've heard so much about you.' (How English was that!).

Gareth wasn't offering or offered a hug and nor was I. It seemed like they intended to remain by the door in stoney silence, blocking our entry like two security guards at a rowdy bar. What's going on here I wondered as I extended my arm for handshakes? Two limp hands touched my own. A reciprocative smile would have been nice.

'Come in,' seemed like a reluctant invitation but I accepted it and followed Mrs Edwards with Gareth and his father behind us.

I had no expectations but this house was dire and in an appalling state. As we moved from hall to living room to dining room, each of them tiny, it looked like nothing had been decorated, no furnishings replaced or added to since … well, perhaps since Gareth had lived there twenty or more years ago.

Beige and brown were the colours of choice on the striped wallpaper, the velour armchairs, the floral carpet and the velvet curtains. Brown, brown, brown! And next to me stood Mrs Edwards in her brown tweed skirt and beige shirt.

We sat through lunch, a traditional Sunday roast, with me the driving force for conversation, getting increasingly angry because it shouldn't have been that way.

'How long have you lived here?'

'Since you got married. How interesting.'

'What was Gareth like as a child?'

'Naughty! I can't believe that.'

'There must be lovely spots for walks around here.'

'Arthritis? Oh, I am sorry to hear that. A physio might help relieve the pain.'

'Yes, I appreciate it would be expensive if it's not on the NHS.'

'A car is essential in these parts, isn't it?'

'No car. Well, at least you have a bus service.'

'I agree, only three days a week is a bit limiting.'

Fuck, fuck, fuck! I was done, I'd run out of things to say. Or maybe not. "Did you know your son was sacked for stealing?" or "Do you have any joy in your lives? Television? Watching the stars at night? Intoxication? Wild sex?"

Mrs Edwards, who did have a first name – Joy (her mother must have had a sense of humour) – began gathering the plates.

'Let me help you,' I offered.

'No, you stay there. John will assist me.'

Mr Edwards was handed a couple of bowls and he followed his wife into the kitchen.

'God, Gareth, you're hardly being a help.'

'You're doing a great job.'

'But it's not fair. They're your parents, this is the first time I've met them, and I'm struggling to find things to say.'

'We won't stay long. Puddings then we're off.'

I was not happy. It was *his* family so it was his responsibility to make an effort whatever he thought of his parents. If things were that bad why had we bothered visiting them? I picked up what was left to clear up from the table and left Gareth sitting alone in the dining room.

'What do you think of this American woman of his?' I overheard Mr Edwards ask his wife. I froze out of sight.

'She's no Judith, is she?'

'No, she's definitely no Judith. Our son is an idiot.'

I coughed as I entered the kitchen.

'Oh, you really needn't have bothered, dear.'

Agreed – and for that matter I needn't have bothered coming to their house. To our village. To Cardiff. To Salford.

'Who's Judith?' I asked Gareth on the way home.

'Judith? It's a common name in Wales.'

'But do you know a particular Judith?'

'I don't think so.'

~

After my career progression in the States, the change to care home employment in Salford and then Cardiff had been a big let-down, but I had now reached as low as it could get with the part-time job in a dead end café in the nearby town. I do believe Gareth was searching online trying to find work, but nothing was coming up, even in the Aber-something town he'd mentioned, so me having a job was essential. At least with Gareth at home all day I could use the car to reach my workplace.

We were barely managing on my pittance of a wage and I couldn't see much scope for improvement. I felt trapped, except of course I could have walked away from this. But where would I have gone? LA? Salford? Idaho? Cardiff? Portland? I'd reached the miserable conclusion that I didn't have a place to call home and I wasn't doing great on friends either.

Driven by loneliness coupled with boredom, late one evening I got to searching on Facebook to see how things were going for those I hadn't seen or heard from in years. How clever of Facebook to call the people on your contacts list "Friends" – yippee, I did have friends, almost two hundred of them!

I started with my brother, Daniel. He didn't post much but there were photos of his children and I was struck by sadness that I wasn't around to watch my two nieces and two nephews grow up. Maybe I would have been able to provide them with an alternative perspective on life because his few other posts were quotes from the bible with commentary about all the evil and sin out there. Poor kids. Hopefully they'd rebel.

I waded through my LA girlfriends' posts. Angie had made it into a streaming channel movie and Kimberley, having returned to LA, had featured in a couple of daytime TV shows. Nothing more as far as I could see so I assumed they were still waitressing. They'd be heading towards forty years old so wasn't it futile to still be chasing their dream of stardom? Mind you, who was I to judge considering my own state?

I continued my search, finding six others who had been in our feisty group of naïve hopefuls all those years ago. They'd quit LA and were suburban wives, defining success through posts about their families – a child doing well at a swim meet, a husband getting a promotion or winning a golf tournament. Clearly I was bitter and cynical because that wasn't a one hundred percent truthful description of what I was reading. Some had great jobs, one did volunteer work, one played in a high level tennis team. And me? Well, I'd travelled across the States and then thousands of miles to reach Britain, not bad going except that every move, every choice, had been made by Gareth, not me.

I visited his Facebook page. Way back there were selfies of the two of us – on a beach, at a concert, in a restaurant. The last one, posted over a year ago, was of us drenched on a hillside in the Lake District.

I thought about what my life might be like had I not met Gareth which got me searching for Kurt, the boyfriend before him. He was a regular poster, sometimes several a day. The guy was a jerk, dissing anyone in the news he didn't like. There were photos of a peroxide blonde woman, large breasted and showing plenty of cleavage. Poor thing being stuck with Kurt –

or maybe she was happy. Maybe she was happier than me.

Gareth was already in bed.

'Coming up?' he called out.

'Sure.'

33

The emailing back and forth with Bridget had helped me think things through. I couldn't continue working at the hotel, that was obvious, and on balance I could see no good outcome if I told Melissa what had happened. The couple had always seemed to be very much in love and my hope for Melissa was that Shaun had made one stupid mistake and it wouldn't be repeated. If that wasn't the case, well, at least I'd be out of it.

When I called Melissa to hand in my notice I said I was going through a personal crisis and on doctor's orders needed to stop work with immediate effect.

The conversation went on for longer than I wanted, on reflection unsurprising because Melissa and I had developed a strong bond.

'Naturally I'm upset to lose you but more importantly, I'm worried. What can I do to help?'

'Nothing really, though it's so kind of you to offer.'

'Have you thought about taking some time out then coming back? We can get a temp in and leave the job open for you to return to.'

'I'm not sure how long I'll be out for. It's best if you get a permanent replacement.'

'You're not just an employee, Jennifer, you're a good friend. Let's make sure we stay in touch. Maybe come over for a meal when you're feeling up to it. I'm sure Shaun would also love to see you here.'

That seemed innocent enough, but was it? The pause before mentioning Shaun and then the tone made me suspicious. Did Melissa suspect the real reason for me leaving? Did she know what Shaun was like in which case should I be telling her the truth? Shaun didn't deserve to get away with it and might well try the same with someone else.

I was too fragile to work out what to say beyond sticking to my original story. 'Sure, that would be great. I'll be in touch.'

'Jennifer?'

'Yes?'

'Oh, nothing. Take care will you.'

Later that evening I got a texted apology from Shaun along the lines of having no idea what came over him, he was embarrassed, deeply, deeply sorry and would never do anything like it again. Apparently he loved Melissa.

I thought he was pretty dumb to confirm his behaviour in writing; I now had proof. But still I wasn't going to do anything and I certainly wouldn't be replying to him.

The next morning there was a ring of my doorbell and I was confronted by Shaun. Someone must have let him in the front door of the block.

'Get lost!'

He had his foot against the door to prevent me from shutting it.

'I'll scream if you don't leave.'

'I'm here to check on what you told Melissa. She hardly spoke to me last night.'

'If you mean did I tell her that you made a pass at me, the answer is no.'

'Thank you for that.'

'It has nothing to do with you, it's because I don't want to hurt Melissa. You had better not try it on another woman, Shaun. She deserves better.'

He didn't say anything more, he simply turned and walked away. The selfish, conceited bastard.

Great, I was jobless and paying a ridiculously high rent for the worst accommodation in one of the most expensive parts of London. I had enough money to survive for a maximum of four months.

I was a recluse for the rest of that week and into the next, my only excursions being to the mini-market to stock up on food and alcohol, and to the chemist for pain relief tablets. A pity you couldn't get Valium over the counter. Maybe I should have seen a doctor but what exactly would there be to tell them – I need a job, I need friends, I need advice on where to live, I need a purpose in life, I need you to tell me whether I should make contact with Gareth?

Kelly, Emma and Cecelia, the women on Brookland Gardens, were texting and leaving voicemails but I wasn't engaging. I felt particularly guilty when Bridget texted to see if I was OK, being the one I'd contacted after the incident. I deleted her message as I was doing with all the others.

One mid-morning when I was still in my pj's Kelly buzzed the intercom.

'You haven't been around for ages so I thought it was time to see how you're getting on.'

'I'm fine thanks.'

'So are you letting me in or not?'

'Maybe not today.'

'Jennifer, I think today would be good.'

'Alright. Just for a few minutes though.'

I pressed the buzzer to open the main entrance door.

34

The café had seen a steady trickle of customers during the summer and fall months, passing through on their way to locations for trekking, hiking and climbing. Now, with winter setting in, we were getting hardly any takings outside of weekends and it came as no surprise when the café owner told me that she would be reducing my hours and that she couldn't guarantee keeping me on.

She knew about my situation, about Gareth not having a job and me desperate for one.

'You could try the restaurant, dear. It's mainly evening work though; would you want that? Then there's the three Airbnb houses. If you're alright with cleaning there's always work at those.'

'Thanks for the suggestions,' I said, appreciating her concern. 'I need to think about what to do next.'

'Of course, dear. Why not take the rest of the day off and have a wander round town to see what's available. Sometimes people put notes about vacancies in their shop windows.'

I had to smile, casting my mind back to past confusion with statements like, "Why not take the rest of the day off …" in fact meaning, "Take the rest of the day off". A command, not a recommendation.

She misinterpreted my smile. 'It's the least I can do, dear. You go now, it's not as if we're busy. And I will pay your full wage for today.'

The café was empty, it had been all morning. I accepted the offer and did as suggested, wandering through the town in search of anywhere advertising for staff. It was a random walk and I ended up in a neighbourhood that I hadn't seen before. It all looked rather attractive, the stone on the buildings a soft honey colour in the mid-afternoon winter sunshine (sunshine being a bit of a rarity).

For no reason that could be perceived as in any way logical, I felt clear-headed and positive about the situation. I was about to be made redundant, Gareth was yet to find work, the place where we lived was grim, being close to his parents didn't matter because we never visited them. So why stay in the area? It was time for us to move.

All that mattered was that Gareth and I were together. What we had to do now was straightforward. We would move to a city where there were bound to be plenty of employment opportunities. We'd both find work quickly, maybe online before we moved. I'd even do waitressing to start with. We'd stay in a cheap hotel; I'd use my credit card to pay for that and necessities like food. As soon as our first month's wages came in we could start looking for better accommodation. It was all so simple; why hadn't I thought of it before?

I couldn't wait to get back to Gareth to tell him what we were going to do.

Passing the butcher, I went in and bought a couple of their best quality steaks, adding a good red wine from the Co-op. I continued my meandering for a while, coming to rest at the edge of the town where I sat on a bench to admire the hillside view. Bye-bye sheep.

I collected the car from the small space at the back of the café and set off towards our village.

I had never liked the journey, a difficult drive at the best of times what with the narrow roads and sharp bends. Recently it had got more unpleasant being dark by the time I set off from work, with rain lashing down on most days. Today, at a little before three o'clock, there was a new challenge, the low, blinding sun. I pushed the visor down and was humming as I drove.

Dazzled by the sun as I turned into our street, I was initially unsure that what I thought I was seeing by my front door was correct. I pulled up and used my hand as a shade. I hadn't imagined it, there was a woman next to Gareth by our open door. They were facing each other, close. Too close. Part of me wanted to drive up, slam on the brakes, jump out and demand to know what was going on. Instead, I turned off the engine and sat in the car at the end of the road, watching.

The open door presented several possibilities. She could be on her way out. They could be on their way in (Gareth thinking that I wasn't due back home for another three hours). She could be a stranger going door to door campaigning for a political party, selling raffle tickets for some local charity or delivering parcels. But why would they be on the path facing each other, and so close?

The hug said it all, instigated it seemed by the woman who flung her arms around his shoulders with Gareth responding by slotting his arms around her waist. There was no kissing, just a drawn-out hug. Then the attractive woman skipped up the drive all smiles, turning and waving before Gareth closed the door.

~

I waited for the woman to be out of sight before parking outside our house and storming in.

'That woman I've just seen in your arms, is she the Judith who you've told me you don't know or is she a Judith who you do know?'

It didn't take a genius to realise that I'd seen them together and was being sarcastic. Gareth was quick to answer. 'She's a friend.'

'A friend – I'm guessing called Judith – who happens to turn up when I'm supposed to be at work earning just about enough for us to survive on. Did you have sex with her?'

'Sex? No, of course not.'

'So who is she, Gareth? The one your parents said you should be with because she's better than me?'

'I was at school with her, that's all.'

'If that's all why didn't you invite her over when I was here? Since I'm utterly friendless it might have been nice to meet someone new.'

'We had a quick catch up. I was telling her how difficult it is to find a job –'

'Which is more than I've ever got to hear from you. You only tell me you're working on it and I have no idea how that's going.'

Gareth remained silent.

'And that doesn't explain the hug I saw just now. Are you fucking her?'

'I've told you. No. It was ages ago when we had a relationship, we were still in school when it started. She's remarried; she's got a couple of kids.'

'Hang on, remarried? Are you saying what I think you're saying? Look at me, Gareth.'

'We were married for a short while but it didn't work out.'

I had two choices, walk away to gather my thoughts or take this through to the bitter end. How could I stop now?

'You know what? I wouldn't care if you'd had six wives as long as you told me, but you aren't too good at telling me things, are you? So instead of hearing that you lost your job on the day it happened, I don't find out until ten months later. And when like an idiot I feel sorry for you for being made redundant, I discover that you were fired because you'd been cheating on expenses. And now this. Tell me, Gareth, how many other things are there waiting for me to uncover?'

'None. Of course not.'

'And here I am stuck in this shit place trusting you to get us out of it … actually I'm not stuck because I'm off. I'm leaving you.'

35

I burst out crying the second I opened the door to face Kelly.

'The usual reaction when people see me,' she joked and I smiled for the first time in quite a while.

'Come here,' she continued, giving me a firm hug. 'I'm dying for a coffee. You sit down and I'll make it.'

'No, I can do it. Wait in the living room.'

Kelly followed me into the kitchen which I really didn't want her to see. Plates were piled high in a dish bowl filled with tepid, mud-coloured water. Two saucepans with food remains were on the stovetop. Last night's half-eaten dinner was on the table along with two empty bottles of wine.

'Sorry about the mess,' I said, followed by the absurd, 'I've been too busy to clear up.'

'Let me help,' Kelly said, opening the dishwasher. I watched as she unloaded it, piling things up on the countertop. 'I've got no idea where anything goes. Can you do that?'

'Sure.' My involvement was slow and robotic.

She tipped out the filthy water from the dish bowl, rinsed the dirty plates and reloaded dishwasher.

'Honestly, Kelly, let me do that.'

'You make the coffee; I'll have earned a cup after this.'

She worked at a lightning pace, well beyond my speed even when feeling good.

'Where's Lily?' I asked, starting the conversation in the hope that I'd be able to deflect from any talk about me.

'Darren's in charge. He's got a bottle of expressed milk, three nappies, a tub of wipes, a change of clothes and books to read to her, so hopefully he'll be able to cope for an hour or so.'

'I'm sure he will. He seems like the perfect dad to me,' I said, keen to stretch the conversation about Kelly, Darren and their baby for as long as possible.

'True and I'm lucky to have him, he's a good man.'

I handed Kelly her coffee and steered her towards a chair by the kitchen table.

'Talking of good men,' she said as she sat down, 'there are rumours flying around about a bad man. Called Shaun.'

I reddened. 'Not started by me.'

'No, and not even about you. Mind you, based on what I've been hearing, possibly including you after all.'

'Don't they say about rumours that putting two and two together gets you to five?'

'Maybe. Maybe not.'

I liked and trusted Kelly. If I explained what had happened I believed she wouldn't be gossiping to anyone and everyone. Even if she did let Darren and maybe Emma, Cecelia and Bridget know why I had to quit the job I loved so much, I was beginning to think so what? Shaun deserved it.

I described what had happened and how I'd responded to Shaun's pathetic attempt to get me to have sex with him.

'I never felt threatened but I was furious that he was betraying Melissa. What I'm still unsure about,' I concluded, 'is whether I should be telling her.'

'That's a hard one. As far as I know she already has a good idea what Shaun is like so on balance, if it were me, I think I'd do the same as you. Keep quiet about it, at least for now. What's such a pity is that you enjoyed that job so much. Was it impossible to stay on?'

'If I did I'd have to tell Melissa. So no, even though I loved working there. And now I need to find work quick if I'm going to stay here.'

'Is staying here what you want?'

'Great question and I don't know the answer.'

'I've never quite understood how you ended up in Muswell Hill.'

I decided to tell her – it was so easy to chat with Kelly.

~

After finding out that Gareth had been married, I'd stormed upstairs. He followed me into the bedroom, begging me to stay, sobbing, as he watched me pack. I remained calm on the outside, refusing to discuss his twisted reasoning for not telling me about his marriage. On the inside I was traumatised. I'd made up my mind to leave Gareth but feared the thought of life without him. I had absolutely no idea where to go or what to do.

Bizarrely, I paused the packing to cook the two steaks. We sat in silence as we ate, Gareth having finally accepted that there was nothing further to discuss, that I wasn't going to listen to his excuses. I retreated to the bedroom and he slept on the sofa downstairs. As soon as I was awake I did the final packing and carried the large suitcase and a duffel bag downstairs. There hadn't been enough space in my bags to fit all my stuff. It didn't matter, I'd sort that out another day. Now all I wanted to do was escape.

Gareth hovered by the front door, his meek, half-hearted plea for me to reconsider suggesting that he knew I wouldn't be changing my mind. His lies had done me in and I wasn't going to listen to further excuses.

'Where are you going to go?' he asked.

'To the station.'

'I mean to live.'

'I'm not sure yet.'

'So at least stay until you have a plan.'

'I can't, Gareth. I don't want to.'

There was a lull as he looked down at my suitcase before lifting it up. 'Right, I'll drive you to the station.'

'There's no need.'

'Don't be silly, Jen, you can hardly walk there.'

I'd been thinking of getting a cab but that would have meant using some of the little money I had, which I really didn't want. 'OK. Thank you.'

He put the case back down. 'Sort out some food and drink for the journey.'

'I'll get something at the station,' I told him, a little shaken by his thoughtfulness despite the situation.

'Will you at least let me know when you've arrived safely at wherever you're going?'

I nodded, fighting off tears. Part of me wanted a final hug but that couldn't happen. We sat in the car in silence. As soon as we reached the station I stepped out and my goodbye was curt. I wheeled my case to the entrance without looking back.

Where was I going? I decided to take whatever happened to be the first train to arrive, which would take me to either Birmingham or Cardiff. I didn't have to wait long, there was just time to cross the bridge to get to the platform. I was on my way to Cardiff despite the unpleasant memory of our time together in that dismal neighbourhood well away from the city centre. I booked into a budget hotel close to the station, bought sandwiches at the Greggs nearby, and sat in my bedroom wondering what to do next.

As far as I could see, at the highest level, I had two options, either stay in Britain or return to the States. The cost of a plane ticket would wipe out my savings and besides that, where would I fly to? LA? Idaho? Maybe Wilmington to stay with Mom and my aunt? Or Portland? I'd loved living there but had no connections, so what would be the point? The choice was made, for now anyway, I'd be staying in Britain.

I felt duty bound to let Gareth know that I'd arrived. He'd always looked out for me, was always concerned for my safety.

Arrived in Cardiff I texted.

Thanks for letting me know. I'm desperately sorry and sad.

I didn't reply.

36

'So you ended up in Cardiff,' Kelly said, ahead of taking a sip from the second coffee she'd made. 'But by the sound of it you weren't keen to stay there for long.'

'You're right. I needed a job quick though, so the day after I arrived I was out and about looking for restaurant work. It was the same as in other places I'd been, finding a management post seemed impossible unless you already knew the owners. That left waitressing and I was back to where I was twenty years earlier, right at the bottom of the pile.'

'Did Gareth make contact?'

'Just the once. I'd moved to a room that was an awful place but at least I could afford it. He came over to drop off the rest of my stuff and begged for a chance to put things right, but it was too late. I was hurt and I'm sure what I said was cold, even cruel while he was being nice, saying things like, "Of course I understand how you feel and I don't blame you, but at least let's keep in touch – as friends."

I remember telling him there was no point, or something like that. It was true, there wasn't, but he kept trying.

"What about having a last lunch together today?" he asked.

"No, Gareth. Just go back to your Judith, will you. I never want to see you again."

Those were my last words. Not very nice, were they?'

'No they weren't. Understandable maybe, but tough.'

'I reckon I was in the middle of the worst six months of my life, stuck in that bedsit staring at a TV screen when I wasn't doing temp jobs waitressing in dives. There wasn't a single person to talk to, to socialise with.'

'But something changed to make you move to Muswell Hill,' Kelly continued.

'I had one of those *I woke up this morning* experiences, I think that's a line from an old blues song. I thought right, if I'm going to stay in Britain I want to be where the action is – and that meant London. Based on my experience in Salford and the first time in Cardiff, I knew there would always be vacancies in care homes. Even though I wasn't enthusiastic about it, I applied for management posts in London. I was choosy because Gareth had once told me that there were great places to live but also no-go areas, which of course is no different to LA or any other big city. Anyway, ahead of applying for something I researched to check out if it was safe and highly rated.'

'That was sensible.'

'I got three offers including one in Muswell Hill which happens to be listed as one of the top ten places to live in London.'

'Not surprising, it is lovely here.'

'It is, though I'll tell you something funny, I only picked Muswell Hill because it's a kinda weird name. Muswell. I liked it.'

'I can't say that's ever crossed my mind.'

'I got the job to manage the catering teams at four care homes. The pay was a shock, way higher than anything I'd ever had, but when I started looking for a place to rent I could see why they needed to. Everything is madly expensive here so I've ended up in the smallest apartment in the ugliest building around.'

'It's not that bad.'

'Come on! Andrew's told me about the bomb that created the hole between the lovely houses and how they filled it without much thought.'

'You've made it look nice inside. This room's got a lovely feel to it.'

We'd moved to the living room and Kelly was being kind because it was a dump.

'Thanks. IKEA and a local secondhand furniture store did the trick.'

'So you worked at those care homes until you got the hotel job and now Shaun the Rat has ruined everything. What next then?'

'Good question. I guess I'll have to move.'

There was a high-pitched ping.

'That's my special Lily notification,' Kelly said as she glanced at her phone. 'Aw look, Darren's sent a video.'

She turned her phone towards me to show the baby lying on her tummy lifting her head with an expression that was either a smile or a grimace.

She put her phone back down onto the table. 'This Gareth of yours, tell me about him.'

'What's to tell?'

'Obviously you were close enough to be prepared to come over to England with him.'

'We were close, yes.'

I told Kelly about how we'd met while I was waitressing at the LA diner; about our travels across America chasing the various projects he was working on; about what was good and what was bad in the cities where we'd lived; and finally about the move to Britain, Salford then Cardiff then the village whose name I still couldn't pronounce.

'That's a pretty factual summary, Jennifer. What about the *relationship*?'

So I explained how sweet and considerate Gareth was, sexy too, the fun we had together, how he encouraged me to get a catering qualification. The tears were flooding down my cheeks as I spoke.

'But then came all the lies,' I cried out. 'I couldn't handle his lies.'

'They weren't exactly lies though, were they? It seems more like him being unable to tell you things that had happened until you discovered them. I'm wondering whether he might have had a reason for that. Shame? To protect you? For fear of losing you – mistakenly as it's turned out?'

'I've never thought of it that way. I'll never know.'

'Let me tell you something. Darren and I went through a really tough patch, so much so that I was thinking of leaving him. We'd stopped communicating. Fortunately Emma was around and between you and me she wasn't getting on well with Andrew either. The two of us fled to Scotland which gave us time to reflect on things. And there was a meanwhile to the story. Cecelia had moved here and she got Darren thinking about our marriage in a new light –'

'Cecelia!'

'I never have found out exactly what they talked about but by the time I got back from the trip with Emma, determined to make things better, Darren was set on trying too. It's been great ever since, Lily's the proof.'

'I'm pleased for you. You're lucky.'

'More than luck, we had to work at it. Tell me, if you crossed paths with Gareth would you be willing to give it a second go?'

There was another ping on Kelly's phone. She read the message. 'I'd better go soon, Darren's running out of ideas. Or patience.'

'In answer to your question, no, I don't think I could.'

Kelly had stood up. 'You might want to reconsider.'

'I won't do that. But hey, thanks for talking, I'm feeling human again.'

'You do know you've got friends here; we've all missed seeing you. Join us for something soon.'

When Kelly left I got started on household chores, beginning with tidying the living room. I vacuumed and dusted and did a load of laundry. The purpose of all this activity was to take my mind off Kelly's question, but of course it was impossible. Spoiler alert – vacuuming doesn't prevent you from thinking about things.

Would I be willing to give Gareth a second chance?

My reply to Kelly had been instant and categoric: no. He'd lied too much; big fat lies that made everything seem wrong. Kelly had given her marriage a second go but that was different. I wasn't stupid, I knew every relationship had its ups and downs, but there comes a point when a split is inevitable and irreversible despite the past happiness.

Despite the past happiness … we'd been together for ten years and for much of the time it had been great.

Could I ignore that? Could I ever find a new man in the same league as Gareth?

I was unable to push him aside as if he'd never existed even though it was a full year since we'd been together. Here I was, looking at the fortieth birthday card he'd sent me, still on display months after the event.

I sat on that armchair in my pj's, surrounded by cloths, cleaning products and the vacuum cleaner, with the realisation that my resolve was weakening. I'd be fine to catch up, happy to introduce him to my friends in Muswell Hill and I think they'd like him. Maybe we could go to one of those music or literature events at Dream Café, he'd enjoy that.

Yeah, if it came to it, catching up could work.

Nothing more though.

37

Soon after my heart-to-heart with Kelly (which I appreciated) there was another attempt to find me a partner (which I didn't appreciate). This time I was paired with one of Andrew's colleagues from school. When I accepted Emma's invitation I had no suspicion that a blind date was on the agenda.

'It's such lovely weather and there's no way it's going to last much longer,' she said when she called me. 'So we're having some people over for drinks and nibbles in the garden tomorrow afternoon. Nothing fancy, just the usual crew. Please join us.'

"The crew" Emma had called them, which I took to mean her and Andrew, Kelly and Darren, Cecelia and Julien and possibly Bridget and David.

'I guess we're in one of your Indian Summers.'

'Exactly, well remembered. It can't last though, not with the clocks going back this weekend. Tomorrow will be it for the year.'

'I'll see if I can make it.'

'Please try. Hard.'

What the hell, I accepted. It would be the first socialising since the Shaun episode.

It was time to snap out of my lethargy, time to make an effort. I managed to get a last minute cancellation at the hairdresser and took the stylist's advice to go for a dramatic crop and highlights. Looking at my reflection in the mirror when it was done I saw a weary face crying out for some colour. Dismissing the usual places where I bought make-up, I visited the specialist store on The Broadway where a beautician dedicated half an hour attempting to make a difference, before selling me ridiculously expensive vermillion lipstick, charcoal mascara and a rejuvenating face cream. I came away with a big negative on my credit card and little likelihood of being able to pay it off.

Back home I tried on three dresses rarely worn because there had never been an opportunity to dress up in Salford, Cardiff or Muswell Hill, except for the Mayfair restaurant visit with Melissa and Shaun – and there was no way I was going to wear that outfit again.

I have to say I did feel good about myself as I headed round the corner towards Emma's house and it didn't bother me when I saw everyone else was wearing jeans while I'd dressed up.

If I'd thought it through I might have realised that it wasn't only going to be the crew in the garden that day. They were still out to find me a man and that day's contestant had a name that sounded like Jointie or Jonty or Jeanté according to who was speaking. I didn't care what he was called; I wasn't interested.

You know that game kids play, we had it on the farm, the one where you have pieces of face that you arrange to make a weird image? Well this guy made me think of that. He had a large, bulbous nose that absolutely didn't go with his closely set, piggy eyes. Then there were the elephantine ears that he really should be concealing with longer hair. But no, this guy's hair was cropped. Finally, a thin-lipped mouth, making his nose more pronounced than it might have been had proportions been right. As we spoke, all I could think of was how dreadful it would be to kiss him. This thought became obsessive; even when he was talking to the others I couldn't take my eyes off that mouth.

I suppose I was being hugely unfair. Maybe he was OK and (not that he knew it) suffering the consequence of my opposition to being set up. Thinking back, I was pretty rude.

'What do you do, Jen?' was one of the first things he asked – and yeah, I had noticed everyone else melting away to observe from a distance.

'I prefer Jennifer if that's OK.'

'Fine. What do you do workwise, Jennifer?'

'Actually I'm between jobs.'

'What's your profession though?'

'Catering. Do you mind if I get a drink?'

'I'll go. What would you like?'

I could hardly refuse. 'A white wine, please. Large.'

Andrew came up to me while the find-me-a-partner candidate was in the kitchen. 'I'm glad you've met Jointie. He's a colleague at school. He teaches music; you should hear him play the bassoon.'

Emma called out. 'Andrew, get a drink for Noah, will you?'

'Will do, Emma. See you later, Jennifer. Good luck.' Good luck!

Kelly was by my side. 'What do you make of Jonty?'

'Not much.'

'I didn't think it would work.'

'Have you met him before then?'

'Just the once. I heard him perform; he plays the bassoon.'

'Great. I've never met a man who plays the bassoon.'

Kelly laughed; she and I were on the same wavelength. We watched as J and his mouth came towards us carrying two glasses of wine. 'I'll leave you to it.'

'Come on, you're joking. Don't go.'

'No, I have to, I need to feed Lily. By the way, you look gorgeous. I love the new hairstyle.'

'Thanks, Kelly.'

J had reached me. 'She's an interesting one, that Kelly.'

'Interesting? In what way?'

'She – and her husband – are hardly typical Muswell Hill residents.'

'Same as me then.'

He frowned; I guess he had no idea what I meant. That frown though, it seemed to reduce the size of his mouth and eyes to make his blob of a nose still blobbier. Jeez, I was being nasty but I really didn't want to be there getting acquainted with a guy I wasn't interested in. I didn't want to be at this garden party at all. And to be truthful, I didn't want to be over-dressed when everyone else had gone casual.

'Jennifer, bon après-midi.'

'Bonjour Julien.' That was the limit of my French.

'Et bon après-midi, Jeanté.'

'Bon après-midi, Julien. Ca va bien?'

'Oui, ça va bien merci. Et toi?'

'Excuse me, guys, I have to see Darren about something.'

Darren was my first line of escape, standing alone as he watched Kelly making her way indoors holding the baby.

'Help, rescue me, Darren. They've started to speak French.'

He smiled. 'I could give you the lowdown on the new burglar alarm equipment that's voice activated if you'd like.'

'Anything's better than –'

'Jennifer.'

'Hi, Emma.'

'Have you met Jointie? Would you like me to introduce you?'

'It's OK, we've already met. And I do know he plays the bassoon.' That was so impolite. 'Look, I'm not feeling great. I think I'm going to have to head home and lie down for a bit.'

I did the rounds offering apologies, including to J, before leaving. Although relieved that I could escape early, I wished there had been someone to go home to.

38

There's this song I first heard on the radio when I was a kid back home in Idaho. It must have been during those pretentious teenage years when you grab hold of words that you think are meaningful, write them down and then recite them to all the disinterested nobodies who you want to impress.

I even remember the words of the DJ when he was introducing the song. 'This is a golden oldie from way, way back. The band is Sunshine.'

Bad news travels like wildfire
Good news travels slow
They all call me bad news
Everywhere I go

Those words have stuck with me big time even if they might not be the exact ones. I guess when I first heard the song I was thinking that everything around me was bad news, the zits on my face, hair that was never straight enough, Daniel always putting me down, losing a grade at school, being forced to do sports, being stuck living in the middle of nowhere.

And here I was, a quarter of a century later, thinking that those words were truer than ever. The hotel had been my dream job until Shaun messed everything up. Now unemployed I couldn't face returning to care home work, but if I didn't get a job quick I'd have to move. And so what because the apartment was getting me down – the cramped living space, the ugly building, the ridiculously high rent. I didn't like being single but I had no enthusiasm to try dating and wasn't happy with Kelly and the others' hopeless attempts to find me a guy. Yeah, I know they were trying to help.

Whenever I saw a guy, and I don't mean if I spoke to them, I mean like even if they were walking past me on the street, it made me compare them to Gareth. I couldn't help it. I'd probably remain single for the rest of my life.

So there was plenty of bad news for starters, but then I got the email from Mom. This was how we communicated, never a phone call, never a text, and she didn't do Facebook.

She was kinda formal when she wrote, which always made me smile but I wasn't smiling this time.

Dear Jennifer

I do hope all is well with you.

I write with some sad news. Your Aunt Maisie passed away this morning. She has been such a shining star in my life and I will miss her dearly. In fact, it's hard to contemplate what life will be like without her.

With much love

Mom

Visiting Mom in Wilmington to see how she was getting on had been what I'd wanted to do for a long time. Trouble was, until I was working at the hotel I didn't have the money to pay the fare. Finally, I'd been able to save a bit and now I was going to use most of it for the flight I booked for the very next day.

Mom, I'm coming over. I'll see you tomorrow, my email started.

I gave her the details of the flight.

Mom met me at the airport. I needed a double take to realise that the woman standing by the arrivals exit beaming in my direction was her. She was dressed in yellow pants and an orange shirt; her wrists were crammed with bracelets and there were two rings on one hand and three on the other. I checked – her marriage ring finger was free. She'd added a few strands of dark to her greying hair and she'd cropped it short. It suited her.

We hugged as passengers in a hurry tutted and pushed past us.

'It's wonderful to see you, Jennifer.'

I was crying, it was so good to be with her.

'It's alright, darling,' she continued, cradling me like I was a child, and that's how I felt.

She drove us back to her condo, the one she'd shared with Maisie. In Idaho I'd never seen her drive, that had been Dad's job. Now here she was, slaloming between lanes, hooting at vehicles she claimed were obstructing our progress, cussing other motorists' bad driving.

When we stepped inside her place she told me to drop my case in her bedroom and come straight back down without unpacking. 'Mine's the room with bright colors, honey, and like I said, you come right on down.'

I met up with her in the kitchen. There were two tumblers of deep ruby red wine on the glass-topped table. Was this the Mom who was teetotal as far as I could recall?

'No rush to do anything, honey. Let's sit and chat.' Was this the Mom who had been task-obsessed, constantly on the lookout for jobs to do?

'To life – even though it always ends in death,' she said and we clinked glasses.

'And then on to heaven?' I tested.

'Maybe. Maybe not. Probably not.'

'I didn't think I'd ever hear you say that.'

'Living with Maisie got me thinking about things in a different way.'

She spoke about how wonderful Maisie had been, exposing her to so much that enriched her life. Mom had joined a tango class, (I'm the worst in the group), was learning to play saxophone, (you wouldn't want to hear me practise), and was busy writing short stories, (that no publisher would ever consider touching).

She was so lively I could barely get a word in.

'Maisie was a lesbian,' she came out with. 'Did you know that?'

'Well, I knew she hadn't married but I suppose I've never given her sexual orientation any thought.'

'At first I was shocked, but she was so comfortable with her choice it made me think it's fine for everyone's preferences to be different.' She was pouring her second glass. 'More?'

I nodded and she topped up mine.

'I took on lots that she enjoyed though the lesbian thing wasn't for me.'

I'd never thought about Mom and her sexuality, ridiculous of course because she'd had two kids. But why was she bringing it up now? Then I guessed. 'You're dating, aren't you? You have a man.'

'I am seeing someone; Jeff is his name. You'll meet him at the funeral and I think you'll like him. He's the second person since Dad died, the first didn't work out at all well but this is looking good.'

'Where did you meet?' With all these surprises I was wondering whether she was a silver surfer on a dating app.

'At my dance class. He's a divine dancer. The first time he took hold of me as we tangoed he swept me off my feet. Literally.'

'I'm pleased for you, Mom. Real pleased.'

Our glasses were near empty and Mom topped them up again. Jet lag plus alcohol was making me light-headed.

'And tell me what's been happening with you, Jennifer, now that lovely man is no longer part of your life.'

'I will tell, but not tonight. I'm exhausted; I need to sleep.'

'You're in my room and I'll be in Maisie's old bedroom.'

'Is that Ok, sleeping in there?'

'It's a room, Jennifer. Just a room.'

She led me upstairs. She was my Mom again, showing me the bathroom and where to find towels. Then we went into her bedroom where she pulled back the patchwork quilt, the one she'd made long ago for her bed in Idaho. I used to sneak in and choose which of the squares I liked best, it had to be a different one each day. Apart from the quilt this room couldn't be more different to the one on the farm. It shouted Mexican with its brightly coloured walls, geometric patterned fabrics and dark wood furniture, the mix reminding me of Frida Kahlo paintings. Her Idaho bedroom had been sterile off-white, the furniture functional rough pine.

'I love this room,' I told her as we hugged once more. I didn't want to let go because she was my Mom and I was that kid again.

She was the one who pulled away. 'Get that rest, Jennifer, because tomorrow's gonna be a busy day.'

Seconds after getting into bed I had drifted off into a restful sleep.

39

I was up at 4.00 am the next morning, body and brain on UK time. I made myself a coffee and replied to the text Kelly had sent to check that I was OK. Kelly had set herself up as my guardian angel and I liked that. I put on the TV and caught up with what was going on in the States; too much intolerance and hostility for my liking.

When Mom was up I helped her sort through the paperwork that the living are left to deal with after a death. We started to clear out my aunt's possessions. I anticipated an awful job and as far as clothes were concerned it was. We had one large bag for the charity shop and one for what was going to be thrown away. All those careful choices of what to wear that Maisie would have made, now relegated to the contents of Walmart plastic bags.

'I think I'll keep these,' Mom said, fingering two silk scarves. One was plain, a deep turquoise, the other a Mondrian pattern of yellow, navy, red and white blocks. 'Maisie loved scarves so this will be a nice memory even if I never wear them myself.'

I used steps to reach the box of photographs on top of Maisie's closet and we stopped rushing through sorting to leisurely look through the pictures. They went back to when Mom and Maisie were children, ones I'd never seen. We discovered two boxes with photos of Maisie with different women, arms entwined, somehow the affection radiating off the pictures. My aunt looked the same age, in her forties, in both sets.

'It was tragic,' Mom explained. 'Both loves of her life died young, one soon after the other.'

'And no one since then it seems,' I said having rifled through the rest of the pictures in the box.

'She did have partners later on in life but I guess all photos are kept on the cloud these days.'

When Mom was in Idaho a cloud was the grey mass in the sky that brought much needed rain in summer and unwelcome snow in winter.

'What's so funny, Jennifer?'

'You talking about clouds.'

She let it pass and went across to the low cupboard by the window. 'There is this one though.' She picked up a photo in a dark wood frame and passed it over, a selfie with Mom and Maisie sitting at a seafront café, huge smiles that were firing their warmth at me.

I smiled back. 'You seem so happy here.'

'I am. I loved your father and I miss him terribly but Maisie taught me how to move on. I hope you don't think that sounds selfish.'

'It doesn't. You gave Dad everything.'

'When Maisie knew she was going to die she reminded me how difficult she'd found it to cope with the loss of her two close friends, her lovers. She'd done what they would have wanted and she was making me promise not to dwell on any sorrow, including her death, but to always live life to the full. Of course, agreeing is easier than doing, but I get what she meant and I'll do my best to keep that promise.'

'It looks like you're doing just fine. Tell me about your man.'

'Yes, Jeff.'

'And …'

'And we get on wonderfully well. You can meet him later on today if you come along to my tango class. I know it's close to Maisie dying but she would have wanted me to carry on as normal. "Absolutely no mourning, you promise me that too," she said on the day she lay in bed near to death. I will understand if you don't want to come though, Jennifer.'

'I will. To see you dancing. To meet your boyfriend. What other surprises will I discover?'

~

Bloody hell, as Gareth would have said.

After spending the rest of the day sorting and making a list of what was left to do, Mom went into her bedroom to get changed. She reappeared in a black dress embossed with a red, yellow and orange flowery pattern. She had on open-toed heels.

'You look stunning,' I said.

'I don't know about that but it is fun dressing up for class. There aren't many other opportunities.'

Jeff, a wiry man with tidy salt and pepper hair, met us in the lobby. Mom seemed nervous as she introduced us.

'It's fine,' I whispered as we followed Jeff into the hall.

He might have been a few years older than Mom but was a bundle of energy as they danced away, spinning, clicking heels, doing moves that I didn't think I would ever be able to master.

'You're both brilliant,' I said during the break. 'Have you been dancing for years and years, Jeff? It looks like it.'

'No, I only signed up a few weeks ahead of your mother. I wanted to do something way out of my comfort zone. I'm an electrician so this sure is that something. As soon as I caught sight of this woman I knew I'd be staying even if I couldn't get on with the dancing.'

'But we did improve,' Mom chipped in. 'We're practising outside of class ahead of our trip to Argentina for a program in the fall.'

'Brilliant.'

'Why don't you give it a try, Jennifer,' Jeff suggested.

'No way.'

'Beginners get to dance with Felipe!'

I looked across at Felipe, young and dishy Felipe, who happened to catch my eye and come across.

'This is Jennifer, my daughter, Felipe. She's visiting from England.'

'And she wants to dance,' Felipe said with a mischievous smile.

'Absolutely not!'

His assistant had started up the music, Mom and Jeff were off, and I was left facing Felipe who took hold of my hands and steered me onto the dancefloor.

I can't say I loved the experience to begin with but being guided by Felipe soon changed that. He twisted and turned me, his arm round the base of my back, mine across his shoulders, our hands clasped. My cheek brushed against his. This was crazy, I was in Wilmington for a funeral and I was getting hot.

'I must move on to others,' Felipe said as a second piece of music came to an end. He gave a little bow. 'We swap partners.'

Before I could say anything or escape from the dancefloor, a male student was next to me, then another, then another, and finally I was dancing with Jeff who, admittedly based on inexpert judgement, seemed the most competent of the lot.

Following the class the three of us went to a bar and drank Argentinian red wine. When Jeff was away to order more drinks Mom asked if it would be alright for Jeff to stay the night. 'After tango we always want to spend more time together.'

She hadn't quite said, "It makes us real horny and desperate for sex", but she didn't have to. After Filipe I knew what she meant.

'Sure. No problem.'

I was restless that night; Mom had given me plenty to think about. Now in her early sixties, her life had altered beyond imaginable and yet here I was, thinking my life had reached a dead end at the age of forty. Somehow things had to change and it was up to me because no one was going to do it for me.

I liked Jeff, the electrician from Flint who had moved to North Carolina to escape the decay in his home town. I liked how he cared for Mom, respectful and valuing her opinions. The ex-farmer's wife from Idaho and this man were creating a powerful energy that was mighty impressive.

Daniel didn't feel the same way.

My brother and his family joined us at the church on the day of the funeral. He was the one in charge, giving out the orders, his children silently obedient and Ashleigh much quieter than I remembered.

I was determined to avoid conflict but it was a close thing after Jeff put an arm round Mom's shoulders at the graveside.

Mom had introduced Jeff as "my friend" but I don't think Daniel had put two and two together until that moment.

'That man and Mom, are they …' he whispered.

I didn't want to be hearing all the God stuff about living in sin and I didn't want him laying into Mom or Jeff so I kept it nice and easy. 'Jeff's a lovely man. They're real happy together and he's looking out for her.'

'Is he now?'

'Daniel, what would you want Mom to do, live alone in misery for the rest of her life? She was a wonderful wife to Dad but he's dead.'

He called across to Ashleigh. 'Round up the kids, we need to get going soon.'

'Aren't you going back for the social?'

'There's too much to do on the farm, I booked an early flight back.'

I looked across at his kids chatting to Mom and Jeff, smiles all round. Jeff dipped his hand into his wallet, pulled out dollar bills and handed them over to the children.

'I thought you might at least stay over tonight,' I said.

'We were in a motel last night so that we could make it to the church on time. One night away is enough.'

What he probably meant was that one short meeting with me was plenty. He wouldn't have known about Mom and Jeff when he booked those flights; didn't he care enough about her to want to stay longer?

'Do you get to see Mom much?' I asked.

'She's been out to the farm a couple of times. I don't think she misses it.'

I bet she doesn't, I thought.

I suppose this meeting was an improvement on the bitter previous one; we even got to hugging each other, a bit like hugging a totem pole.

'What a strange man my son is,' Mom said as we waved them off.

'It's always kinda tense at a funeral,' the ever-diplomatic Jeff said.

It was quite some party, a grand gathering organised by the tourist office and hosted by the city mayor. Everyone was speaking highly of Maisie as the food and drink came and went. We'd intended to get on with sorting Maisie's possessions as soon as we got home, but overwhelmed by the buzz of the reception, and the effect of the alcohol too, meant that wasn't going to happen that day.

'I really like Jeff, Mom,' I said as we were looking through Maisie's jewelry the following morning.

'It means a lot to me you saying that Jennifer.'

'Are you planning to live together?'

'It's early days, we'll see. But we are spending a lot of nights together. You OK with that?'

'OK? Much more than that; I think it's cool.'

'Which is not the case with your brother. He told me so before leaving.'

'I guess he is what he is. Does he help you? Financially?'

'He doesn't have to; I've got my job. I haven't told you about it, have I? I was working for Maisie, on reception at the Visitors Bureau.'

'Also cool.'

'I'll carry on with it for a while, for as long as Jeff's working. One thing I do know is that Maisie's left everything to me, including this place. I won't be short of money which has got me thinking that I'll be able to help you out.'

'There's no need, Mom. I'm doing fine.'

'But I want to. You haven't said where you're working now.'

'I'm not, I've just left a job. I'll get something else as soon as I'm back.'

'I'm paying for your fare over here and a bit more, that's not for discussion, and I'll be paying for you to come here as many times as you can. I've missed seeing you, Jennifer, it's been much too long.'

'I know. I've missed you too.'

Maybe we'll come across to see you in England.'

'I'd love that. Both of you.'

I wanted to see her lots and I was thinking what was there for me in England? Why not move back to the States, to Wilmington, to be near Mom?

I wasn't ready to suggest that. 'Let's get on with the sorting; I've only got another two days here.'

We lifted up pieces of jewelry, adding a description of each onto a list ahead of getting it appraised. Mom decided to keep two rings and a bracelet, I took a

236

sapphire pendent with matching earrings. The rest she'd be selling.

'I guess you're not planning to see Gareth anymore,' Mom said as she placed a string of pearls back into its case.

I'd been wondering when this would come up. 'No.'

'That's a shame.'

40

A few days after leaving the Wilmington sunshine to return to the London drizzle, I received a one line text from Bridget.

Can we meet about something?

I was happy to go over straight away but Bridget wanted to delay for a short while. We settled on meeting at Dream Café on the Thursday at ten o'clock. She wouldn't tell me what it was about.

Bridget was impressive. She was friendly, laidback and fun-loving whenever we were socialising at the Brookland Gardens crew's get togethers. Beyond those times our only contact had been when she was working at the café. I'd formed the opinion, based on instinct alone, that when it came to business she was shrewd, quite possibly the decision maker out of her and David.

I strolled over to the café on the Thursday morning having given close to zero thought about what she wanted to talk about. My sole guess was that it was to arrange a surprise celebration for someone.

There was a new guy behind the counter, young, tall and thin with untidy dyed blonde-white hair. He was chatty as he led me to the office, informing me that this was only a temporary job while he considered what he wanted to do full time.

The door was ajar but still he knocked. 'Your appointment, Bridget.'

'Thanks, Ed.'

I hadn't seen the office before and was surprised by how untidy it was. A desk was piled high with papers and the nearby waste bin was overflowing. The little spare floor space in the small room was filled with boxes – wine, soft drinks, crisps, granola bars.

'Hi. Take a seat, Jennifer, then give me a minute to clear the desk.'

I watched as she pushed papers aside to make space, wondering whether she intended to keep pushing until everything fell onto the floor around the bin.

She caught my smile. 'It's not usually as messy as this but we're having a kitchen reorganisation so all the dry goods have ended up in here. And I've got a year's worth of invoices and receipts to wade through.'

'That's fine. No rush.'

She was gathering loose sheets and piling them up into stacks. A painting on the wall caught my eye; easy to recognise as one of Bridget's own. It was of a single leafless tree on a hillside with sheep grazing around it. A low sun cast an orange tint over the landscape. Her paintings all had a hint of fantasy.

'That's beautiful. I love your paintings, Bridget.'

'Thank you. I put that one up to remind me what life outside the city is like.'

'It could be in Wales.'

'Wales?'

'I lived there for a bit.'

'Did you? Right, I'm done,' Bridget said, placing one of her piles of paper onto the floor and pulling out a folder from a drawer to take up the space. 'What would you like to drink? The usual?'

'Yes, that would be lovely, thank you,' I said, the True Brit accent in an instant obliterating the American drawl that I had resurrected back in Wilmington.

Bridget got up and went over to the doorway. 'Ed, could we have a flat white and an espresso please?' She closed the door before continuing. 'You must be wondering what this is all about.' She had returned to behind the desk.

I nodded and waited for her to tell me.

She opened the folder, took out some sheets and glanced down at them before addressing me. 'When you were emailing me about your difficulties at the hotel, I admired how you stayed discreet even though it must have been awful for you. What you were hinting at was no surprise because Shaun's inappropriate behaviour wasn't a one-off. I'd been hearing all about it from Melissa and as soon as you told her you were quitting she knew why. I think she tried to contact you –'

'That's right but I was hoping that what Shaun had tried was one stupid act. I didn't want to mess things up for them if that was the case. I ignored her calls because if I'd spoken to her it would have meant either lying or telling her what had happened, and I wasn't happy to do either.'

'She guessed why you wouldn't speak and appreciated that.'

Ed knocked on the door and Bridget stopped talking. He was carrying a tray with the two coffees and a plate of mini patisseries. Were they made in-house or bought in I was wondering as Bridget spoke.

I wasn't fully attentive because the hotel job was history, the memory hurt and as far as I was concerned there was nothing further to say about it. Melissa appreciating how I'd handled the incident didn't solve my problem. I was out of work. I was not going back to care home management. I couldn't get a job in a local restaurant because senior vacancies never came up. Stuck without work and no money, this conversation with Bridget was not going to solve anything.

Half-listening I picked up how disappointed Melissa was that I'd been forced to leave; that I'd done a great job. Had I misheard? Was she saying that Shaun had left?

'Sorry, Bridget. Did you say that Shaun isn't running the hotel anymore?'

I got a frown and felt guilty for not concentrating.

'Like I said, Melissa has kicked him out. Finally. So yes, he's left the hotel, he's left the house, in fact he's moving well away from here. It happened quickly but when Melissa decides on something you don't want to hang around arguing your case.'

'But what about the hotel? They put in such a lot of work to set it up and I know how much effort is needed to run it. They shared the load; Melissa's great but it's too much for one person.'

'True. She's determined to carry on but she'll need help.'

I was aware of a further issue because Melissa and Shaun had always been open with me about finances. 'They had to borrow loads to buy and renovate the property. It was a fifty-fifty split so how is that going to be sorted?'

'Good question. As far as who owns it goes, you're right, it's fifty-fifty plus of course the mortgage from the bank. Although they used savings to pay for most of the renovations, there's an additional loan, again from the bank.'

I picked up the small cube of passion fruit cheese cake and popped the whole thing into my mouth, blushing with embarrassment on realising that I hadn't been offered anything. But then Bridget took a mini muffin and the much needed break in the conversation allowed me to gather my thoughts. Why was she telling me all this?

'So yes, everything – the property, the debt, the expenditure, the revenue – has been in their joint names. Melissa is going to settle with Shaun by taking on all the debt and passing over half the deposit they put down to buy the place. That's very generous because most of the money was hers, but she wants to rid herself of him as quickly as possible. He'd be an idiot to refuse the offer.'

The owners had been so trusting of me that I knew the amounts we were talking about, hundreds of thousands of pounds. I'd always regarded them as a full on partnership, as solid as a rock, a happy, loving couple. I didn't know who had contributed the most, but on reflection it could well have been Melissa. She'd spoken about having gone to a private school, she spent a fortune on clothes, she drove a Land Rover: maybe she came from a mega-rich family who provided the money to help her. But hundreds of thousands?

'I've been using the future tense which isn't strictly correct.'

'Sorry, Bridget. What do you mean?'

'I mean Melissa's plan isn't a plan anymore, it's happened. Here's some news hot off the press so I'd appreciate if you keep quiet about it for a few days. David and I have taken on Shaun's share of the hotel so we're part-owners. We'll be able to help out a little with the management too, but only if there's a good team in place.'

'That's great news. Congratulations! Melissa must be so happy and it's exciting for you two as well.'

'It is exciting. The café has done better than we could ever have dreamed and it's given us the confidence, and the money, to go in with Melissa. We signed the papers yesterday which is why I didn't want to meet you until this morning. We know there are risks so it's vital to have reliable and competent people in the team.'

I must have been slow because I still wasn't getting it. "The penny hadn't dropped" Gareth used to say.

'Jennifer, have you picked up why I'm telling you all this?'

'No. Not really.'

'We want you back as deputy manager at the hotel. In fact, with Shaun gone there'll be additional responsibilities, so it would be a promotion.'

'I … but what does Melissa think?'

'You must know the answer to that. She's desperate to have you back.'

'And David?'

Bridget was laughing. 'David is a list person and as soon as the idea of ownership was suggested he had a spreadsheet up and was filling it. The first thing he wrote was getting you back as deputy manager.'

'I'm pleased to hear that, but why the laughter?'

'Mention of a list brings back a memory that still makes me fall about laughing.'

'What happened?'

'I shouldn't say really. Well OK. It was soon after we met, before we started our relationship. He invited me over for a meal and for a complicated reason he hadn't had time to get the food in. I volunteered to go to the supermarket and he said he had a list of what to buy in his coat pocket. I shouldn't be saying, you're not going to go round telling everyone, are you?' I shook my head, wide-eyed and all-ears. 'The piece of paper I pulled out wasn't a shopping list, it was his action plan of how he intended to move on after his wife had left him.' Bridget was laughing again. 'Have sex with Bridget was written down.'

'No!'

'And the next point he'd written down was to have more sex with me with the date added – by the end of the first week in March!'

Her laughter was contagious.

'That's so embarrassing.'

'He was inconsolable when he saw me holding it up even though I told him it was alright, in fact funny.'

'And did you … oh, I can't ask that. But it has all worked out.'

'It has. And yes, we did.' She giggled like a little kid. 'There was other stuff written on the list, including quitting his accountancy job to open an arts café. At the time I thought it was no more than a wild dream but look what's happened. I've kept that scrap of paper. God, I don't know why I'm telling you all this.'

'It's cool; I'll keep it secret. But a huge well done to David and you – for the café and now the hotel.'

'I hear my name. What are you two saying?'

I swung around to see David behind me. He was beaming. Surely he hadn't overheard our conversation.

'I've explained the situation to Jennifer, David.' Bridget looked back towards me. 'I imagine you need time to think about our offer.'

'No, I don't, I'm hugely happy. I'd love to work at the hotel again and having you two there along with Melissa will be even better than before.'

'Great. Let's set up a meeting to go through contract details,' David said, 'but as far as I can see there's nothing to stop you starting as soon as you want.'

'Thanks, David. And thanks, Bridget. I'm over the moon.' (As Gareth used to say).

41

Having agreed to work at the hotel, our group hug brought back the unpleasant memory of another hug, the one with Melissa and Shaun after I'd accepted the deputy manager post first time round. I'd thought that a warm and welcoming couple were showing their delight that I was joining the team but look how that turned out. I knew this hug was different.

Over the moon, over the moon, over the moon. The expression stayed with me as I made my way from the café to the florist on The Broadway to buy a pricey bouquet, a present to myself. I walked past the supermarket, the usual place where I got wine, and turned into the side street where the expensive wine merchant was located.

The inside of the store was like an ancient college library, all dark wood panelling and creaky floorboards. And just like a stuffy library it was austere with an intimidating near silence as the few customers pulled out and replaced bottles with the faintest of clinks. The meticulous placement was by country of origin. I set off in search of American wines, which I found in the furthest aisle from the entrance, and selected a bottle of the expensive Californian white that Gareth and I used to drink in LA.

'I'll take this one, please,' I whispered, sticking to the library code and coming out laughing as I imagined returning the bottle like a book even though it would be empty.

At home I put the flowers in a vase, opened the wine and collapsed into my favourite seat, setting aside the thought that it would be nice to have someone there with me to share this moment.

How quickly things can change. Life had been an absolute disaster only days ago ahead of leaving for Wilmington and now there were plenty of positives to savour.

Over the moon, over the moon, over the moon. I had an unbelievable job lined up. I had bosses who treated me as a friend. But top of the list was having Mom so happy with plans to see more of each other. Briefly I thought of Gareth, about what he'd be thinking. He'd be pleased that I'd met up with Mom, pleased about my job too.

It was the cow! The cow jumped over the moon in the nursery rhyme. It didn't add up though, why was it an expression of delight, why would a cow be happy to be jumping over the moon? I googled and came across Charles Molloy, the man who had written it in the eighteenth century. He must have been on something, maybe opium. There followed an internet journey, taking me to a further expression of joy that must have originated from those weird English: Pleased as Punch. Why am I wasting my time doing this, I wondered. But I knew why – because I had nothing better to do and no one to tell about my success.

That evening I got a text from David asking if I could see him the next morning to discuss contract terms. We met at the café and by the end of the half-hour I was close to complaining about the over-generous salary he'd offered.

'It's not too much, Jennifer, because the three of us know that you'll be working hard to earn it.'

'Then I accept and I'm hugely grateful.'

'Excellent. Melissa's told me she'd like to see you. She's at the hotel.'

'Sure, I'll head over now.'

Having welcomed me back, Melissa quickly moved our chat past anything to do with the hotel. She provided a cutting overview of her life with Shaun, letting me know that he was a weak-willed, two-timing shit and that his pathetic attempt to get me into bed with him had been the final straw.

'But how did you know about that?'

'It was hardly a challenge to work it out and there was no denial. As soon as I accused him he went through all that "I couldn't help it" crap again.'

She seemed to have got over Shaun real fast because she was seeing a new man and reckoning it was going brilliantly.

'But what about Shaun? What's he doing now?'

'Who cares? Anyway, me and my gorgeous man are going away for a few days. To Paris of course, Romance City. We're back on Tuesday so let's make Wednesday the day you start. Sorry, I must dash now, I've got loads to do before we leave.'

Is something wrong with me I wondered as I was walking home? Melissa had been with Shaun for years and as soon as it ends she's off with someone else, whereas it's over a year on and I still can't let go of Gareth.

When I opened my emails back at home there was one from Mom, a long message with information about her inheritance from Maisie. It was way more than she'd expected and enough to send me a monthly allowance so that I could have a nicer place to live.

No! I wrote back, the single word.

Yes! It's either that or the money goes to an abandoned cats charity!

She knew I didn't like cats.

I'd better think about it then, but seriously, I'm not saying definitely yes.

Her reply email consisted of two emojis, a black cat and a smiley face.

I took out the vacuum cleaner, hoovering having recently emerged as my default activity for reflection.

Should I accept Mom's generosity? It struck me that what she proposed wasn't only to make me happy, it was to make her happy too. I would take up her offer. Adding her money to my substantial salary, I should be able to afford an upgrade to my current home.

Jeez, things are good I was thinking as I thundered my bad news anthem in sync with the throb of the vacuum cleaner.

Bad news travels like wildfire
Good news travels slow
They all call me bad news
Everywhere I go

Would something turn up to bring everything crashing down?

~

I was apprehensive on my first day back at *On the Hill* because I'd been given way more responsibility than when I'd previously worked there; they were relying on me to deliver. I felt the pressure of having to justify the hike in salary together with the five percent stake in the company that had been included in my contract. As a shareholder, David had told me during our contract meeting, if things went well there would be a substantial annual dividend coming my way.

And from Day One things were going well. The business was booming; we were having to turn people away.

Melissa was doing a great job with the marketing, getting us featured in newspapers and magazines.

'Look at this, you're world famous, Jennifer,' she declared, swivelling her laptop towards me. We were in the office that afternoon, reviewing what to stock in the bedroom mini bars.

The ten best boutique hotels in London ran the headline in the online weekend magazine of a leading national newspaper. There I was, greeting four guests in reception, broad smiles all round. You know when you see a photo and think that's not me because surely I don't look that awful – well that's how I felt. But when I complained Melissa assured me that I was stunning.

'Stunning enough to have loads of men chasing after you,' she added. This wasn't the first time she was pushing me to be out there in the marketplace for a partner. 'They'd die to see that body of yours.' At the time, everything she was saying oozed sensuality and her heart-to-hearts with me about her relationship were shockingly explicit.

Stunning or not, when I got home I emailed the link to the magazine article to Mom.

It was Jeff who wrote back later that evening, praising his star step-daughter. Hang on though, I wasn't his step-daughter because they weren't married. Or were they? Surely I would have been told. The fact that it was him who replied meant that he had access to Mom's emails which I didn't like because there were things I wanted to ask her, including whether she was living with Jeff full time.

I decided to call her and during that first conversation it took Mom a while to accept that phoning from England wasn't going to cost a fortune.

'Something else Mom, are you and Jeff married?'

'Married? No, of course not. Why do you ask?'

'Because in an email from your account he referred to me as his step-daughter.'

'Oh, that's just him being friendly. I showed him the article.'

'But he wrote the message from your address.'

'Yes, and he did ask first. I suppose I could have forwarded him the link; I didn't think it mattered. There's nothing fishy going on, honey.'

'OK, but you still haven't told me if you're living together.'

The answer was yes. Apparently it was a recent decision and Mom had been about to let me know. Jeff was selling his place, Mom had already sold Maisie's condo, and they were in the process of buying a bungalow with a good amount of land around it. They intended to spend lots of time out in the sunshine working on the garden.

'I'll get Jeff to send you some photos of the place or maybe the link to the real estate agent's website.'

'I'd like that.'

'Talking about real estate agents, listen up. I've been looking online at rentals in this Muswell Hill of yours. There's this great website that lists everything in a district so you don't have to visit each company separately.'

'Really?' I teased though she didn't pick it up.

'Yep. You were right about rentals there; the prices are wild. I guess that's because you live near the palace.'

'What palace?'

'Just you hang on there and I'll get Google Maps up. Here we are. Alexandra Palace.'

'That's not a palace,' I said. 'It's called a palace but no royalty live there. It's expensive around here because it's a great place to be and not far from the city centre.'

'Maybe, though from what I've researched there isn't much of a difference to other districts nearby.' This was my Mom speaking. I had to remind myself that as far as technology was concerned, she had never even been able to master the TV remote.

'True enough,' I said. 'Everywhere in or near Central London is crazy prices.'

'Well hear me out. You told me what rent you're paying and I reckon you need to at least double that to get a decent apartment.'

'Mine is decent.'

'It's tiny, those photos you sent me don't lie.'

'I agree it is a bit on the small side –'

'And you told me it's the ugliest building around. So this is what I'm gonna do.'

When she said how much she was going to send across each month, threatening me with supporting the stray cats charity again if I said no, I didn't argue. I gave her my bank details.

'Here's another idea, Jennifer. Why don't we see each other next time we speak? You'll need to download something called WhatsApp.'

'I might already have that one. And yes to a live chat next time.'

'You make sure you start looking for a new place right away, Jennifer.'

'I will Mom.'

42

Each day before and after work I was onto the property app, the one I hadn't needed Mom to tell me about. Apartments were coming up at an affordable rent now that I could at least double what I currently paid. They were the sort of places that you'd want to live in, the sort of places you'd happily invite people over to. My tenancy agreement had a month to run and I didn't intend to renew so I needed to get moving.

The four of us – Melissa, Bridget, David and me – had regular weekly meetings at the hotel on Monday mornings. At the end of the one following my conversation with Mom, I mentioned that I intended to move and Melissa volunteered to join me at any viewings. I accepted; I'd value her second opinion. She had expensive tastes though and got me to push up the maximum I wanted to pay during our searches.

'No harm seeing what a place is like,' she urged.

'Except a waste of time if it's too expensive.'

'Owners might be prepared to take a reduction, Jennifer.'

'This is Muswell Hill.'

'You never know what someone's personal circumstances are like. Let's take a look at this one,' she suggested as she cursored through the photos.

We did and it was a fabulous top floor apartment in one of those Victorian villas that I had always loved walking past. It was fully furnished with subdued, calming colours throughout – the walls, the kitchen units, the carpets, the curtain fabrics, the seating.

'It's very white,' Melissa whispered as we were being shown round.

'It makes it tranquil. I can see myself chilling out here every night.'

'I suppose you could always add splashes of colour; I'd help you choose. Look, if you're interested in this place, let's start negotiating.'

'I want to think about it first.'

'No time for that; it'll be gone. Excuse me,' she called across to the agent who had politely stepped away to give us time to chat. 'It's a nice flat but it's way more than our budget.'

Melissa offered a rent twenty percent lower than the asking price and the agent didn't laugh. He said it was unlikely to drop by anything like that amount but he would talk to the owner.

'Jeez, Melissa, how could you do that?' I said when we were on the street outside the property. 'I haven't worked out if I can afford it even at twenty percent less.'

'You haven't signed anything. If he comes back with a yes, you can say sorry but no. Fancy a drink?'

There was a pub on the corner of the street, far enough away from the place I'd viewed to not be a nuisance because of noisy crowds. God, I was already thinking I was living there.

Melissa dismissed my anxiety about the cost of the place before switching topic to her holiday plans with her man.

I cut her short. 'I need to get home to work out the math now that you've made an offer for me.'

'I'm only trying to help.'

My comment had come across as critical when in fact I was excited by the possibility of living in the place we'd seen. 'I know – and thank you. It's just that I'm nervous.'

'OK, you head off to do your calculations and let me know what the estate agent says.'

At home I set up a spreadsheet. Adding Mom's contribution to my own salary I could easily afford the place, even without the twenty percent reduction that Melissa had asked for. There would be money left over for everything else. How lucky I was. If I saw something nice in one of the mid-priced clothes stores I'd be able to get it. If I felt like a new hairstyle or a spa treatment, no problem. Even a vacation was possible, but without someone to go with that wasn't going to happen.

I was on reception duty the next morning when the real estate agent called.

'My client won't go to a twenty discount but she is prepared to accept fifteen percent if you're willing today to sign a one-year lease with no escape clauses.'

'Sure. I'll take it. I'll be over around midday.'

As soon as the call was over, I rushed to the office to let Melissa know.

'Brill, Jennifer. Now you can start planning the housewarming party. Take the rest of the day off if you want, I can do reception.'

'No need, I'll come back after I've signed. I've got too much to do.'

'You know, I'm grateful to have such a hard working person as deputy manager, but maybe you need to think a bit about life beyond the job. That might sound like an odd thing for a boss to say, but I know you'll always be conscientious so I don't need to worry on that front.'

I had no idea how to respond so nodded and smiled before returning to reception to deal with the imminent wave of guests leaving and new ones arriving.

Wealth is a relative concept I was thinking that morning as I signed guests in and out. I might be considering myself rich but it was nothing against the well-off tourists paying for their comfortable bed and nice shower at our hotel. OK, the bedrooms were cool with their trendy fabrics and furnishings, their giant TV screens, and bathrooms with the latest jet and rainforest shower heads. I suppose I was adding to their positive experience, making sure that everything was spotlessly clean, that the breakfasts were good and that the service was impeccable. We were getting brilliant reviews, averaging 9.5 ratings on the vacation websites. Even so, a starting price of two hundred and fifty pounds for a single night's stay in Muswell Hill, three hundred and fifty over the weekend, seemed way over the top.

That wasn't my problem though, was it? The guests kept rolling in, praising the place, paying up, and vowing to return when they were next in London.

And I was all set to move to my lovely apartment.

~

During our Monday management meetings I could see why Bridget and David were making such a success of running the café and now the hotel. Bridget was bursting with suggestions and David was razor sharp on anything to do with accounts. It wasn't that simple though because David also had great ideas and Bridget was hot on money.

We were a good team with Melissa focusing on marketing and what she kept referring to as the customer experience. I suppose I was the practical one, making sure that everything ran smoothly. I appreciated being treated as an equal.

Collectively, the enthusiasm and goodwill were contagious. When something cropped up each of us gave our opinion and usually by the time we made a decision there was full agreement.

Only usually though because there was one exception, anything to do with Rachel and Andy, David and Bridget's older children. This is when Melissa and I liked to keep out of it, leaving the others to decide. I vaguely knew both youngsters having seen them behind the counter at the café. According to Kelly they didn't get on which might explain why I rarely saw the two of them together. Apparently, Kelly explained, Bridget thought David's daughter had him in the palm of her hand and David thought that Bridget's view that her son could do no wrong was mistaken. 'Bridget's seen Rachel drunk and disorderly,' Kelly told me, 'and David's caught Andy smoking dope.'

That Monday's meeting, the one after I'd signed the contract for the apartment, was not going well.

Item One on the agenda: Revamping the hotel website.

Bridget was suggesting using her son to do it, reminding David that Andy had done a great job with the Dream Café website.

'Agreed, but the hotel website is far more complex. The café gets a few hits a week whereas the hotel gets hundreds.'

'Andy's sure he can do it. He'd work flat out during the holiday to set it up and then back at university he can manage it remotely.'

'I'm not sure.'

'But why not?'

'I've just said. Because it's complex. The bookings function needs to be spot on.'

'He's studying computing at Oxford, for God's sake.'

'Melissa? Jennifer? What do you two think?'

'Sorry Bridget, but I don't think it's a good idea to get a family member involved. Say it goes wrong, it would be hugely awkward.'

I was pleased Melissa had said what I was thinking, meaning I could keep quiet. I simply nodded in agreement.

'Fair enough,' Bridget said. 'We've agreed in the past that if we don't reach a consensus view on something we don't do it.'

Item Two on the agenda wasn't going to be any easier.

'Rachel's been a big success working at the café during her holidays,' David began.

I nodded. Lookswise she was a crazy cat, but was a bundle of energy and efficient, too. I rarely spoke to her but my impression was that she did great.

David continued, addressing Melissa and me. 'She'd like to add some night shifts here. What do you reckon?'

I waited for Melissa to answer. She didn't which I suppose was fair enough because it was my responsibility to sort out reception duties at the hotel.

'Only night shifts?' I asked.

'Yes. She'd finish at the café then come across to here.'

'That's a lot of hours of work.'

'She's saving up for a visit to New Zeeland next Christmas. That's expensive.'

'I think not, David. Nights can be threatening so I prefer using more experienced staff for those shifts.'

'That's what I think. David and I talked this through ahead of the meeting and disagreed. Being able to raise the issues but not have the responsibility for deciding is appreciated. Thank you, both of you.'

'I agree with Bridget.' David paused. 'It's never easy getting it right with children from a previous relationship. So yes, thank you both for helping us out.'

Were there issues beyond whether or not their children should work at the hotel? I seemed to remember Kelly telling me that David and Bridget lived in separate homes despite being partners and that disputes about the older children was the reason why.

What impressed me that day though was how friendly subsequent discussions were once we'd shifted to less contentious items. By the time the meeting had come to an end there were smiles all around.

'Is anyone doing anything interesting this evening?' Melissa asked.

'Not us,' Bridget replied. 'We had such a busy weekend at the café we're shattered. It'll be early to bed. What about you, Jennifer? Anything exciting?'

'Hardly. Also an early night.'

'And you, Melissa? You always seem to have something on.'

'I suppose it'll be another wild night with my man! I really do think I'm in love.'

'Love? Good on you, girl,' Bridget said. 'We must meet this mystery man soon.'

'You will. At Jennifer's housewarming party.'

'Are you having one?' Bridget asked.

'Not as far as I know.'

I smiled but I wasn't finding things that amusing. The talk of love unsettled me. Bridget had David to love and there was that funny story about his list. Melissa had her new man and was acting like a teenager. Mom had Jeff. And me? Nobody since Gareth. OK, I'd had sex with Blind Date Will but that didn't count. It definitely hadn't been anything to do with love.

Love. A word chucked around like confetti. Had I loved Gareth? I'd loved being with him, sharing experiences. I'd loved the thought of us spending the rest of our days together. Yes, of course I'd loved him until it went wrong.

The thought of trying to find love again was exhausting even if Melissa was proof that a new relationship could be exciting. Maybe I should get out there as Mom had done, signing up for some activity. At her dance class she'd found Jeff, the man who was making her happy.

It struck me that there was an obvious getting out there place for me.

43

I typed in Muswell Hill Community Theater, changing it to Theatre before hitting Go. The two listed at the top of the search were the sweetly named *Muswell Hill Amateur Dramatics Society* and the more hip *Am-Dram@NEL* (which I later discovered stood for North East London). Which one would a forty-year old fit in with?

I was set on taking action immediately to counter a growing feeling of what was the point. The obvious thing to do was to try out both options.

The Am-Dram website had short headlines above photos of youngsters on stage performing. I zoomed in: maybe they weren't that young. Or maybe they were.

No need to let us know in advance, simply come along and enjoy the fun! ran one caption. It needed quite a lot of further searching to discover that they met on Wednesdays. I was reading this on a Tuesday evening.

Sitting on the bus the next day for the short journey to the local college venue, I was feeling that rush of adrenalin like I'd had ahead of auditions back in school.

My first thought when I entered the rehearsal room was wow. The stage was an impressive size with banks of lights and a control booth at the back of the hall stacked with electronic equipment.

I stood by the door as others pushed past me. Apart from the guy busy welcoming everyone I was, as anticipated, considerably the oldest. Does that matter, I wondered, as I took a deep breath and approached the person running the show?

'Hi. I'm Jennifer.'

'Max.'

We shook hands.

'I'm thinking of doing some … am-dram, so I'm here to see what it's like.'

'Great. Have you done any acting before?'

'No.' I was hardly going to tell him that I'd been a rising star in school twenty-five years beforehand and that I'd had unsuccessful auditions in Hollywood.

'Not a problem, not a problem. Let me explain how we work.'

As Max spoke, youngsters kept interrupting with "Yo Max" followed by high-fives, which was pretty distracting. He explained that the college offered performing arts programmes and this was the opportunity for students to do more acting than their courses provided.

'So is everyone here a college student? Apart from me.'

'No, we get students dropping in from the university down the road.'

'What about locals who aren't at university or college?'

'Occasionally. And there's me, of course.'

I got a run down on Max's acting career, mainly radio work with a recent uplift as a voice on audio books. He was a freelance tutor at the college, too.

'Let's get started,' he called out. 'Everyone over here, please.' The tightly knit circles of friends broke up and around twenty participants headed our way. 'You've come at a perfect time, Jennifer, because we're starting a new play tonight.'

'Anything I'd know.'

He paused and smiled and I had a flashback to my Hollywood days when everyone was out to self-promote. I must have been psychic. 'In my spare time I'm a scriptwriter,' he explained, his blasé tone implying that writing a script was the easiest thing in the world as long as you had a few spare minutes. 'This is my latest.'

'Sit down in a circle, guys,' he instructed and I had no choice other than to join in. He took a bundle of papers out of his leather satchel. 'You're about to get the first act of my new play, but I'll start with a plot overview before we begin reading. Actually before that, let me introduce Jennifer who's come along tonight to find out what we do.'

There were a few "Yo, Jen" calls.

'Are you a journalist?' someone asked.

'No.'

'Are you an agent?'

'No.'

That marked the end of any interest in my presence.

'Let's get going, guys. OK, the background. We all know about our appalling history, the colonialism, the racism, the slavery, the way women were treated.'

'And still are,' someone called out and there was laughter.

'But what if in the future it was reversed? What if women ruled, particularly women from black communities, and they began to subject white men to the same levels of oppression? Would they really do that? Would they have remorse? Those are the themes of my play.'

Even though a fair number of the females in the room were from the ethnic minorities addressed in the play, I didn't spot much interest when I looked around. Maybe they were merely there to act, sing, dance and have some fun.

The scripts were handed out and we took it in turns to read. I assumed Max was deliberately allocating male roles to females, females to males, white to black, and black to white. I was a male, a middle aged cotton factory owner. I guess you can't always judge a script by a first read, the whole thing could be brought to life once on stage, but I wasn't hopeful.

There was a break and I followed some of the others to a bank of vending machines in a nearby corridor.

'Shit isn't it?' the girl next to me in the queue said.

'Oh, I don't know. It has promise.'

'Nah, it's shit. His stuff is always shit and he's a crap teacher, too.'

'Are you hoping for a career in acting?'

'You bet. It's Hollywood for me.'

'Good luck,' I said as she walked off, spilling some of her drink onto the floor as she went.

Since I wasn't going to be joining the group there was no point staying for the second session. Slipping away was tempting but I decided to do the polite thing and tell Max that I had a bit of a headache.

'No probs, Jennifer. See you again maybe?'

Max was schmoozing with a pretty young thing as we spoke. Hollywood beckons for the poor girl!

~

The Muswell Hill Amateur Dramatics Society met on Thursdays. In for a penny, in for a pound, another of Gareth's sayings, came to mind as I dashed home from the hotel, and with zero enthusiasm got ready for my second night out in a row.

It was a short walk to the hall at the side of the Methodist Church, this a modern building unlike other churches in the area. I was anticipating a complete opposite to the Am-Dram kids, a fuddy-duddy group of enthusiastic though talentless oldies, the sort of people depicted in those Marigold Hotel movies. They would be selecting old faithful plays, perhaps *The Importance of Being Earnest*, or if there was ambition and at least some capability, *My Fair Lady*. It could even be a dating service for dapper men and lonely, last chance saloon women. Yay, here's my chance!

Silently, I reprimanded myself. If you're in that mindset there really is no point going, Jennifer. But since you ARE going you'd better make the most of it.

My alter ego fought back. It'll be a waste of time. Simply don't go. Turn round and head home.

But I was there and two women of around my age were holding the door open for me and smiling.

I was welcomed by Daisy, the person running the group. She was in her fifties or maybe early sixties with bunched up henna-red hair, grey roots showing through. She was wearing a brightly coloured patterned skirt that in my opinion clashed with the brightly coloured patterned shirt. I'd seen that look and image on the in-your-face journos and PR people in LA and for an instant was surprised to hear a softly spoken woman with a refined English accent rather than a laid back Californian one.

So much for negative first impressions because that evening I saw a charisma that made her a born leader and later on I was to discover that she'd had an acting career of considerable success.

One "Sshh" and the group fell silent. 'We have a visitor,' she announced. 'Welcome, Jennifer.'

There was a chorus of hi's and hello's with not a single yo to be heard. Presumably for my benefit, Daisy explained that *A Raisin in the Sun* was the play the group was working on, that the cast had been selected and we were towards the end of the first reading of Act Two.

'I know this,' I said. 'We studied it in my last year at high school.' Our English teacher had been broadminded in a school that was ultra-conservative. She had introduced us to novels and plays that were controversial, particularly on racism. I remember her telling us that we were all racist even if we didn't recognise it. That had got me thinking. I used to chat with her after school, sharing thoughts on what we were studying and discussing the books that my friend Rebecca's sister, Clara, had been passing on to us.

There were fifteen of us sitting on chairs in a circle that evening and we all did some reading, even the ones who had joined the society to do the lighting, sound and stage design.

I liked the informal but serious approach, the talent of these amateurs, their enthusiasm, and the fact that the age range went from teens through to eighties. I was comfortable; this was a group for me to sign up to.

'Have you enjoyed it?' Daisy asked as the others were noisily stacking chairs.

'Yeah, loads.'

'If you decide to join I have a job for you.'

'Sure. What?'

'You'll have noticed that the cast's Chicago accents leave something to be desired. I'm hearing Southern drawl, New York brash and even hints of Gangsta Speak – and sometimes all in a single sentence! Would you be prepared to be voice coach?'

'I'd love to do that. Thanks for asking.'

'Another thing. Could you be the understudy for Susan, she's the one playing Ruth Younger? Susan's having tests for something or other at the hospital next week and although she's certain that it's nothing serious, I do like to cover all risks.'

'I'm sure she'll be fine but I'm happy for you to put me down.'

'Brilliant. We usually go to the pub after rehearsals. Would you like to join us?'

'I'll give it a miss tonight; I've got a busy day at work tomorrow.'

Walking home alone I regretted saying no to the offer of a drink with the group. Next time I'd join them. It had been a great evening; I'd had a lot of fun. I was looking forward to the voice coaching and I would learn the Ruth Younger lines for the challenge of it even though it wouldn't be needed.

44

The curtains closed and there were smiles and high-fives all round before we shuffled back into line as the curtains reopened to further applause. It had been a great three nights; I was exhausted but exhilarated.

Yep, you've guessed it, Susan's tests revealed a thyroid problem, requiring more rest than taking on a lead role in a play was ever going to allow. So I was Ruth Younger. The month had been manic, learning the lines, providing one-to-one voice coaching, endless (it seemed) dress rehearsals in the local school hall, and on top of all of that, getting everything ready for my move. The job too, of course.

It had all been worth it. After that last show I was joined at the reception in the foyer by the group of people who had shifted from being acquaintances to friends – the crew. I no longer felt that they included me because they were sorry for me; instead, they genuinely liked my company as I did theirs.

'You should have stayed in Hollywood,' Kelly said having planted a firm kiss on each cheek, 'though then I'd never have got to meet you.'

'Did you see what the local rag wrote about you?' Bridget asked.

I had, and gee, did that bring back memories of my brief stardom in Idaho.

A stunning performance from Jennifer Kroll ran the headline.

'We are so lucky to have Jennifer. She had under a month to prepare,' Daisy was quoted as saying.

People I knew and people I didn't know were coming up to congratulate me during that reception.

'Well done, dear, I loved you,' an elderly woman said.

'Seeing that play gives me hope for our future,' a black woman said, tears streaming down her cheeks.

'That was so fucking cool, Jennifer,' was David's daughter Rachel's assessment.

I stayed on until the reception came to an end – how could I leave early? I definitely drank too much – how could I not?

The late night and the alcohol were an unwise combo because I was moving into my new apartment the following morning. I'd managed to get everything packed and ready to go during the hectic month, helped by being given generous time off from hotel duties, but that still left all the sorting and unpacking I'd need to do on arrival.

Actually, it didn't go too badly – bloody English again – actually, it went brilliantly well. The moving team were efficient and helpful, not that there was much to transport, and Melissa came over in the afternoon to help me. When she'd volunteered I was worried that she'd take over and put stuff away without asking me where I wanted things to go: she is a bit of an express train. But it was all fine and by the time the take-out pizzas arrived at six we were done.

'So, when's the party, Jennifer? I can help you plan it.'

'Hold on a bit, let me recover from the play and the move first.'

'I'm not saying have the party tomorrow, but surely you can at least set the date.'

I was happy to see Melissa leave. Exhausted as I had been the night before, I was now mega exhausted.

Melissa's suggestion stuck with me though and I was coming around to the idea of having a housewarming party. With Mom and Jeff planning to visit, maybe they could join in. However, I was still waiting for Mom to finalise dates.

I decided to do some more chasing and WhatsApped her late that evening.

Her face popped up on screen after a single ring. 'Well, Jennifer? How did it go?'

'I'm pretty well settled in. I had a friend to help me.'

'I don't mean that. I mean your play.'

'Not bad at all.'

'Why are you laughing, Jennifer?'

'More than not bad, it was brilliant, Mom. Brilliant and I loved it.'

'I'm real pleased, Jennifer.' She paused. 'Do you think you gave up trying to make a go of acting a bit too quick?'

I'd been thinking about that. I had tried in LA, at the studios, with agents, through open auditions, without a sniff of success. But I was a naïve kid back then with no awareness of the games you needed to play to get noticed (except the one which I was not going to play). Would it have been any easier as I got older and wiser? Hell, no, because I'd visited LA friends years later and none of them were making it. Their talents and determination had counted for nothing.

'No, Mom, I don't think that, but I am happy to be back doing some acting. Anyway, more important, have you sorted out the dates for your visit?'

'Almost. Jeff reckons we could spend some time with you and then maybe take a road trip. Scotland he thinks.'

'That sounds nice. I need to know the exact dates you'll be here though because I'm going to have a housewarming party.'

'A Party! We love parties.'

Back in Idaho Mom had been a stay-at-home. She regarded a trip to the stores in town as a major social outing.

'Nothing grand. Just a quiet event.'

—

The thrill I got from being part of the drama group made me realise what a loser I'd been for not making more of an effort to socialise. My head was now flooded with thoughts about what else I could do.

Enrolling in a gym or maybe asking Kelly and Emma if I could join them on their runs were possibilities, this sudden interest in exercise in recognition of my lack of energy and fitness during the performances.

I was wary of the gym idea following my disappointing experience in Salford and the idea of being with two experienced runners was intimidating. They'd be welcoming; I'd be embarrassed.

There was a tennis club near my apartment, so close that I could hear balls whacking against rackets and the screams of frustration or joy, and I could see the glow of the floodlights at night. I'd walked past the entrance but there had never been a reason to continue up the private lane to reach the club.

When I was a kid back in Idaho I'd spent time, a lot of it, hitting balls against a barn wall. I played a bit in school too. I was doing fine and liking it. Daniel was doing better though and was in the school team. Didn't he let me know it. "Take it in turns hitting against the wall, Sis," sounded like a friendly enough invitation, but winning was on his mind, hitting balls so hard I couldn't return them. I gave up playing which might have been because of Daniel's behaviour, but if I was being truthful it was more likely because I'd reached those teenage years of mine when sport wasn't cool and all that mattered was acting and stardom.

Twenty-five years on and I was wondering whether I should try playing again. It was more appealing than the gym or running and I was stuck with a determination to do something. So, on a Saturday morning a couple of weeks after my move, I walked up that lane and reached the clubhouse, a wooden structure

277

in severe need of repair. The roof sagged and many of the planks running along the walls were warped and untreated.

I went up to the woman in tennis gear standing behind a counter.

'Hi there,' I said, all smiles. 'Who can I speak to about joining?'

'Have you looked on our website?'

'No, not yet.'

'If you had done you would have seen that we're full and there's a waiting list.' It was reasonable to let me know but it did seem like I was being told off.

'Oh, it didn't cross my mind to check first. Well, can I add my name to the list, please?'

'Best to do it online, then you can include details of your LTA rating.'

'LTA?'

'Lawn Tennis Association.'

'Rating?'

'You need a rating to be able to play matches against other clubs.'

'I won't be doing that; I haven't played for ages. In fact, I'll probably be needing lessons.'

'You don't need to be a member to take lessons, the coaches take anyone they can get.' Her tone suggested disapproval. 'Coaching information is also online.'

'OK, I'll take a look then. I might as well have a coffee while I'm here. Or do you have to be a member to get a drink?'

I'd sort of promised myself that I'd quit sarcasm, but I reckoned it was deserved.

I got a coffee and sat on an ancient armchair by a chipped wooden table.

Two men and two women came in and sat close by. I'd guess they were around my age which I saw as a plus – the club didn't only have whizz kid members.

'I'm slowing down,' one of the men said. 'No energy at all.'

'You know the old adage, Brian. You need to get fit to play tennis rather than play tennis to get fit.'

They were all nodding in agreement which left me confused. I was hoping to play tennis to get fit.

'Quite right,' a woman said, patting the man on the knee. 'Fit for other things too, eh Brian?'

Now three of them were laughing. Perhaps the jibe had hit a raw nerve because Brian wasn't joining in.

Having gulped down my coffee I left, hardly feeling good about the place. Maybe I'd look at the club website. Maybe I'd add my name to the waiting list. Maybe I'd investigate coaching. Or maybe I'd go running with Kelly and Emma.

45

'Have you had a good weekend?' Melissa asked as I joined her in the office ahead of our Monday morning meeting.

'Not bad,' I replied. 'I tried to sign up at the tennis club.'

'And?'

'There's a waiting list. I can't say I found it a particularly friendly place although that's probably unfair because I only saw a few people. Hi, Bridget. No David today?'

'He's got some sorting out to do at the café so it's just me.'

The meeting turned out to be no more than a check list that everything was going to plan and was soon over.

I went to reception to take over from the man on night duty. With the early morning rush of departures over and a pause before the new arrivals, I was able to take things easy. There was a game I sometimes played, looking through the names of current and pending guests and imagining what they might look like. Mr

Lotherby-Smythe would be a beanpole with horn-rimmed glasses and a mane of white hair. Lucy Lockshaw would be on the large side with an enormous bust and a squeaky voice. Who next? We had a Kees van de Beek, a Luca Ricci and an Ahmed Fayez due in.

And a Gareth Edwards!

Gareth used to joke that everyone in Wales was called Gareth Edwards, David Jones or Rhys Williams, so joking aside, our guest could be one from a large pool.

I could see that Melissa had been on reception the previous late afternoon when this man arrived. I went back to the office to speak to her. 'A Gareth Edwards booked in yesterday for two nights. Do you remember what he looked like?'

'Yes, and how! A good looker, tall, slim, boyish face.'

'Anything else? Anything unusual?'

'I wouldn't say unusual though I did think his hair was interesting. Tight golden curls with maybe a hint of red.'

'Glasses?'

'If you mean was he wearing glasses then yes, he was.'

'Thick black plastic frames?'

'No, his were thin metal ones. Why are you asking? Do you know him?'

'Maybe, though I don't think it's the same person.' But I almost certainly did think so. Changing glasses was easy, changing hair wasn't. 'I'll see you later,' I muttered and left Melissa to it, returning to reception.

What if he was still in his room and he came downstairs while I was at the front desk? I couldn't get my head round whether I wanted that or not. After a few calming breaths I concluded that it would be fine if I saw him since I was well past anger (definitely so) or regret (I think so) or sadness (sort of). Catching up would be fine.

However, that left open the far bigger question of what he was doing in Muswell Hill.

I didn't have time to think that one through because there he was at the foot of the stairs heading towards the exit, which would be taking him straight past me.

'You!' my tone accusatory.

There was a look of surprise before he nodded, smiled and approached. He was in front of the counter facing me like he was an ordinary guest with an ordinary inquiry.

'I'm taking a couple of days' break in London,' he explained.

'In Muswell Hill just by chance.'

'I was hoping you'd be willing to have a catch up while I was here. The plan was to find the nearest hotel and then come round to yours, ring the bell and hope you'd let me in. This place is the closest to your flat but of course I had no idea … I assume you're working here.'

'That could explain why I'm standing behind the desk.'

He didn't smile. 'Yes, of course.'

'Actually I've moved so you wouldn't have found me.' I looked for signs of down and out or financially secure in his dress but it was impossible to judge. 'Why stay here though?'

'Like I said, it's the nearest.'

'But it's the most expensive hotel around.'

'You can say that again.'

'But it's the most expensive hotel around.'

Again no smile, not that my pathetic wisecrack deserved one. 'The prices here are ridiculous though I suppose that's London for you. I'm working so I can afford to pay if that's what you're worried about. I won't do a runner.'

It was my turn not to smile.

There were two women behind him waiting to be served. 'I'm working, Gareth.'

'Yes, sorry,' he said, glancing behind him. 'Can I take you out to dinner tonight?'

No.

Yes.

No.

Yes.

No.

'Yes, if you want to. I finish at six but will need to go home to freshen up.'

'Tell me where you live and I'll come round at say seven.'

'No, I'll walk back to meet you here. Seven's fine though.'

'Thank you, Jen. That makes me happier than you can imagine.'

'It's just a catch up, Gareth. Nothing more.'

'I understand. I'll leave you to it now. I'm going to be a full on tourist today, to South Kensington for the Natural History and V&A Museums.' He turned to face the two women. 'Sorry to have taken so long.'

They turned out to be all-smiling, hero worshipping Americans. One replied with a sugary-sweet, 'Gee, that ain't no problem,' and the other with an even more sugary-sweet, 'You be sure to have a nice day now.'

Gareth was a good looker who oozed charm, I suppose that had helped win me over, and he hadn't lost it if these captivated women were anything to go by. 'That's most kind of you. I'm sure I will.'

'Whoa, he's some guy,' the woman with too much make-up said as she approached me after Gareth had walked off. 'And I couldn't help overhearing that you're meeting him tonight.'

'Yeah, we're old friends.'

'Shame you ain't new friends!'

'How can I help you?'

~

Could I do a thing right that day at work? Hell no. Half of me was hating Gareth for turning up without warning, half of me was hating myself for agreeing to have dinner with him, and half of me was excited by the thought of being with him. OK, so that's three halves, which gives an indication of the state I was in.

Mess Up Number One: I hadn't put together a duty schedule for the cleaners, so when they came up to me I told them just to get on with it however they wanted.

'This is not as you like,' the Polish leader of the team said. After we'd engaged her I'd taken on the challenge of helping to improve her English vocabulary and word order, a bit of a joke what with me being American.

Right then I wasn't in the zone to correct her. 'You're right, it's not like me.'

Her big smile in anticipation of an explanation and a brief tutorial evaporated when I told her to get started before turning away to face the computer screen.

Mess Up Number Two: I forgot I had a meeting with Bridget scheduled to sort out the breakfast supplies we'd be ordering from the café for the following week.

She found me at reception. 'Where were you? Our meeting?'

'Oh, sorry Bridget, I completely forgot.'

'It's too late to squeeze it in now, I must get back to the café. Do it yourself and let me know what you'll be needing from us.'

'Will do. I'll send the order across to you this afternoon.'

I knew Bridget wouldn't be making a big deal of me forgetting, but it bugged me because I was usually on the ball and eager to do everything right.

Mess Up Number Three: Melissa was not happy when I opted out of our coffee time chat. I'd been her confidante regarding the relationship with her new man, (who wasn't that new anymore but it was still how she described him), receiving a day-by-day account of how things were progressing. Whenever I was on duty and she was in the office we took a break together for her to provide me with updates.

Where are you? Melissa texted, half an hour after our usual eleven o' clock break.

Can't today, too much to do.'

Not even ten minutes? You'll want to hear about last night.

I couldn't face her. She was so wrapped up in her own drama that she had probably forgotten my interest in one of the guests, but she'd still recognise that something was up as soon as she saw me. I'd either burst out crying or fall about laughing depending on which of my two wildly fluctuating moods was dominant at the time.

Tomorrow. I promise.

Somehow the end of the day arrived and I could go home and get ready to see Gareth.

46

So how come a guy can just slip on jeans, loafers and a tee, polo or shirt and he's all set to go, maybe after running his fingers through his hair as a half-hearted gesture that he cares about his appearance? And there's us gals pulling out clothes from cupboards and drawers, mixing and matching, remixing and rematching, putting on make-up then wiping it off and starting again because it was too come-and-get-me.

I had no idea what Gareth would be wearing that evening, but since this was a catch up and definitely not a date, I wasn't going to dress up. I showered – that was fair enough – then slipped on blue jeans and a white shirt, simple and casual. I did put on some make-up, but only because I always did when I went out, absolutely not for Gareth's benefit.

The nervous anticipation of the day had gone by the time I was walking back to the hotel. I was calm and curious, that was it.

Gareth was already waiting in reception even though I'd arrived early. He sprang up off the leather sofa by the window and came bounding across to the hotel entrance to greet me. I let him hug me, pleased that it was a brief one before he pulled away. He did smell nice though, it reminded me of the fragrance when walking through a pine forest after heavy rainfall. I was facing a man in a light grey linen suit and a navy shirt, his shoes navy too. So much for my theory about men not caring what they wore for dates (even though this wasn't a date).

'Hi Jen. Shall we go straight out?'

'Sure. Where to?'

'I thought we'd just wander down to that main road and find something. I walked around there earlier; there's plenty of choice.'

'But have you booked a place?'

'No, but it's not the weekend so it should be fine.'

'Wrong. Everywhere here is always crowded.'

'Really?'

'Yes, really. It's Muswell Hill, not mid-Wales.'

His scowl indicated that he was unimpressed with my dig and I regretted saying it. 'Come on then, let's see if we can get a table somewhere.'

He set off and I was left chasing after him. This was not a good start and I wasn't helping. I caught up and we walked towards The Broadway.

'I'm sure there'll be something,' I offered as an act of appeasement.

After being turned away at our fifth attempt, Gareth looked thoroughly miserable. 'Any bright ideas?' he asked.

He was leaving the next day so postponing wasn't possible. Abandoning was an option, of course, but we'd got this far and it would be disappointing not to chat for a bit.

'Come back to my place and I'll cook. It won't be grand but –'

'I couldn't impose.'

'No problem.'

'Are you sure?'

'Come on, Gareth.' I was smiling, he was frowning, as we stood facing each other. 'Start walking.'

'Let me buy some wine then.'

'No need, I've got a stock at home.'

'But I'd like to.'

'If you insist. We'll be passing a metro supermarket on the way back.'

'Is there somewhere local with a more interesting choice?'

'A ridiculously expensive wine merchant down that street,' I said, pointing.

'Let's go in there then.'

He homed in on the American aisle and picked up two bottles of that Californian wine that had been our favourite. Part of me wanted to insist that he put them back and chose something different. This is not a date I could have said but didn't.

We paused outside my house while I searched for the key.

'Wow, this place is amazing,' Gareth said.

'It's a rental and I've only got the top floor.'

'Even so.'

There was another "amazing" from Gareth when we entered my apartment. 'This style is so cool.'

By then I had added splashes of radiance to the light-coloured interior, scarlet cushions and a bold rug in the living room area and red appliances in the open plan kitchen. He would have seen lavender in the bedroom.

'Take a seat and I'll get going cooking.'

'Let me help,' and before I could say no he was by me in the kitchen.

I handed him a knife and got him chopping up the vegetables. It was a small kitchen area and we were close to touching, bringing back memories of our time together when we would cook as we chatted. One evening early on came to mind. We were full on preparing the meal – yep, he was chopping vegetables – when we looked at each other, laughed, dropped everything and took off our clothes, not in a rush, just real slow and sexy. Was he recalling that moment because at the exact time it was on my mind he paused and looked across before carrying on with his chopping.

No way was there going to be a repeat of that racy night; instead he was asking whether I wanted the carrots cut in thin strips or chunky blocks.

'Whichever way you want, Gareth.' I could tell he was nervous and strangely, I wasn't.

He asked how I'd ended up with the hotel job. I played it down, leaving out how senior my role was, and with no mention of the gap in employment there because of what had happened with Shaun.

'Where are you working, Gareth?'

As I asked I did wonder whether I'd be getting a truthful answer, or more lies like the ones that had brought an end to our relationship. How many months was it before I found out that he'd been fired for cheating on expenses? If he'd told me I would have done anything to support him, even after knowing the reason for his dismissal. Anyway, there was nothing left to say, I'd got over it.

He opened a bottle of wine. I pointed to the cupboard above the worksurface and he took out two glasses and filled them. 'I've changed careers. I'm a teacher now.'

'Whoa, I didn't expect that.' He could be lying, but on balance I believed him.

'After you … after we split, for ages I couldn't think about what to do. Then I was in the pub with an old friend who teaches and he mentioned that schools were desperate for IT staff. So that's what I did, a QTS to get the qualification, and then a job. I haven't been going for long but I'm loving it.'

'I can see you being a good teacher. You're patient and you've obviously got the knowledge.' In saying this I was thinking of how much Gareth had helped during my catering management course. Abruptly I stopped talking; I needed to go easy on the compliments.

'I don't know about that but I do my best and so far it's going well.'

'Are you still living in Wales?'

'No, I've moved to Buckinghamshire.'

'Buckinghamshire! God, you Brits with names. That sounds like a place full of castles with knights in shining armour. Where is this Buckingham-Shire?'

'It's pronounced *sheer*.'

'Sorry, m'lord!'

We were both smiling – was that good or bad?

Gareth poured out a second glass of wine and took a slug. 'I was sorry to hear about your father, Jen. I liked him a lot.'

'And he liked you. I regretted not asking you …'

'You don't have to apologise.'

This was like the old Gareth, sensitive and thoughtful, charismatic too. The man I had loved. A pity it was too late.

I grabbed hold of the bottle. 'More wine?'

He held up his glass. I was pouring the remains, a drop for me, a drop for him, evenly distributed. We'd been drinking it like soda.

'I think that's probably it, Jen, it's empty.'

'Good thing you bought two bottles then,' I said as I unscrewed the cap.

The oven timer beeped and I got him to sit down while I served up. Our dinner table conversation was impersonal, with Gareth describing his day at the museums like he was a tour guide.

'Highlights?' I asked him.

'I think a photography exhibition about 1960s London at the V&A. And at the Natural History Museum it has to be the dinosaurs. I know that's a cliché, a regression back to my childhood, but they have a brilliant display.'

'It's nothing to be embarrassed about, dinosaurs are cool.' Dinosaurs – Cool! Yep, I did realise that must sound stupid as I was saying it. And I carried on. 'When I was a kid they found some fossils in Idaho. It was from a Tenontosaurus, though how on earth do I remember that name?'

'Will you be at the hotel tomorrow?'

That was an abrupt change of topic. 'Yeah, but not until after lunch and not on reception.'

'So you won't be around for checking me out then?'

'Afraid not, but there's a pretty girl who'll be on duty to look after you.' I'm not sure why I said that.

'What do you do there apart from being on reception then?'

'I'm Deputy Manager so there are loads of responsibilities.'

I told Gareth about the setup, how I'd got promoted, how it went wrong for a while because of Shaun, how I was rehired after Melissa had kicked him out.

'I'm glad you're doing well. I suppose you have to be to afford the rent for this place.'

'I am doing well but I couldn't live here without Mom's help. When Dad passed away she went to live with her well-off sister Maisie. I don't think I ever told you about her. She died not long ago and there was a big inheritance coming Mom's way.'

'Is your mother coping OK without having your Dad around? Emotionally I mean.'

'More than coping, she's having a whale of a time. There's a boyfriend who seems like a nice guy; the pair of them are planning a visit here. When I went over after Maisie died I couldn't believe how much she'd changed.'

'Good, and I'm sure that makes you happy. I wish I'd got to know her better when we visited the farm but I was too busy spending time talking with your dad.'

There was a pause. 'Look, I didn't finish saying it earlier but I want to apologise for not letting you come to Dad's funeral.'

'I can understand why you didn't. And on the subject of sorry, I've got far more to be sorry about than you. There's a lot of apologising to do but perhaps not this evening.'

Yes, there was a lot of explaining and apologising required, but I also didn't want to open up old wounds that night. But did that mean he was expecting to see me again?

47

We slept together that night.

OK, I was drunk, but not drunk enough to not know what I was doing. It was me who suggested it. 'You can stay here tonight if you'd like, Gareth.'

If he would have questioned me with, "Is that alright?" or "Are you sure that's what you want?" I might well have changed my mind, but he didn't. He simply nodded. We left the plates, serving bowls and wine glasses on the table and went into my bedroom.

What would it be like to have sex with this man again? What if it was completely different, a desperate, frenzied lunge like you sometimes see in the movies when two lovers are reunited?

Of course, I had an equal part to play in what was to happen and as we sat on the bed kissing in between taking off clothes, I was unsure where my thoughts would be taking me – taking us.

The sex was that same glorious mix of intensity and tenderness that had been so good when we were in the States; the sex that was increasingly wanting during our time in Britain. We came together with a shudder then rested in each other's arms and it was as if we had never parted. We used to be quite chatty after love-making, but now Gareth was quiet and I wasn't going to break the silence. It was not the time to talk about the past or the future or even the here and now. It was simply the time to lay together as we drifted into slumber.

Gareth fell asleep before me. Listening to his gentle breathing, I fought off the urge to weigh up the implications of what I'd done, of where having him there by my side could possibly lead. Here he was and I was content.

My restful sleep was followed by more love-making in the morning, with happy memories of our lazy weekends together flooding back.

I was in the kitchen while he showered, making coffee, toast and jelly just like I used to do.

'Where's the marmalade?' Gareth asked as soon as he joined me, replaying the ongoing joke from when we were in the States and I'd never heard of the stuff.

'If you were at the hotel for breakfast I'm sure there'd be marmalade on offer. A bad choice coming here and staying overnight!'

We were forever teasing each other during our relationship. Now my attempt to be funny seemed clumsy and out of place.

'Being here with you is the best choice,' Gareth said as he took hold of my hand. 'I didn't think this could ever be possible.'

At the start of the evening neither had I and now I was wondering where this was leading. We'd had our catch up alright, catching up on sex too, but what next? Maybe this was it and we'd be going our own separate ways.

Gareth released his hold. 'I'm back at work tomorrow, a staff training day.'

It struck me that he must be as unsure as I was about the future.

'Back to Buckingham-Palace-sheer, is it?' I said with an attempt to lighten things to avoid the tension from spiralling.

'Yep, that's the place.'

'It sounds posh. Are all the kids you teach like the Hogwarts ones?'

'Actually, no. There are some wealthy parts of the town but some desperately poor areas too, so the kids are a mix. Some have got every gadget going – iPad, laptop, the latest smartphone – and they've been brought up with IT around them since birth, but others are in families that can't afford to buy anything. They're at a huge disadvantage when they start in my class and I'm trying to make sure those kids don't miss out.'

'That's a good objective.'

I was pleased to be talking about neutral stuff rather than anything personal.

'Maybe you could visit to see where I live. It's a small town, not exciting, but there are some great walks nearby.'

'Perhaps.'

'I hope so because I want to see you again.'

I was all set to say that I wanted to see him again, but I kept quiet. Nothing would be easier than slipping back to where we'd left off, but would it work? I needed to sort my head out before making any decisions.

I shifted to practical matters having noticed the digital display on the Alexa speaker showing 11:01. 'Since you're leaving today you should have vacated your room minus one minute ago. No worries though, I'll sort it now.'

I called hotel reception.

'Hiya, Melissa. Can you keep the cleaners away from Mr Edward's room until we get there at around one or half-past? ... That's right, he ... Everything's fine, I'll explain later ... I'm not saying over the phone. Bye.'

I turned back to Gareth. 'Don't worry, I won't be charging you for an extra day.'

'I might have done a runner if you had.'

He stopped abruptly and maybe unsurprisingly because it must have got him thinking about our last few months together full of money difficulties.

'Tell you what, we've got a couple of hours more. Let's head over to Alexandra Park for a walk and then

I can take you to the brilliant café round the corner for lunch.'

'Great. Whatever you'd like to do.'

'OK, first the park.' The park was fine but I was wondering whether the café was a good suggestion. Having mentioned it I was stuck with it, but if Kelly or Bridget were on duty I'd have some explaining to do afterwards. So what though. Melissa now knew that something was going on so the chance of keeping it secret was zero.

Now outdoors and holding hands, Gareth started talking about our past and I was ready to listen.

'Jen, I have so much explaining and apologising to do I'm not sure where to start. I'm aware that whatever I tell you can never be enough to justify your forgiveness.'

'As long as it's the truth, Gareth.'

He paused. We watched some student-aged boys and girls throwing a rugby ball and on the other side of the path, a more sedate, older group doing tai chi.

'Yeah, the truth.' He sighed. 'I've always been known for my honesty so how I got into such a fucking mess with you I'll never understand.'

We stopped walking and Gareth turned to face me. I kept silent, waiting for him to continue. Recent conversations with Kelly, Cecilia and Mom were on my mind, each of them in their own way having got me thinking that while it might be impossible to forget, forgiving was altogether different.

In the end it was me who broke the silence. 'I'm listening. Go on.'

'I want to explain how I ended up in such a terrible state. Can I do that?'

'We're here, you're talking. So yes.'

'There aren't any more surprises, I promise you.'

I was glad to hear that. If there were further revelations it would have meant I knew still less about the true Gareth.

'It's the reasons that I might be able to give you,' he continued, 'even if I'm still not sure about them myself.'

'I can take reasons. I couldn't take more surprises.'

Gareth was nervous and I could understand why. This was his one and only chance to convince me that all the lying was justifiable – a huge ask. I assumed his purpose for coming to Muswell Hill was to restore our relationship and it was up to me to decide whether that was going to happen.

It was best to get straight to the point. 'Gareth, can I check that you being here is because you're hoping we can get back together?'

'At least that we can be good friends.'

'Good friends! We had sex last night.'

'Of course I want us back together again, I'm desperate for that. For now though, I don't want to do anything that might scare you off.'

'You don't have to worry about that. I'm a big girl, I can make up my own mind. Come on, let's head to Dream Café, I'm starving.'

~

We stepped into the café and Kelly immediately caught my eye.

'Grab this table, Gareth, I'll get the food. We're slightly ahead of the main lunchtime rush which is fortunate; it'll be packed soon.' I handed him the menu and he chose a tuna and mayo baguette. I picked up our lunches from a shelf and went across to the counter to pay.

'And he is?' Kelly asked.

'Gareth.'

'*The* Gareth?'

'That's the one.'

'He looks dishy as hell. Should I be putting two and two together?'

'If you want, but today's only a catch up.'

'Crumpled clothes, him unshaven, you glowing. My extraordinary sixth sense is kicking in and telling me –'

'Look, can we talk later?'

'Sure, but can I add that by the way he's looking at you I'd say he's besotted. Don't lose him.'

I wasn't happy with Kelly's comment; I didn't need that pressure.

I must have looked miserable or angry when I got back to Gareth because he asked if everything was alright.

'I'm fine.'

'This place is cool. It reminds me of where you worked in Pasadena, that deli and café. And I like these paintings.'

'They're Bridget's, the owner. She also part owns the hotel.'

'A talented lady.'

'Yep, she is that.'

'You have nice people around you.'

'I do. I'm happy here.'

There was an awkward silence as we ate our sandwiches. What was he waiting to tell me that I didn't already know? Wouldn't it be better to chill out for the remaining hour or so without ruining it with difficult stuff?

'Maybe now isn't a good time to drag up the past,' I suggested.

'When is? I want to tell you a couple of things. The first is about Judith, the woman you saw me with before you left. You need to know that there was nothing going on between us, it was over years before. That village where I lived, it was an awful place for teenagers. Nothing to do except bitch about each other and you were either part of the in-crowd or the victim of it. I was an outsider and Judith was too. She knew what was going on in my family and was kind about it while

302

others were spiteful. We were around seventeen and everyone was dating and boasting about the sex they were getting. Judith and I started messing around but she was close to her parents and didn't want to hide anything from them. We wanted to have sex and in our simplistic teenage minds reckoned that getting married was the best option. And there was no reason to wait beyond turning eighteen because we were in love and knew there would never be anyone else.'

'Was it a shotgun wedding?'

'Absolutely not. Nothing on that front until we got married.'

'Did you have children with her?'

'No. We weren't rushing to start a family.'

'So what went wrong with this perfect match?'

'Almost immediately Judith felt that it had been a terrible mistake to marry so young, not specifically to marry me, but to marry without having had the chance to experience more in life. I was thinking the same. I had the chance to go to university and being there married didn't seem to fit. There were no rows; we just decided to separate and then down the line we got divorced. The funny thing is, although she wanted her independence, a couple of years later she was remarried and pregnant.'

I nodded in acceptance of his account; there would be no reason for him to lie. 'You mentioned that she knew what was going on in your family. What was that about?'

'That's the second thing I want to tell you. It's harder, much harder to talk about.'

I knew Gareth's father had been a postman serving the nearby town and a string of villages along the main road and I knew that he'd lost his job. What I now discovered was that he was sacked for stealing post, a serious enough offence to land him in prison. The family were left in turmoil, disgraced and ostracised by the local community and in dire poverty.

'I vowed never to behave like my father and I do think I stuck to that because despite what I did, exaggerating expense claims was hardly the same. Yes, I upped them a bit, things like including the cost of your dinner at a restaurant with my own meal. That was wrong and the fact that everyone else was doing it wasn't an excuse. At the time the company was using any reason they could find to get rid of the higher paid older staff and contractors, replacing us with cheaper new graduates. So that was it for me and several others.'

'If that's the case why didn't you simply tell me?'

'Stupid male pride? I was embarrassed, ashamed to be letting you down, terrified of losing you. Anyway, none of them are proper excuses, are they?'

'Thank you.' I hesitated. 'Yes, thanks for telling me.' There was a further pause. 'Look, I need time to think things through.'

'I've told you because I think it's important you know. I have no expectation of a particular consequence.'

I smiled. No expectation of a particular consequence. What a weird way of saying that he didn't know whether what he'd told me was enough to get us back together.

'We need to head off to the hotel. I start work soon.'

I took hold of his hand as we walked along.

'You'd better go up and grab your stuff otherwise the cleaners won't have time to get the room ready,' I said as we entered the hotel.

'Will do,' he said and together with Melissa who was on reception, I watched him bound upstairs.

'I am impressed!' Melissa said. 'You and I have got a lot of catching up to do.'

'Maybe.'

'Definitely.'

A few minutes later Gareth returned carrying his luggage.

'I feel terrible charging you so much,' I said as Melissa, all flirtatious smiles, handed him the card reader.

I walked to the door with him.

'Jen, I was thinking. When your mother visits, do you think I could come over to see her – and you?'

'Yes. That would be nice.'

48

Following the success of the Muswell Hill Amateur Dramatics Society's recent performances, Daisy was keen to maintain the momentum.

'We do two big productions a year,' she told me when the post-mortem meeting was over, 'but I'd like to run some smaller events, possibly with one-act plays. The trouble is, we can't get further use of the school hall so we're stuck for a venue.'

'Have you ever been to Dream Café?'

'Of course I have.' Silly question, everyone in the area used the place.

'They have events nights, poetry, music and other things. Maybe they'd be interested in holding theatre nights.'

'I wrote to them to enquire but got a rather curt note letting me know that there was no availability.'

'Maybe I have an in. I can try if you'd like.'

'It would be great if you would.'

The next morning I met David and asked if he'd be willing to run drama evenings. He said that a once a month event might be possible.

'Did you get an inquiry from someone called Daisy? She runs the group.'

'Her,' he scoffed.

Apparently she had told him that her society didn't expect to be charged for the venue but would want to sell tickets and keep all the revenue.

'I told her that if she intended to charge an admission fee we'd organise the tickets and keep the income. I never heard back from her.'

'I can't make the decision myself but I do think we'd need to issue tickets to cover expenses. It increases the chance of having a genuinely interested audience too. I appreciate there'd be preparation for you but the café would be making money on drinks sales.'

'And losing revenue from customers who would have come in for a drink if it were an open house.'

'Yeah, I didn't think of that. What about if we charged for tickets and split the revenue fifty-fifty?'

'I'd be happy with that though I need to run it past Bridget first.'

Bridget called me into the hotel office later that afternoon. 'David's told me about the theatre events, but I'm not sure,' she began. 'We've already got so much on. I wish David wouldn't agree to every request.'

'I don't want to cause any trouble. If you say no that's fine, but what about giving it a three-month trial then reviewing it?'

'Fair enough, let's do that then, though only because you're involved.'

'Brilliant, I'll let Daisy know.'

'Mmmm, Daisy. Could you be the liaison rather than her?'

'I'm not sure what she'll think about that.'

'Perhaps tell her that it's the easiest route because you and I meet at the hotel all the time.'

I had no idea why Daisy was to be avoided as far as Bridget and David were concerned. She could be a bit in your face and at times cantankerous, but she was full of enthusiasm and put in a lot of hours to make the society a success. Anyway, she was happy for me to deal with the venue and clearly something was going on when she told me that she had no interest in working with "those awful people."

We had a venue and the date for our first performance. I let Mom know and she booked her flights.

I texted Gareth. *Mom visiting in April and I'm on stage on the 17th. You're welcome to come along.*

An instant reply. *Absolutely. Can't wait!*

~

Why had I invited Gareth? When we'd last met he'd opened up about the reasons for the lying and I believed him. We'd got on OK and yeah we'd even had sex, but did that mean we were heading back into a relationship? If they had their way, Kelly and Melissa would be pairing us up without question. Both had told me I'd be mad not to commit, but with three weeks to go before he returned I remained hesitant. Immersing myself in work and rehearsals for the Dream Café performance, I put deciding on the back burner.

There was an irony when Daisy allocated roles for the one-act plays we were to put on. Mine, a grim domestic drama, was set in Salford. I'd barely understood the accent when I'd lived there but now I was immersing myself in YouTubes and podcasts to get it right for the performance.

Mom and Jeff would be arriving a couple of days before the event and I was thinking about accommodation.

'Is it easy to get from Barnet to Muswell Hill using public transport?' I asked Melissa the Monday morning after their plans had been finalised.

'Why?'

'There's a reasonably priced hotel there with good ratings.'

'Don't be silly. They can stay here for as long as you want; they can use the room we keep free for last minute bookings. No charge, of course.'

'No, that's too much.'

'You'll be fired on the spot if you don't accept!'

'But is that OK with Bridget and David?'

'Of course. The three of us have discussed it and we agree.'

'That's so kind.'

'Just give me the dates so we can block them in,' Melissa said. 'And didn't you say your man is visiting, too?'

'Gareth? Yeah, though I'm not sure he's my man.'

'Are you going to pretend that you aren't back sleeping together or will you be upfront and have him staying at yours?'

'That's a good question. I don't know the answer.'

'Let me know when you do. I'll hold a room free for that weekend until you decide, though why on earth would you not want him in your bed?'

'It's complicated.'

'Then uncomplicate it.'

I put the decision about Gareth on hold and turned my attention to planning Mom's itinerary. Having made a list of the must see places in London, I WhatsApped her.

I needn't have bothered because she and Jeff had already worked out their itinerary. They'd be with me for three days before taking a road trip to Liverpool, Jeff being a big Beatles fan, then on to the Lake District and Scotland before swinging back via Newcastle where Jeff seemed to think his family originated. Finally, they would have another three days with me to see those London attractions that I hadn't needed to tell them about.

'That's one hell of a drive you're planning,' I explained.

Jeff was in on the conversation. 'Come on Jennifer, we live in America. Here one helluva drive is up to a thousand miles down Florida way or across to the Mid-West.'

True enough. I remembered some of the long journeys needed to get from the Idaho farm to anywhere worth going to.

'I'm so looking forward to seeing you, Mom. Both of you. I'll be at the airport when you arrive.'

I texted Gareth; we hadn't got into calling each other.

Dates finally confirmed for Mom's visit. She's arriving on the 15th probably jet-lag shattered. You're welcome to come here for dinner on the 16th and then the play on the 17th. Don't expect much though, it'll be a laid back performance.

I pinged it off, aware that an important piece of information was missing. We'd slept together once so why was I hesitant about this second visit? I would leave it up to him to decide – I chased the first text with a second one.

There are a couple of sleeping options. The hotel owners have said that it might be possible to stay there free of charge for a couple of nights which is incredibly generous. Another possibility is to stay with me.

Jeez, I was turned on thinking of him in bed with me. I texted again.

My preference would be for your to stay here.

I reread my message and sent a further text: *your=you*

He didn't reply.

I kept looking, still nothing.

It was after eight when my phone pinged. *Only just picked up your messages, was teaching then parents evening. At you=yours. Definitely.*

With that sorted, Gareth having selected the option I was hoping for (lots), I worked on my Salford accent well into the early hours of the morning by binge

311

watching episodes of Coronation Street. It was going well; I was happy.

Despite the late night, sleep was impossible. As dawn approached, worries about Mom and Jeff's visit, about coping at work, about getting the Salford accent right and remembering my lines, about whether there was a future for Gareth and me, came and went then came round again. Somewhere in the middle of all that fretting I reached one decision. I'd been putting off holding a housewarming party despite Melissa's nagging, but it struck me that organising one on the night of the drama evening made sense. The performance would run for about an hour and a half, leaving plenty of time to clear up and get to my place sometime after nine. Everyone I knew in Muswell Hill would be at the event so we could set off together.

I must have got to sleep in the end, waking late and drowsy like I was hungover. I called Melissa to let her know that I would be late in to work.

49

'A party, brilliant!' Melissa said when I let her know what I was planning.

'Yep, I've taken the plunge thanks to incessant nagging by someone. I've got my list of who to ask so I'll send out the invites after work.'

'Will I know everyone or might there be some exciting guests?'

'I'm not sure about exciting but my mother and her friend will be coming, Gareth too. The rest are the usuals – the Brookland Gardens crew, David and Bridget – and I'll also be inviting the drama group.'

'Great.'

'And you of course, so I'll finally get to see this mystery man of yours.'

'I'm afraid that won't happen. We've split, it wasn't working out.'

'I'm sorry.'

'No, it's fine.'

Melissa was so good at playing the optimist that I couldn't tell whether she was devastated or delighted or somewhere in between.

'I'll still be coming to the play and the party though, and if you decide not to go for Gareth I might take him off your hands!'

'That reminds me, he won't need a room here. He'll be staying at my place.'

'Oh, it sounds like that's it then and I've got no chance. Does he have a brother?'

'Afraid not.'

'Shame. Maybe there's someone nice for me in the drama group.'

'No one comes to mind.'

~

When I collected Mom and Jeff from the airport I expected to see a frazzled pair following their sixteen hours of travel including two flights. But no, they were full of beans, Mom rushing towards me before throwing her arms around me, with Jeff striding up behind her pulling two large suitcases.

I'd borrowed a car from Kelly and we were soon loaded up, ready to set off.

'Are we going straight to the hotel?'

'That's what I was planning, Mom.'

'Couldn't we do something first?'

'Like what? A tango class? A marathon?'

Mom didn't pick up my humor. 'No, I'm too tired for anything energetic but I thought we could drive through the centre and see the sights. What were the ones you've looked up, Jeff?'

'Buckingham Palace, the Houses of Parliament, The Tower of London, Soho. That's some for starters.'

'And I thought maybe we could stop off for a drink somewhere,' Mom added.

I'd had a busy day at work, had some preparation for the party to finish off, and was keen to store up tranquillity ahead of the performance. Added to that, I'd never driven through the centre of London and had no idea what route to take to reach those sights Jeff had mentioned. I felt like the exhausted adult trying to rein in a couple of overactive kids. 'It's best to reach the centre using the underground, the subway. Tell you what, you two can do that tomorrow while I'm at work, but if you want we can have a drink tonight at somewhere near your hotel. Let's check in first though.'

Jeez, was I hoping that they'd collapse with tiredness once they'd reached the hotel. But no, they were determined to go out and were in the lobby waiting for me after I'd returned the car I'd borrowed from Kelly.

'Ready, honey. We've freshened up and we can leave unpacking until later.'

'OK, there's a café nearby, the one we'll be at for the plays.'

'We'd rather visit one of your pubs, wouldn't we, Pat?' Jeff said and Mom nodded.

'Fine,' I said, the word laced with resignation as we walked towards The Broadway.

'This one,' Jeff announced, stopping in front of *The Famous Royal Oak.*

'Are you sure here?'

'Sure as can be, Jennifer.'

We were greeted by a mix of raucous laughter, cheering and shouting.

'This is great,' Jeff said. 'I'm gonna get one of your pints. You should try one, Pat.'

He'd forgotten they weren't *my* pints, I was American, but I was happy to go along with his high spirits. It turned out to be a quick drink because they were beginning to crash. By the time we got back to the hotel they were as eager to get to their bedroom as I was to get home.

'Are you sure you're OK for tomorrow?' I asked.

'You bet. There's more than enough to do.'

'OK. Call me if you need to, but if I don't hear anything I'll see you back here late afternoon.'

'And then we'll get to see Gareth again.'

She said it like they were long lost friends. 'Yeah, and then you'll see Gareth.'

~

Gareth reached the hotel the next afternoon ahead of Mom and Jeff returning from their sightseeing. I was still working but there was no problem stopping when he arrived.

'Good journey?' I asked.

'Yes, fine.'

There was a reticence as we faced each other, broken by me with a 'Come here you.'

We hugged, limiting it to formal since we were standing in the middle of the lobby with guests around us and Melissa on her way to introduce herself. Her hug was definitely more intense than mine and ridiculously I felt cheated. At least she didn't hang around.

'Melissa is one of the owners,' I told Gareth. 'Look, I'm not sure what's best. We could head to my place and then come back when Mom and Jeff return, but I don't think they'll be much longer so it's probably sensible to wait here.'

I was imagining a passionate session broken by a call from Mom to let me know that they were ready to be collected.

'Can't you text or call them to see when they're coming back?'

'I've tried but Mom's not picking up or replying to texts and I haven't got Jeff's number.'

'Let's just go for it, head to yours now. When they get back they won't mind having time to unwind if you're not here waiting for them.'

'I'm happy with that.' I knew what Gareth was thinking and I was thinking it too.

'I've hated not being with you, Jen.'

Over the few weeks since that last time we were together I'd been thinking things through non-stop. Finally, I'd reached the conclusion that there was no more thinking things through to do.

317

'And I –'

'Gareth!' Mom was in sprint mode, falling into Gareth's arms. 'It's so wonderful to see you.'

'Hello Mrs Kroll.'

'Pat. You must call me Pat.'

And there I was, an observer as Jeff joined the other two and they were chatting about their London adventures. Gareth was all charm with his smiles and polite questioning, and Mom was beaming non-stop. Hey guys, what about me?

I snapped out of it and joined the huddle. 'So, you had a good time, did you?'

'Oh, it was great. And Gareth's just told us … and Gareth's explained … and Gareth reckons we need to visit …'

'Let's head back to my place, I need time to get the meal ready. And then I suggest an early night because you two must be exhausted and I need lots of sleep ahead of a busy day tomorrow.'

'Agreed, an early night for all of us because I'm shattered too; it's been a hectic week at work.' I caught Gareth's eye and there was no doubt that we were sharing the same feeling – and it wasn't tiredness.

We had to survive another three hours with Mom and Jeff, hearing about their jobs in Wilmington, what they had planted in their garden, what they planned to plant in their garden, and what it was best not to plant in their garden. Gareth was playacting the horticultural specialist while I zombied out, desperate to be alone with him.

I faked a yawn and Mom got the hint. 'It's been a long day, Jeff. Let's head back to the hotel. It is lovely there, Jennifer.'

'Yep, I know.'

'I'll walk you back,' Gareth said.

'There's no need, I'm fairly sure we know the way.'

'No, I will,' he insisted.

'And you could get ready for bed, but please don't fall asleep,' he whispered when they were out of earshot. His lips tickled my ear, sending shivers through my body.

'Don't be long.'

'I won't, I'll be running back.'

'Take the key on the cabinet by the door.'

Maybe he did run because I'd only just got into bed when he came upstairs. And yep, it was a good night. A great night.

50

There was no stage, no proper lighting, no props, and the audience was tiny even though the café was full, but I was getting a buzz and a half performing. Everything I needed to convey was coming across exactly how I'd wanted.

Sitting on the chair recounting the domestic violence I'd been subjected to, I was focusing on the minutest of details – nervous glances, wringing of hands – to transmit my pretence of tension to the audience. It was working, I could sense it.

That Salford accent needed to be consistent and it was. Those Coronation Street reruns were paying off.

I was connecting with the other actors to pick up the beat of the script. Daisy had helped with that and had told me I was a natural.

I was in floods of real tears because my character was in floods of tears.

Loved it, loved it, loved it all.

And finally there was the applause to savour. Receiving the acclaim was like a drug; I didn't want it to stop.

But it did stop and suddenly a bit of me was sad, wondering whether I should have kept on trying back in LA after all. As I looked up at the smiling faces in the audience, reality kicked in and I was fine again, happy to be where I was with Gareth coming towards me clutching a giant bouquet. Maybe the kiss was a bit wilder than appropriate for public display.

'That was very good,' Gareth said. 'I won't call you *a* star because I know you don't much like the word, but can I call you *my* star?'

'You can and I'm very happy you're here this evening.'

Others were coming towards me and Gareth dissolved into the crowd as people gathered around to hug or shake hands. The compliments were flying and Mom was by my side crying.

'It wasn't that bad, Mom.'

She smiled. 'It's taken all this time for me to understand why you wanted what you wanted.'

'And do you know what? I think this, being here, is finally what I do want.'

Daisy had clapped her hands to quiet everyone down and was saying a few words, including thanking the owners of the café for providing such a wonderful venue.

'I believe that as soon as we've cleared up we're invited over to Jennifer's home.'

'Everyone can head off now,' David called out. 'There are enough staff here to sort things out.' He turned away and was giving his team instructions before I could check if he was sure.

'OK. Follow me if you don't know where I live.'

I led with Gareth, Mom and Jeff by my side.

Tiredness hit me so hard that it almost struck me down. There hadn't been much sleep the night before (thanks Gareth), the performance had left me emotionally and physically drained, and now I had a party to host. If I could press a magic button to reach the end of the housewarming with everyone gone, I would be pushing it like mad.

I shouldn't have worried because Gareth, Mom and Jeff were the perfect hosts. Earlier that afternoon they'd helped prepare, so they knew what food needed to go in the oven, what was stored in the fridge, where the glasses, plates and cutlery were – in fact everything.

'I have done parties, honey, I think I'm doing fine,' Mom said when I checked if she was coping.

Gareth was next to her. 'So chill out, Jen. You take in all the compliments about your acting and we'll sort the rest, won't we, Pat.'

So I was an observer as Gareth, Mom and Jeff did the entertaining, pouring the drinks, handing out the canapés, keeping the music playing. I assumed Gareth had put together the playlist because the tracks were things we used to listen to together. That left me in a bit of a daze as I chatted to the guests, repeating the same things over and over again.

'The performance was all down to Daisy's brilliant directing.'

'Yes, I'm really lucky to have found this place to live.'

'Mom lives in North Carolina. She's here for a few days.'

The party went on longer than I would have liked but finally people were drifting off. The farewells from my female friends were variations of "That man is gorgeous, make sure you hold onto him." ("Thank you, Kelly." "Thank you, Emma." "Thank you, Melissa.") Even members of the drama group were asking me, "Are you and Gareth together? He's absolutely wonderful."

Mom was getting ready to leave and was standing next to Melissa who had offered to walk her and Jeff back to the hotel.

'Step into your bedroom for a minute can we, honey?'

'Sure. Is anything wrong, Mom?'

'Nope. I just want to tell you something in private.' I led her to the bedroom and she closed the door behind us. 'All I'm gonna say is that you must get back with Gareth –'

'Thanks for the advice. I still have some thinking to do.' Actually, I didn't, but this wasn't a conversation I wanted to have.

'I'm not advising you, I'm telling you, which is different.'

'OK, thanks. Let's go back out.'

'No! Wait! Since the day you was born you've been making up your own mind, not listening to me or Pa. We accepted that, we admired you for it. But this is different, this is your Mom saying you *must*, do you hear me? And if Dad was here I know he'd be telling you exactly the same. If you don't stay by Gareth you'll regret it for the rest of your life. That's all I have to say so you can go back out now.'

'There you are!' Cecelia shrieked as I reappeared. She edged towards me stumbling. Julien caught hold of her. I'd never seen her drunk. 'Great theatre, great party. I've had a chat with Gareth, he's so interesting. Did you know he's a teacher?'

I nodded and smiled as Julien edged her towards the door, followed by Melissa with Mom and Jeff.

Then it was just me with Gareth.

'What did your mother want?'

'Nothing much.'

'I think she had a good time; I think everyone did.' He put an arm around my shoulder and I leaned into him. I wanted to stay like that but he pulled away. 'The place is a tip; shall we do some clearing up before bed?'

'No.'

'At least put the chilled stuff back in the fridge.'

'No. Gareth?'

'Yes?'

I'd already decided what I wanted ahead of Mom's uncharacteristic outpouring, but her words had sealed it. She'd made it all sound so simple and it was – Gareth wanted me back and I wanted to be back with him, so what was the problem?

'Are you aware that everyone thinks you're wonderful?'

'Alcohol does strange things.'

'The thing is, they're right. I'd like to go to bed with you now.'

'Is this a date?'

'I smiled. 'Could be.'

'Is it a one night stand?' he asked between kisses.

'I don't think so. Who knows? It could be for a lifetime.'

Epilogue

Three months have passed since the housewarming, three of the happiest months of my life. Gareth and I are getting along great, back to what it was like when we first met. No, even better because it's an equal partnership now that I'm working and I don't have to rely on him supporting me. I'd always found that difficult.

In the end there were several reasons why our relationship had fallen to pieces first time around. Possibly things started to go wrong while we were still living in the States because the frequent moving from one side of the vast country to the other at short notice was so hard. As well as being stressful, it had never seemed worthwhile to make friends because we'd soon be leaving a place. When it comes down to it, whatever else might be going well, isn't it true that the most important thing to keep you happy is the people around you?

Yep, all is good with Gareth but we aren't rushing things, meaning we don't live together. I'm sure that will happen but for now practical considerations have put it on hold.

Where would we live? Gareth is tied to his teaching job in Buckinghamshire, at least until the fall. He's happy to be in that cosy little town but he's not hung up on the place. He thinks it would be easy to get work in London, so it's likely that he'll be the one moving, not me.

But is Muswell Hill realistic? I do love it here; I have a great set of friends who adopted me with open arms and warmth soon after I arrived. I'm particularly close to Kelly, and more recently to Melissa who calls me her agony aunt as she moves from one relationship to another. I'm having loads of fun with the drama group, socially as well as during the rehearsals for our forthcoming show. I joined the tennis club, too, despite the uncomfortable first visit. What with my hectic job and being with Gareth most weekends, I don't play as much as I would like, but there are a few regulars who I enjoy being with and chatting to after a match. I'd be hard pushed to find a better job than the one I've got. I'm partly responsible for the great reputation we've acquired in such a short space of time and there's going to be one helluva bonus coming my way soon. I'm going to use it to travel to North Carolina with Gareth to visit Mom and Jeff.

Gareth's been here since Friday and will be heading home tomorrow. Sometimes I stay at his place but mainly we're here during weekends because there's so much more to see and do. He had never told me that he'd lived in London for a while, which means he's taking me to places I would never have discovered by myself. Today we were at the Sir John Soane's Museum, a crazy house jam-packed with paintings, books, sculptures, furniture and architectural models. After the visit and a meal out we headed back to my place. Whenever I step into my apartment I'm overwhelmed by how lucky I am to be in such a beautiful place in a great location.

This evening we once again broke our unrealistic resolution not to talk about where to live, and once again we ended up with the depressing realisation that we could never afford to buy a house in Muswell Hill or anywhere nearby. It's no big deal though; if we have to go on renting forever, well, we'll do that. What's important is that we're together again.

I'm looking forward to our lazy Sunday morning before Gareth leaves. We'll be joining Kelly and Darren, Emma and Andrew, Cecelia and Julien, and Melissa, possibly with a new man, for Sunday brunch at Dream Café.

To bed first though.